BOILING

A CROSSING THE LINE NOVEL

POINT

BOILING

A CROSSING THE LINE NOVEL

POINT

NEW YORK TIMES BESTSELLING AUTHOR

TESSA BAILEY

Entangled Publishing, LLC
2614 South Timberline Road
Suite 109
Fort Collins, CO 80525
Visit our website at www.entangledpublishing.com.

Select Suspense is an imprint of Entangled Publishing, LLC.

Edited by Heather Howland
Cover design by Heather Howland
Cover art from DepositPhotos

Manufactured in the United States of America

First Edition January 2016

Chapter One

Austin Shaw hardened his jaw and slid onto one of the plush leather chairs lining the bar. With his left hand—the one sporting a Rolex he'd just nipped from a trusting pawn store owner—he reached under the opposite arm, removed the copy of *Crain's Chicago*, and tossed it onto the bar, nodding at the nearest group of businessmen as he did so. As expected, they nodded back, sitting a touch straighter in their seats, thus reminding Austin he was having a brilliant fucking hair day. What else was new?

In Austin's peripheral vision, he saw the red-vested bartender jolt from his post watching the Chicago Bulls game on an expensive flat-screen and stride toward him. *Good man.*

"Something to drink, sir?"

Austin cast a discriminating eye over Red Vest's shoulder toward the top shelf, rolling his tongue in his mouth, anticipating his employment of the New England accent he'd been practicing. "Johnnie Walker Blue." He laid his arm across the neighboring chair and watched the bartender's eyes light on the Rolex. "And a round for those hardworking gentlemen across the bar, too. Their boss is an asshole."

Red Vest quirked a blond eyebrow. "How'd you know?"

"You're looking at him." Austin tilted his head. "But let's keep that between us, eh? My office is on the top floor for a reason."

The bartender laughed and went to fulfill the order. Austin leaned back in his chair, his confidence solidifying now that he'd accomplished the two most important objectives when walking into an establishment. Thanks to the combination of his Rolex, the financial journal, and the easy lie he'd told, the bartender had now assigned him a worth. And that worth was high. If Austin needed information—and he *did*—valuable words would roll right off Red Vest's lips now, smooth as smoke.

Secondly, he'd made friends with everyone in the room without breaking a sweat. Pleasing others meant they'd do the same for him. Do it with a smile and the arrogance he'd been born with? He'd have those stiffs jumping through flaming hoops before they finished their drinks.

Right. Now that he was in charge of the landscape, the business at hand bled in, like an uncapped ink pen against white cotton.

Polly Banks. Hacker extraordinaire. Ex-convict. And the first woman who'd made his acquaintance without noticing or commenting on the silver flecks in his eyes. A ghastly oversight, really.

With a discreet check of his watch, Austin began a

mental countdown until the untouchable Ms. Banks strolled through the establishment's doors. Tonight wasn't the first night he'd followed her to the upscale bar in Chicago's financial district. It was merely the first night he'd chosen to insert himself into the frame, rather than hang back and observe Polly's amateur operation from the darkened back corner booth. At least, he'd assumed the operation was amateurish. He hadn't quite figured out what angle she was working, which gave him a beastly case of nerves. On top of a festering volcano of irritation, wrought by her increasingly diminished attire.

Low-cut silk tops and flashes of garter belts that likely accounted for the unusually populated bar. Austin kept his expression mild even as his features ached to threaten each and every arsehole in the vicinity with a look. One that said, "Ah, gents. Put your wedding rings back on. The sleek beauty you've been ogling five nights straight is mine. She just hasn't come 'round to the idea yet."

Bit of an under-exaggeration, unfortunately. When Polly looked at him, Austin could feel her disdain like a blast from a fire hose. It was jarring, really. He'd encountered many reactions from the fairer sex. Astonishment, attraction, nervousness. What he wouldn't give to inspire nerves from Polly. He'd know just what to do with them, and his process involved a distinct lack of clothing. Possibly a piece of leather for her to bite down on when overcome by pleasure.

Austin took a sip of Johnnie Walker to stifle the groan building in his throat. He and Ms. Banks were nowhere near nudity and leather—*yet*—unfortunately. Instead, he was in disguise, watching her play a game in which he could easily assist her. If she didn't liken him to pond scum.

Really, he'd had no chance to make an alternate impression on the sassy bit of goods with a mind that rivaled even his own. Both of them had been brought to Chicago upon being issued ultimatums. Prison time...or working undercover to put criminals—such as themselves, but with significantly fewer accolades—behind bars. He and Polly, along with four other victims, had been sent to purgatory. "Atoning for their sins," their leader, Captain Derek Tyler, had put it.

Austin disguised his snort with a cough. Sins were only sins if someone was watching. And he was usually long gone before his marks caught on.

Do unto others...then disappear. A motto that had served him quite well.

Until recently, when the law had put a target on his back, making the world that was once his endless playground a damn sight smaller.

Sometimes he even let the cops think he hadn't orchestrated his own arrival in Chicago. That he hadn't been drawn here by news of a loose end, left undone during his last con. A living, breathing loose end named Gemma.

Austin showed zero reaction when the door at his back opened, allowing the bite of fall to swirl into the bar, cooling his neck. When Polly clicked past in high heels, however, reacting was a necessity. Any man who *didn't* show a reaction to a modern, sexualized version of Snow White...well, that man would make the chess pieces in place around him suspicious. Suspicion was the enemy to cons everywhere. And being a formidable con of great reputation, Austin let the glass pause halfway to his mouth as he considered Polly's ass on her way to the opposite end of the bar. Even threw in a conspiratorial salute to the group of businessmen drinking the liquor he'd paid for as they did the same.

Goddammit, he'd never felt an ounce of possessiveness over another human being in his thirty-one years. But just then, he wanted more than anything to walk up behind Polly, wrap an arm around her hips, and drag her back against his lap. Look those tossers right in the eye as he licked up the side of her smooth neck. *Mine, you pathetic drunks. You wouldn't last a minute up against the brilliance of how she thinks. How she reasons and makes decisions. Piss. Right. Off.*

When the tumbler shook in Austin's hand, he quickly set it down and looked busy going through his cell phone. He put the device to his ear and turned sideways, away from Polly, but at an angle that allowed him to watch her through the bar's back mirror. He'd taken great pains applying the phony beard and gray wig so she wouldn't recognize him, but he wouldn't take any chances. If she made him, there wouldn't be a hope in hell of him discerning her game.

Anxious. The hacker who had once breached the White House's technological firewalls was actually anxious. Which made him...jumpy. Fucking hell, he didn't do jumpy. Rule number one, however, was knowing the lay of the land before running an operation, and he had no clue what Polly's game was.

A gut feeling told Austin he'd find out tonight.

• • •

Here, kitty kitty.

Polly Banks ordered a dry white wine and crossed her legs in what probably looked like slow motion to the handful of douche bags behind her. The bartender had already started to pour her drink of choice prior to her placing the order, however, which was troubling. It told her she'd been here one too many nights, and tomorrow called for a venue change. *Not good.* She was running out of nighttime haunts to locate her mark. After this, she knew of a single nightclub where Charles Reitman was known to frequent when in Chicago. After that, it would be back to the drawing board. Or *keyboard*, as it were.

Her time in Chicago hadn't been designated simply to play house with the undercover squad. No, no. Each and every move Polly made was planned down to the tiniest degree and orchestrated with precise, thoughtful keystrokes. There was a debt that needed settling, and she'd come to Chicago to do just that. If her daylight hours were dedicated to aiding the same law enforcement machine that had ruined her fun and sent her to prison? Well. She'd be free of their confines soon enough. Free to navigate cyberspace at will, locating information and selling it the highest bidder.

Just as soon as she located Charles Reitman and got close enough to take back every penny he'd stolen from her fathers.

Yes, her vendetta against the man who'd swindled her fathers out of their life savings was pretty hypocritical. After all, her bread and butter happened to be blackmail. But Polly had a code that dictated whom she stole from and why. It was simple, really. If the fuckers deserved it, they were open season. Her fathers hadn't deserved it. They'd barely made it into the black with their clothing line before the financial security had been swept out from under them like a rug. By Charles Reitman. The man who'd posed as an investment banker and vamoosed with six hard-earned figures, sending Polly's family spiraling into bankruptcy.

Life had been hard after that. They'd lived in motel rooms, rationed food, and been turned down for assistance from people they'd considered friends. She'd watched the parents who loved her suffer, battle to keep her fed and clothed. Keeping her warm and safe when no one else would do the same for them.

And then it had gotten much, much worse.

Polly had grown up and learned how to get even. Now if only the topper to her revenge cake would come into the bar and proposition her for sex, she could move on with her plans of world domination, secure in the knowledge that justice had been served.

Polly accepted the glass of wine from the bartender with a half smile, curling a hand around the back of her neck in a flirtatious gesture. He coughed into his fist, mumbling that the group of gentlemen had bought her a drink. Polly turned and sent them a fluttery-fingered wave. *Just one drink? How generous among the eight of you.*

Although dressing the part had been necessary, Polly didn't like being ogled. She placated herself with the fact that she could hack into the bar's point-of-sale system and have each man's credit card information by morning.

Polly turned back to the bar and sipped her wine, feeling a kick of adrenaline when the door opened and a slim figure breezed in. His looks were entirely unremarkable, but there was a caginess to him. Slim's gaze swept the establishment's interior in a casual glance that felt...practiced. Without looking at the bartender, he reached out and shook the younger man's hand, calling him by name. The bartender floundered a moment, as if surprised the newcomer knew his name, but recovered by offering to buy him his first drink.

"Beefeater, rocks. Thanks, man," Slim said, his attention landing on her. Staying there. "And whatever the lady is having."

That was when Polly recognized him. It wasn't whom she'd been expecting. Not Charles Reitman, but his face… she explored the recesses of her mind trying to place it. For years, her free time had gone into researching Reitman, following his movements. Not an easy task when you're tracking a slippery con. A snake in the grass, just like all con men. There. Her photographic memory delivered the DMV record her memory bank had been seeking. This man — Slim — was an associate of Reitman's. Did that mean she'd been correct and Reitman was in Chicago? *Yes.* Polly's heart pumped double time. Finally.

She leaned back in her chair, allowing the white silk of her blouse to gape as she smiled at Slim. His name still eluded her, but *he* wouldn't. If she played the situation just right, this guy could lead her to Reitman.

When Slim correctly interpreted the invitation and sauntered forward to join Polly, she was distracted by a man in the corner of the bar. He stiffened in an almost imperceptible manner. Just a subtle tweak of his shoulders. Had he been there the last four nights? No, she didn't think so, but his face was obscured by the fall of gray hair, the collar of his jacket. Knowing all too well how cons often worked in teams, she decided to keep an eye on him while feeling out Slim.

Funny, Slim was busy feeling her out. Typical con. "I assumed you were waiting for someone," he said, sliding onto the chair beside her.

"Oh?" she purred, tucking her short black hair behind her ear. "Why is that?"

"You're the only woman in the room." He dipped his head and Polly could see he'd been good-looking once, probably before alcohol consumption had become his favorite pastime, an educated guess she made based on the tremor in his drinking hand. The raw red skin of his nose. "If you're not waiting for someone, you must like being the exception to the rule."

"The rule being what? Only men are allowed in this big bad boy's bar?"

He smiled into a long swig of gin. "I don't make the rules."

"Good." She gave a dainty shrug, going for a mischievous air. "I won't have to apologize when I break them."

He swirled the alcohol in his glass. "What are you looking for tonight?"

"Tonight?" She tugged the material of her skirt down, knowing it would only spring back up her thighs when she let it go. Which it did. Again, the figure huddled at the end of the bar demanded her attention, but she strove to focus on Slim, who'd finally let his gaze drop to her legs, an action she'd expected upon approach. This guy wasn't bush league, and she needed to remember that. Dividing her attention between him and the gray-haired mystery man would be a misstep she couldn't afford. "I'm just trying to stay warm," Polly continued. "It's a cold night out there, in case you didn't notice."

"I noticed," Slim murmured, scrutinizing her. "If you don't mind heading once more into the fray, I was planning on eating dinner down the street. Join me."

Polly perched her grinning lips on the rim of her wineglass, even as her insides recoiled at the command. She didn't like being told what to do. Not by anyone, but a con issuing demands took the ever-loving cake. And speaking of cake…"Do I get dessert, too?"

"I've never been known to skip the best part." Slim tossed back the last of his drink, set the glass down on the bar and held out his hand. "I guess you were waiting for someone after all, huh?"

Maybe I'll kill him, too, for good measure. "You seem to be good at reading people," she said, allowing him to assist her off the chair.

His hand smoothed into the small of her back. "You have no idea."

Prick. Polly picked up her purse, comforted by the weight of her recently procured nine-millimeter. "Lead the way."

• • •

The best cons included more than just a mechanic, also known as the man performing the con. Austin himself had worked with a partner since he'd turned sixteen and watched his father get taken for five quid in a game of three-card monte during a family trip to Brighton. He'd seen it all take place, like a play unfolding on a stage. At the time, he hadn't known what the term "shill" meant. He'd only seen the silent communication pass between the mechanic—the card dealer—and the man who'd taken a turn before his father. They'd been in on it together. *I won!* The shill had said it loud enough to stop passersby in their tracks. *This guy must be blind...I've already won supper money for the week.*

Austin had scoffed to himself, expecting his father to catch on. To see clear through the pair of wankers who'd pulled the wool over everyone else's eyes. Only his father hadn't copped on, and when it was his turn to guess which bent playing card hid the pebble, Austin's family had walked away minus a fiver. He could still remember the stifling disappointment he'd felt in his father—how it had kept him silent the whole ride back to London. The next day, he'd skipped school and hitched a ride back to Brighton to watch the monte sharks all day, learning their tricks. Before long, he'd set up his own operation on the opposite end of the beach, swindling unsuspecting tourists out of their holiday money.

He'd done fair enough for a beginner, but he'd needed a partner. A shill. A *chiller* to step in when a mark didn't take kindly to being cheated. There'd been no need to seek out a partner, however, because a partner had found him right enough. Found him, sunk his claws in, taught him the ropes...then double-crossed him by making off with his half of a million-dollar score.

Austin's hands turned to fists inside his coat pockets as he followed Polly down the darkened street in Near North Side, just north of the Loop, Chicago's business district. His blood pumped in both temples, creating a heavy drumbeat to match his footsteps. She couldn't know the identity of the man she walked beside. Could she? He wouldn't wager on anything where Polly was concerned, suspecting the undercover squad had only begun to tap her capabilities as a hacker. But this man—one of the best shills in the bloody business—was dangerous, despite his affable demeanor.

Austin still hadn't managed to trap the alarm that had run free when Darren Burnbaum walked into the bar, the familiar swagger tipping off Austin immediately. His anxiety had only tripled when Polly got up to leave the bar with the man. By God, she'd barely made him work for the pleasure of her time, agreeing to dinner in two minutes flat. If that easy agreement had come off suspicious to Austin, it sure as hell hadn't gone unnoticed by Darren, which was only *one* of his aliases.

See, the drawback to needing additional players in a good con meant Austin had crossed paths over the last fourteen years with some of the best. When word went out that a mark was prime for the taking, cons swarmed like piranha around the opportunity. Kind of a fucked-up version of supply and demand. Oftentimes, if anyone wanted to score, it meant organizing the team and working together. So Austin was quite familiar with Darren's skill set, and he didn't want it anywhere near Polly.

She was playing a part, so the fix was definitely in. This wasn't just a random meeting at a bar—it had been planned. Until he knew the particulars, Darren was going down for the count.

Because as dangerous as Darren Burnbaum had proved to be, Austin Shaw was twice as lethal. And not a goddamn hair on Polly's head would be harmed on his stolen watch.

When Darren led Polly to a diner, Austin shook his head. *Still a cheap fuck.* Loath to let Polly out of his sight for even a minute, Austin hung back and waited for them to enter the diner and be seated. Then he sneaked around to the kitchen entrance through the alley around back, nodding to the bored cook who shrugged and flipped over a grilled cheese sandwich. He slipped into the bathroom, grateful to see two stalls, and closed himself in the left one.

If he remembered correctly—and he always did—Darren had a coke habit that would require a trip to the bathroom at some point—

The ancient bathroom door swung open. Austin held his breath and waited for Darren to lock the right stall door and tap out a line of coke…onto the goppin' toilet tank? Austin grimaced. The lengths a man went to for his vice. Darren's came in the form of white powder while Austin's stood five foot two and smelled like fresh-squeezed lemonade. At least Darren's position would make what came next easy.

Austin left his stall, braced his hands on either side of the one occupied by Darren and kicked it open. The door slammed into Darren, sending him crashing face-first into the wall behind the toilet. Austin wasted no time wrapping an arm around Darren's throat, tightening until drawing air was impossible.

"Forget you ever saw her," Austin whispered into Darren's ear, just as the other man was forced into unconsciousness.

He let Darren's dead weight drop onto the floor before moving quickly from the bathroom and back out into the alley, palming his cell phone with a curse. Just like any good con, sometimes other players were needed to pull it off successfully.

Austin scrolled through his contacts and dialed Erin O'Dea. Arsonist, escape artist…coworker. She answered on the fourth ring in a singsong voice. "Aus-tin. Connor doesn't like when boys call, especially on a school night." He could hear the strike of a match in the background. "So make it snappy, before he makes your *bones* go snappy."

"Right." Austin descended the stairs to the Red Line train that would take him back to Lincoln Park. "I need you to call Polly and get her home, please. Set the smoke alarm off in her apartment or something." As if on cue, the train pulled up and Austin entered the half-empty car. "Should be a treat for you, O'Dea. The sound of an alarm without the drawback of being arrested."

"I don't like easy treats. Give me a challenge."

Austin sighed and checked his watch. Only another few minutes before Darren regained consciousness. "I've no time to indulge your whimsy tonight. What do you want?"

"I'm bored with my Ruger. Bring me the shiny, British."

"Done. It stays between us."

An alarm pealed down the line in response.

Austin hung up and fell into a hard plastic seat, staring at his reflection in the opposite window. Only it wasn't him at all, was it?

Really, who the hell was Austin Shaw? Self-designated protector of Polly Banks? Con man? Master of disguise?

And since when did he give two shits?

Chapter Two

Polly paced the squad meeting room, which was essentially a basement in an abandoned youth center in Ukrainian Village. Seraphina, her saintly squad mate, had hung a tapestry and placed scented candles on the concrete window ledges, but it still looked like a dungeon. Which was apt, considering they were all prisoners of their past transgressions.

She'd come early, unable to remain in her apartment while harboring so much restless energy. Her lead—her *one and only* lead on Charles Reitman—had been within her reach last night. She hadn't been gullible enough to buy Erin's innocent story about the miraculous fire alarm deployment. Before she'd left the diner last night, she'd gone to check on Slim and found him unconscious in the men's bathroom. Not wanting to end up the same way, she'd done the smart thing and bounced with a quickness.

Now she was back at square one with the added variable of a third player. A meddler. Someone had choked out her ticket to Reitman, and she was not happy about it. Since childhood, she'd been a sucker for riddles, but this was one time she didn't appreciate having to piece a mystery together. Making another attempt to connect with Slim would be a bad move because of what had befallen him while in her company. The nightclub, Tossed, was the final venue on her list of Reitman's haunts, and she had no choice but to seek him out there after her face had been seen by one of his associates. Chancy, but necessary.

Polly heard a familiar set of footsteps coming down the basement stairs and ordered her features to look bored. She leaned against the wall and studied her nails, even as her heart started to thud. Austin. No one else moved like him, with unhurried steps that were somehow crisp at the same time. Each footfall had meaning, a purpose. She hated having his walk memorized, but there it was. She would hear the handsome con coming from a mile away in a monsoon. He carried awareness with him, foisting it on everyone in his path, daring them not to acknowledge how truly shit-hot he was. Insufferable man. False modesty wasn't in his repertoire, either, Polly lamented as Austin waltzed into the room, shaking raindrops from his rich brown hair.

"Ms. Banks." He made a savoring noise in his throat, dragging his gaze from the tips of her boots upward. "Should I assume from your punctuality that you were hoping to clock some alone time with me? I usually only take scheduled appointments, but you're always the exception."

She knew better than to take the bait. Another facet of Austin she had memorized was his sexual gravity. Step off the ledge when he challenged you with innuendo and, well, *splat*. There was no way to compete with innate charisma like he'd been blessed with. Dammit. "I had no idea you would arrive first. I assumed it would be Connor." Their resident ex-SEAL, who insisted on neat edges and precise plans, was usually fuming by the time all six members showed up. "If I'd known, I would have killed some time in Starbucks."

"Connor *used* to arrive first," Austin said, sauntering toward her. "Until I realized it got under his skin when I do instead. So here I am." He ran a hand over his sculpted mouth, his attention locked on the base of her neck. "And here *you* are."

The hard wall against her back felt more like a trap the closer he came. "You go to such lengths to get under people's skin, but you can't get under mine." She tilted her head. "That must drive you crazy, Shaw."

"*You*. Are the only thing that drives me crazy." The tips of his shoes bumped hers, sending a bolt of energy straight up her limbs. "And you damn well know it."

Okay. *This* was the confusing part. Every so often—like just then, for instance—she swore the constant bullshit exterior Austin wore like armor...dropped. Allowing her what she *might* classify as a brief glimpse at the real man underneath the disguises, accents, and charm. The operative term being *might*. If she were a total moron. Thankfully, Polly knew that the hints of vulnerability that shone through were manufactured. Part of the Austin Shaw Show. There wasn't a hope in hell she would fall victim to a liar, the way her fathers had. The way Austin *expected* her to.

Unfortunately, whenever Austin got this close, a humming started approximately three inches south of her belly button. That humming was only temporary, though, because it eventually turned into a twist....a *churn*. While her brain registered Austin's inability to feel real human emotions such as compassion or regret, her body was turned on by those same drawbacks. If she let him, he'd give her sweaty, feverish sex without any of the pillow talk or round two possibilities. But no. *No.* If she let him get to her, physically or otherwise, he would win the standoff they had going on. A standoff she refused to concede.

When Austin's belt buckle nudged her belly, Polly swallowed a whimper. "If I drive you crazy, then why won't you back off?"

"If I thought that's what you wanted, I might." His eyelids drooped, his breath feathering the hair on her crown. He was so close, she could taste his dark, cultured scent. Honey and spice. Poison disguised as temptation. "Just one go-round, Polly. I need your body."

Good Lord. "No."

"Your pride is getting in the way of my sanity." He laid his hands high above her on the wall, eased close so he could speak just beside her ear. *Move*, Polly commanded herself, but no dice. His thigh muscles chafed her smoother ones, his ripped-up stomach cradling breasts that strained toward him. *Traitors.* He was sinful male and bad intention in one seriously disarming package. Her feet wouldn't move for all the tea in China. "Mmmm." Austin sucked in a slow breath. "There goes the rest of it. Farewell, sanity." He exhaled into her hair. "Even though you continually torture me, I brought you a gift."

She managed to shake her head. "I don't want it."

He only pressed closer. "Yes, you do." His fingers toyed with the ends of her hair. "A few weeks ago, I realized I'd never seen you drink coffee during the meetings. Only tea.

Then you stopped. Now your hands don't know what to do with themselves without being wrapped around a mug." Her interest sufficiently piqued, Polly lifted her chin and met his eyes. Big mistake. Those stupid silver flecks were all but glowing as he spoke. "I realized you must have run out. So I sorted through the rubbish and found out the brand—"

"You can't get Fullings' verbena mint in Chicago. I looked." She narrowed her gaze as he crowded closer, flattening her against the wall. "The specialty places I order from online are all back-ordered."

"A mere mortal couldn't get it, maybe. But we're talking about me." Austin knew better than to kiss her, but he appeared to be considering it. Dampening his lips by rolling them inward, eyeing her mouth like a predator. Polly's right hand bunched, ready to swing, but he kept speaking instead of leaning in that final inch. "They're back-ordered because I bought all of them out. I've a single packet in my right front pocket, same as there will be every day."

"I knew there had to be a catch," Polly breathed. "You're going to dole it out. Conditional gifts aren't gifts at all, Shaw."

"I've graduated to playing dirty, Banks. I'm not proud of it," he said, his voice low and vibrating. "You want to reach into my pocket and feel how desperate you've made me?"

Oh, part of her did. A *huge* part. She wanted to touch this brilliant specimen of a man, just like every other woman who had fallen victim to his game—and witness the effect she'd had on his body. She could excuse the attraction because it was only natural with someone like Austin in your vicinity, especially after a yearlong sex famine. His voice, attire, scent, and speech were all designed to make a woman's womb shake. But Polly wouldn't join the trail of idiots left doddering around behind him. Not in this lifetime.

"That tea is important to me," she said, enunciating each word. "But I wouldn't lower myself to begging someone like you. If you thought I would, that was an adorable underestimation on your part."

She could see cogs whirring behind his eyes, feel his breath fanning her forehead. This is what he did for a living; he read people. Since they'd begun working together, she'd seen him in action several times, and it was impressive, but she prided herself on remaining unreadable to him. "Tell me why the tea is important to you and I'll hand over the whole lot."

Now *that* she hadn't been expecting. His response threw her a little, cutting off the sharp rejoinder she'd had poised for delivery. "Why do you care what matters to me?"

Dammit. There it was again. A shimmer of something *else* beneath the cocky exterior. A parting of the curtains that allowed blue light to shine through. *God, he's good.* As soon as it appeared, though, it vanished without a trace. He cleared his throat and stepped back, running a hand through his *GQ* cover-model hair. "Do you even have to ask? When I know what makes someone tick, I can manipulate them." He winked at her. "I thought you knew that about me, Banks."

She put up her middle finger. "Manipulate this."

An unfamiliar figure filled the doorway. "I must be in the right place."

• • •

Austin didn't think, he simply lunged forward to shield Polly, wedging her against the wall, her front to his back. A fleeting moment passed where he felt her hand curl in the material of his shirt, and it was a glorious goddamn feeling. Finally, some form of a tell from the mysterious Polly Banks. And it had only been six months in coming. So if presented with an unknown threat, she would consider him the lesser of two evils. Right. He could work with that. Some marriages had been founded on less, and he merely wanted to shag her senseless.

Believing your own lies was another necessary skill when leading the life of a con. A brilliant one, at that.

"Who the hell are you?" Austin asked the man framed in the doorway. "A quick answer, if you please."

"I don't," the figure returned.

"Cop," Polly whispered against the back of Austin's neck, warming his scalp and making his pants that much more confining. *Fucking hell.* She'd picked a rotten time to get grabby and soft-spoken, but he'd take it. "Hundred bucks says he's a cop."

Austin tilted his head, studying the man. His clean-shaven head reached the door's top frame, arms jutting out slightly on either side of him, as if they contained too much muscle to hang at his sides, like a normal bloody human being. It was hard to place his heritage, standing as the man was in the shadows, but Austin judged him to be half African-American with some Scandinavian blood accounting for the rest. He actually found it comforting that the chap looked as suspicious of them as they were of him. *Cop* suspicious. As always, Austin was amazed by Polly's astuteness.

"I don't place losing bets," Austin murmured, wishing she would twist up his shirt again, maybe do some more whispering. "Bad news," Austin called to the newcomer. "We only work with one cop, and I've only just come 'round to the idea. If you're here to give us orders, consider this my preemptive fuck-off."

The man appeared unfazed, swaggering into the room in a way that put Austin's back up. He knew deception well, and although the man moved with a casual gait, Austin recognized an ability to defend oneself. A fighter's swagger. "I'm not a cop anymore." The newcomer leaned against the far wall and crossed his mammoth arms over his chest. "And that's the last time you tell me to fuck off, English."

"We'll see."

"It's too early in the morning for a pissing contest." Polly slipped out from behind his back, leaving him feeling cold. "Although there'll be no avoiding it when—"

"Who the fuck are you?" Bowen Driscol asked, coming to a stop just inside the door, his wife, Seraphina, close at his side. "I only signed up for one cop. Not including my wife."

"Good God," Austin grumbled. "The street tough figured it out quicker than me? All this inactivity is making me rusty."

Bowen escorted Sera to a chair before standing guard in front of her like a rough-edged version of a sentry. The details Austin had gleaned about their story were murky, as he never wanted to appear interested, but he knew the highlights. Sera, a freshly minted NYPD cop, had gone undercover to find a way to put her brother's murderer behind bars, all while Bowen—a criminal in his own right—had been working with the NYPD to keep her alive, unbeknownst to Sera. There had been quite a patch of turbulence toward the end of the case, but obviously it had ended well, since one didn't cross the street without the other now.

Austin had a contentious relationship with Bowen, the

former Brooklyn gang leader, but more of it stemmed from jealousy than anything else. Not over his looks, obviously. Austin had everyone beat in *that* department, thank you very much. No, his envy stemmed from Bowen's inability to hide his thoughts or emotions. They flashed in his face one by one. Humor, vexation, anger. What that must be like. Not bothering to expend energy on keeping your hand hidden to the other players.

Underneath the jealousy of having such freedom, however, was a worry that kept him awake at night, when he wasn't thinking about Polly.

What if he dropped his mask and nothing lay on the other side?

Connor Bannon, the ex-SEAL who was usually first to arrive at every squad meeting, strode into the room, stone-faced, as was his custom. Riding on Connor's back was Erin O'Dea, the blond pyromaniac and escape artist who was rarely seen out of Connor's company. Their first mission as a squad six months ago had coincided with Erin's stepfather attempting to institutionalize her and steal her trust fund, but uncle had ended up with a bullet in his head instead, the details of which were still sketchy, but Austin suspected Connor had fired the kill shot. As he was a dishonored SEAL who had turned to violent street-enforcing back in New York, Austin doubted there would have been any hesitation on Connor's end. Especially not with Erin trapped in a cage, teetering over a lake as she'd been at the time.

Leading up to those events, Austin had developed somewhat of a soft spot for Erin, sort of a half-crazed sister who didn't judge him for being a cheat. He'd liked her loony, but seeing her settled made him feel...good. As a result, his animosity toward Connor had thinned out somewhat. Not that they'd be attending some ghastly baseball game together or something anytime soon.

"Who's the pig?" Erin asked, dropping down off Connor's back.

"For fuck's sake," Austin said, disgusted.

"Come on, guys." Sera stood and tried to sidestep Bowen, but he blocked her. She sighed. "Derek will make introductions when he gets here. Try to resist alienating him right off the bat."

"Alienation has worked like a charm for me so far," Austin commented, sending a tight smile around the room. Yeah, he was the resident prick among the group, and the title suited him just fine. He cast a glance at Polly over his shoulder to make sure she hadn't moved from behind the protection of his body. She lifted an eyebrow as if to say, *take a picture, asshole*. Well. Being the resident prick suited him most of the time. He'd made a right bollocks out of the tea bag idea, hadn't he? It had been meant to soften her up, not harden her even further toward him. For the millionth time, Austin wondered why his wits failed him only around Polly. Normally, he rose to a challenge, but the one she presented was proving far more difficult than he would have imagined.

His lack of finesse where Ms. Banks was concerned made up only a small portion of his confusion. In the past, he'd been required to seduce marks. He'd done it fast and he'd done it *well*, if the nail marks on his back were any indication. Perhaps he'd still had an ounce of conscience remaining, however, because he'd begun to feel guilt following the act. Swampy, inconvenient guilt. So he'd shut himself off during sex, moved on autopilot in a way that would achieve his goal, while blocking out the subsequent emotion that came along afterward. By Austin's count, it had been nearly a decade since he'd *enjoyed* sex. Pitiful, that. But true. So why this attraction to Polly? If he succeeded in getting her into bed, who would she even encounter there? What if she looked up at him and saw what he suspected he'd become? Another soulless con beyond redemption.

"Since our illustrious leader is running late," Polly started, "shall we piece together what we already know? He's an ex-cop—"

"Don't talk about me like I'm not here," said the new man.

Austin flexed his right hand. "Don't talk to *her* like *I'm* not here."

"My apologies." Polly came to stand beside Austin, giving him a curious look, before returning her attention to the man. "*You're* an ex-cop, but you're here with us in convict hell, so you've done something to earn it."

Erin trudged across the floor in the man's direction. When she stood within five feet, she leaned close and sniffed him. "Peanut butter." She turned and looked at Connor, who clearly wanted to haul her back, but respected the escape artist's need to be untethered, able to gain freedom at the drop of a hat. "Connor, he smells like peanut butter."

"I heard you," came the ex-SEAL-turned-street-enforcer's rumble. "That means he's harmless?"

"No, it means he's *dangerous*." Erin waved a hand to indicate the room. "Any one of us could have had a nut allergy."

Connor nodded, as if Erin's reasoning made perfect sense.

Bowen scratched the back of his neck, looking restless until Sera settled a hand on his shoulder, stilling him. "Five more minutes. If the captain is a no-show, I'm taking Sera home." He eyeballed the newcomer. "I'm not exactly aflutter with anticipation to make your acquaintance, man."

"Yeah?" The guy's jaw hardened. "I wasn't exactly thrilled to find out a group of criminals and cons have been running free in my city."

Austin gave a slow clap, unable to contain the laughter that escaped him. "You are aware this is Chicago, are you not? Home of the Chicago White Sox—or *Black* Sox as history will remember them for fixing your precious World Series?" He looked around the room for support, which didn't come. "The phrase 'vote early and vote often' originated in *your* city, good man. Rest assured that Chicago's reputation is already too black for a handful of criminals to tarnish it further."

Polly sniffed. "I hate when we agree."

Austin swept her tempting body with a look. "I know one thing we'd agree on if you'd only let me play."

He had the satisfaction of watching her cheeks redden— just a touch. "And wake up fleeced of my possessions? No, thank you."

His stomach knotted, but he grinned through the discomfort. "I'd leave you the essentials."

"Drop dead, Shaw."

Captain Derek Tyler chose that moment to enter the meeting space, shoving a box of doughnuts in Erin's general direction. "Never again, O'Dea," he growled. "You want doughnuts at these meetings, pick them up yourself."

"Captain," Erin responded, her voice muffled inside the

pink box. "Do you have a nut allergy? If you die, I'd rather it were of natural causes."

Derek threw an exhale at the ceiling, then looked at Sera—the only cop in the undercover squad and probably the one with the largest reserve of patience—who responded with, "New guy smells like peanut butter. The men are all a little touchy and it didn't help when Austin dissed the almighty Series. We all knew he was a cop on sight, because, *hello*. Probably best to lead with introductions. I'll pick up the doughnuts next time. You never pick anything with frosting."

Bowen rolled his shoulders. "That's my wife." He looked at the new guy. "Who I'd like to point out is neither criminal nor con, as you put it."

"Then what's she doing here?" New guy rubbed his chin and leaned forward, considering an already-bristling Bowen. "I've earned a guess since you've all taken turns pegging me for a lowlife." He swept Bowen with a discerning look. "Dragged her down with you, huh?"

Connor just managed to intercept Bowen in time on his charge toward the newcomer. Big as Connor was, Bowen knew every trick in the book and was more than capable of getting the drop on Connor, so Austin heaved a dramatic sigh and went to step in. "Now, Driscol. You're upsetting your missus." A fair amount of struggle went out of Bowen, even though murder still existed in his eyes. Thankfully, Austin knew exactly how to defuse the bomb, having started as a chiller when joining up with his partner. The one who calms the mark when he realizes he's been had. "All right. If you insist on fighting…" Austin said for Bowen's ears alone. "He's got a limp on his right side, the pathetic fuck. I'd go right for his knee if I were you. Exploit his weakness."

As expected, Bowen's irritation was handily transferred to Austin. "I don't need to fight dirty to *win*."

"It was merely a suggestion." When Bowen shrugged off Connor's restraining grip and returned to Sera, Austin lifted an eyebrow at the new guy. "Congratulations, you're the new heat merchant in the group. Up until five minutes ago, it was me they hated most."

"Don't worry," Polly said, perching at the edge of a chair and crossing her legs. "That hasn't changed for me."

"If you're all finished ruining my morning, I'd like to get this meeting started." Derek's voice demanded everyone's attention, even though he sounded flat-out bored as he studied the contents of a manila folder. "I don't have a case to assign just yet, but I've got something brewing. So stay close and keep your phones on."

"Don't tell me you brought us down here for a meet-and-greet," Austin muttered. "I could have made plans."

Derek didn't look up from his file. "Oh yeah? To do what?"

"Criminal type things. Clandestine meetings, hatching nefarious plots—"

"As I was saying." Derek finally tossed down the file. "We've made it a policy to be honest with one another. Since day one, we've been open about our strengths, and it will be no different with our new addition, Henrik."

Bowen snorted. "Henrik?"

"My mother was Dutch," Henrik drawled without taking his eyes off Derek. "And I never agreed to this little trust exercise."

"When you chose the squad over jail time, that's exactly

what you did." The captain let that statement settle in the quiet room. "We're already dealing with a lack of trust, but curiosity will pull even more focus." Derek leaned back against the battered metal desk. "Henrik Vance worked under me in homicide before I was promoted. He was a good cop who made some grave mistakes and—"

"—and this is my punishment," Henrik finished, spreading his arms wide. "I don't like it any more than you do. But I'll do my job and do it well. That's *all* you need to worry about."

Erin walked over to Henrik with the doughnut box and held it out. "Touch the bear claw and I'll set you on fire. It belongs to my man." She smiled, looking more like a Girl Scout than a convicted arsonist. "Welcome to the family."

Chapter Three

Polly swirled the blue liquid in her martini glass while discreetly checking her blond wig in the nightclub's mirrored wall. Disguises weren't her thing, to say the least, but now that one of Reitman's associates had peeped her—and been choked out on her watch—she wasn't taking any chances.

Austin could have helped her with the disguise. The thought flitted through her head before she could stop it, making her grimace into the martini. He'd gotten way too close that afternoon. So close, she could still feel the imprint of his sturdy frame, his hard thighs. *Powerful* thighs. Thighs that had likely shoved open the legs of so many duped women, he'd lost count. She didn't want to recall the way they'd flexed and rubbed against her, but her third martini was eroding the mental block she'd erected.

Erected…yeah he'd done that, too. In spectacular fashion.

Polly drained the contents of her glass and set it down

on the high-top table, resolving to focus on why she'd come to Tossed, a nightclub on Chicago's Near North Side where Reitman had used his credit card several times on his last trip into town. The tabs were always criminally low, as she suspected he talked his way into free drinks like the savvy grifter he was. Hell, the research she'd done over the years suggested he could sell someone the Willis Tower.

Reitman had started as a friend to her fathers, but after he'd made off with their "investment" money, they'd confided in her the subtle ways Reitman had earned their trust. He'd bought them lunch on occasion, giving them a false sense of his financial security. He'd given them nicknames. Called them to discuss personal problems that didn't exist, to gain their sympathy. At a time when her fathers' relationship had only begun to be accepted in their suburban community, their raising of an adopted daughter still relatively taboo, Reitman's friendship had been a confidence booster. Given them a sense of hope. It was a long con that had lasted almost a full year. But in the end, her fathers were ashamed to admit, they didn't even know where their "friend" lived, how he took his coffee, or if Charles Reitman was his real name. All they had left to show for the year of opening themselves up to a stranger was an empty bank account and crushed dreams.

These bitter memories—consoling the men who'd given her a home—were what she needed to remember next time Austin tried to run game on her. She'd think of sharing a Subway sandwich among the three of them while sleeping in cheap motels. The broken disillusionment on their faces when they couldn't get Reitman to return their calls. The shame when they couldn't afford to send her on field trips with her class. Yeah. Austin was cut from the same cloth, and nothing could repair those rough edges. Edges that were deceptively smooth and inviting.

Lies. All lies.

Polly ran a hand over her wig and turned from the mirror, intending to perform another casual sweep of the bar. Then she saw him.

Charles Reitman.

He'd aged since the last picture she'd managed to get her hands on, but was still attractive in a way that would carry him to a ripe old age. If she didn't plan to kill him, that is. His black hair was threaded with silver, a complement to the laugh lines around his mouth and corners of his eyes. He wore gray suit pants and a starched white dress shirt, the image of a financial mogul out for some fun. His skin told of a recent tropical holiday, but Polly knew he used tanning beds on a regular basis. Around him, women were already taking notice of the masculine laugh, the confidence radiating from him.

A hint of what appeared to be awareness broke over his features...and then he turned and looked right at Polly. Later, she would say it was shock that rooted her to the spot, holding her legs hostage. Shock that he could feel one woman staring at him from fifty yards away, when others were watching him from a separation of mere feet. Perhaps it was her anger he felt. Whatever the reason, Polly froze. When two girls in metallic minidresses swirled past, a voice spoke up in the back of her mind. *You're the only one not moving on the dance floor. Dance. Do something.* But the fear of failure was too great. Years of preparation and she'd lost her nerve. It couldn't be happening.

Her line of vision was blocked when a man slid into her

personal space. She only caught a glimpse of his tight black T-shirt and throat tattoo before he leaned in to speak beside her ear. "In my country, women such as yourself don't stand alone for long when there is a dance floor nearby."

"I guess it's a good thing we're in Chicago," she returned, trying for a subtle peek over his shoulder toward the bar, but he was too large. A *presence*. Especially when he moved closer, obscuring her view completely. Polly lifted her right hand to shove the roadblock away, but his fingers closed around her wrist.

Slowly, the fingertips of his opposite hand brushed down the inside of her arm, stimulating the sensitive skin with such ease, she sucked in a breath. "Whoever this man is that makes you frown, he cannot do what I do."

The arrogant words, spoken in heavily accented Russian, should have made her scoff, to tell her new admirer to *get lost*. But there was a hint of warmth in his tone that drew her up short. It lit up some receptor in the back of her mind that relaxed her tense body. *Not a danger.* He'd cut through the hypnotic state she'd been in, wrapping her in undesired heat. So much heat, its potency startled her. Why didn't she feel alarmed by his proximity when they'd never met? Allowing people into her personal space had never been easy for her. Only one man had managed to chip away at the invisible wall a day at a time over six months—but she wasn't thinking about him right now. She was in the nightclub to get eyes on Reitman, and this tattooed distraction could blow her chance, if she let it. "I don't...I won't be finding out what you can do. Please move."

He laughed against her forehead, the sound dark and sensual. It bathed her face in mint, mingling with his fresh-smelling cologne. Warm rainwater. He was so *warm*, moving in front of her like they were already in bed, swaying in an almost imperceptible fashion, wetting his lips. Effortless seduction.

Her physical reaction was disconcerting, but not unfamiliar. Hadn't she felt this way just this morning? That lingering yen for rough, pulse-pounding sex with her con-man squad mate was never too far from the surface, but perhaps it was being heightened by the liquor. Perhaps a need to get Austin out of her system? Close as this man stood, in the darkness of the dance floor, she couldn't get a good look at his face. Five o'clock shadow. A nose that appeared slightly crooked, as if it had been broken once or twice. Pointless observations. After years of abstaining, this was the worst possible time to change course. She needed to get away and regroup, watch Reitman at a safe distance until she got her head together. "Excuse me."

The stranger's firm hand pressed to the small of her back, easing her forward against his body. He groaned in his throat when her breasts made contact with his stomach, the sound reverberating right down to her toes. "Dance with me, *zolotse*."

Polly started to decline. Dance? No. She had a job to do…but that note of *something* in his voice was awakening a familiar craving down deep in her bones. Finally, she succeeded in glancing over the stranger's shoulder and saw that Reitman was still watching her curiously. Whether the Russian's forward behavior was inappropriate or not, he'd done her a favor. If he hadn't shown up, she might be staring at the bar like a jackass. A dance floor would be the perfect place to observe Reitman until the time came to follow him from the club. It had nothing to do with wanting the stranger's hands on her or the odd surety that he could pinpoint where desire had built the strongest inside her. How? How did she know that? Why was she so sure? "I haven't danced since middle school, so—"

Her unfinished sentence hanging in the air, the Russian walked her backward, farther into the darkness, his jaw alongside her temple. He murmured something in his language, and even though she didn't know what his words meant, they went straight to her belly, settling and growing heavy. *Concentrate.* She needed to concentrate. But it was growing increasingly difficult to focus. She'd only drunk three martinis, and they'd been poured with a conservative hand—she shouldn't feel her inhibitions loosening with every step.

But…they *were.* And when the Russian's fingers slid just inside the top of her skirt to graze her thong, a pounding started in her chest. *Yes.*

There was no more denying that this mysterious man made her think of Austin. Same height, same masculinity, same sexual prowess. If she closed her eyes, she could pretend it was the con. She could dull the sharpest corners of the inescapable lust.

No one would ever know.

• • •

Blimey. Why hadn't she passed out yet?

Polly had to be made of steel on the inside as well as out. The sedative he'd dropped into her drink was mild, but it damn well should have required him to carry her out the back door by now. He hadn't planned on it—nor did he like going to such extremes—but he'd had no choice. Not when he'd seen the man at the bar.

His ex-partner Charles.

He should have known. Should have trusted the gut feeling he'd been encountering from day one when he started following Polly that something fucked up was 'round the bend. It had been too coincidental, seeing Charles in Chicago the night after Polly's thwarted date with the chap he'd left on the diner's bathroom floor. He hadn't wasted time wondering if Charles was Polly's reason for coming to Tossed dressed like a gorgeous, half-naked club kid, so he'd acted preemptively by doctoring her drink. Polly had no idea what she was up against with Charles, and she wouldn't be finding out, if he had to send Charles out of Chicago himself.

As soon as the sedative took effect, he would take her home, leave her safely on the couch, and spend the night planning. And wondering just what the hell Polly was about, stalking a murderous con on her night off.

If he didn't think she'd go nuclear, he would take off the damned prosthetic nose and drop the accent, so he could shake some sense into her as *Austin*. Right. He was *angry* with her. *Not* turned on. Even though the curve of her arse begged his hand to descend, to grab the flesh that mesmerized him on a daily basis. Push those parted lips wide and appease his monumental curiosity over how she would taste. Maybe slide his tongue down to her cleavage, dipping into her bra to swipe at her always-perked-up nipples.

Down, boy. Taking advantage of a pliant, starry-eyed Polly was beneath him—them—and doing so would make him a right bastard. Just a dance. He would enjoy the single dance they might ever share and try to pretend she wasn't seconds from going lights-out. Or better yet, pretending she hadn't been seconds from engaging somehow with his ex-partner, a fact that unsettled him greatly.

Polly wound her arms around his neck. "What did you call me earlier? In Russian." Austin almost cursed out loud when her curves shifted over his lap, his stomach. *Come on, babe. Go to sleep and stop looking at my mouth.* "I liked the way it sounded."

Austin breathed deeply through his nose. "This word I said...it means *my gold*."

"Hmm. Awfully personal, isn't it?" The pace of the music picked up, bass thumping in the air. Polly's eyes slid closed, and relief—and yeah, some inexcusable disappointment—spiraled through Austin...until those eyes blinked back open and her body started to move. And *sweet fuck*, did she move. Her body churned against his in a slow roll, accompanied by a flash of her eyes. Drowsy excitement. The way a woman might look the morning after several rounds of sex, but wanting to go one more time before breakfast. Only this wasn't just a woman, it was Polly, a woman who until now had only been unintentionally sexy. He hadn't come prepared to withstand her at full measure, her feminine wiles in effect and focused on him.

No, *not* him. Some strange Russian man lacking in boundaries. Austin gave himself a mental shake, trying to rid himself of the rampant jealousy that thought set loose. *Pull back.* He needed to stop absorbing the mind-melting sensation of Polly's body undulating against his and use the opportunity to find out something about her connection to Charles. If he didn't, he would regret it tomorrow, and

Polly would be in further danger. "Who is that man to you, *zolotse*?"

Her fingers played with the hair at the back of his neck. "You're awfully concerned about my business for someone who just met me."

"Perhaps you inspire concern."

Another unhurried grind of her hips against his, one that made Austin's eyes slide closed. "If you knew me, you'd know I'd take that as an insult," she breathed.

Good God. Men weren't built to be tortured like this. Or they *were*, rather. His cock had wasted no time growing long and stiff, giving Polly a place to rub, rub, *rub* with each sensual movement of her hips. His conscience was being swallowed up by the surrounding darkness, the couples around him moving in a similar fashion. A way he and Polly should *not* be moving, but he was having a difficult time getting his body to listen. He'd been dreaming of fucking her for six goddamn months, had watched her ass twitch past, heard that little breathy inhale after she sipped her tea. Witnessed the brilliance of her mind and ached to go head-to-head with her, knowing it would end with them both coming.

You might be a cheat, but you're better than this. Austin's teeth sank into his upper lip until he felt pain, but it did nothing to distract from the feel of Polly. Her tits were a revelation, swelling above the leather of her top, begging for his palms, his lips. He knew how to suction his mouth and work his tongue at the same time, knew it would dampen her panties. Christ. He really shouldn't have thought about what she was wearing beneath her skirt. White silk. He wanted her in white silk...with a string of pearls decorating the center of her backside.

Enough.

Garnering his will, Austin moved to separate their bodies, but Polly chose that moment to slip her hand up the inside of his T-shirt, her nails scoring his abdomen, his pecs. "I shouldn't be dancing with you. I'm supposed to be..." Her head turned toward the bar. "I have to go."

Austin swallowed a groan, grateful for the flare of panic that interrupted the surge of blistering heat. God, he wanted those nails on his shoulders leaving blood in their wake, but that arousing imagery was interrupted by her desire to flee. Go after Charles—something he couldn't allow. Tangling with Charles in her state was unwise in every way imaginable. And he couldn't get that close to his ex-partner or he risked being recognized, disguise or no disguise. The guy was a master, and they'd spent too much time in each other's company.

Focus, you plank.

"You would take yourself away from me so soon?" He eased Polly's hands from beneath his shirt and stepped back, gritting his teeth at the loss. "Stay with me, *zolotse*. We can just talk."

"I..." She shook her head, as if trying to clear it, but couldn't. "I should go, but..."

He hated himself just then. Would hate anyone who stifled her impressive mind for a single second. The fact that it was *he* who had done it was insufferable. *No choice. You had no choice.* When her gaze strayed to the bar again, her attention beginning to pull away, denial gripped Austin. He needed to keep her occupied until the sedative kicked in and he could remove her from the situation.

Against his better judgment, Austin brought his mouth within an inch of Polly's and backed her off the dance floor, placing them in an even darker corner. There was no denying the satisfaction that surged when her lips parted and he felt her quick little puffs of breath against his mouth. Their bodies were plastered so closely together, he swore he could feel her heart pounding double time. Or maybe it was his. He couldn't tell, nor did he have the wherewithal to guess, because he and Polly were alone for all intents and purposes. Alone and pressed together, chest to knee, mouths poised in that moment just before a kiss. That taut section below her belly button started to writhe with the music again, shifting his cock right to left, right to left. And fuck, Austin had never come close to sainthood, but the fact that he hadn't nailed her to the wall already had to qualify him.

"Why aren't you dancing?" she breathed into his mouth.

"I can't—" Accent. *Accent*. "You make concentration difficult."

Polly studied him from beneath her eyelashes. "Funny. I was going to say the same thing about you." She dipped down and dragged their hips together with a sweet, feminine moan. "It's probably because I haven't been with anyone in so long."

Fucking hell. This was it. This was where he died. "Is that so?"

"I don't know why I told you that. I'm not thinking straight."

Shame harpooned him, enough that he pulled his mouth away from the perfection of her. Over the years, he'd become quite adept at numbing the feeling of shame, but he couldn't seem to accomplish it around Polly. Austin swallowed heavily and let out a rush of unrehearsed words beside her ear. "Let me think for both of us."

After a moment wherein he held his breath, she nodded, and the foreign good intentions she'd inspired in him solidified. He'd come here to save her from herself, and now he'd have to pull double duty. Keep her safe and resist her body when she wasn't in full possession of her faculties. Just a little longer. *Just until you can get her out of here.*

Austin braced both hands on the wall above her head. "You touch. I won't touch back. Even if it's all I'm thinking about."

She appeared to absorb their position for a second, those luscious tits lifting and falling between them, driving him fucking mad. Then she took him off guard by wrapping a leg around his waist. Thank God the loud music disguised his vile curse, because it wasn't in character. It was all Austin now, discerning the shape of her pussy through his jeans. Sweating under his shirt with the effort of staying still when his neglected sex drive shouted *fuck her.*

"You remind me of someone I'm not supposed to want."

The rushing of testosterone inside him whipped faster until it moved in a frenzy. *She means me. No.* No way he could beat this. "Don't. Don't tell me his name."

A line formed between her brows at his odd command. "Austin," she whimpered. "Touch me, Aus—"

He broke, lunging forward until their lips were interlocked. "You need to be touched by Austin?"

Her whispered reply might as well have been a shout. "Yes."

Austin savored the single damning word before bringing their mouths together in an imitation of fucking, more impassioned than anything he'd ever been a part of in his life. Without pretending. Without games. For the first time in his life, someone had wanted *him* instead of the mask he wore, and that revelation pounded in his temples. The leg around his waist tightened and he growled into her mouth, shoving her roughly up against the wall, thrusting his hips up into the cradle of her thighs. They both broke away from the kiss on a groan that melded together, taking the place of the club's music and ingraining itself in his brain forever. The sound was desperation and pleasure...and relief. For a fleeting moment, he thought he might have the strength to pull away and do the right thing, but every thought fled when Polly went up on her toes and bore down on his cock with a swivel of her hips.

"*Fuck.*" His accent broke again. *Maintain. Have to maintain.* "Give me permission to lift your skirt in back. You will feel my hands and you will love, P—" He cut himself off before uttering her name. "So beautiful. I must touch you. Please, you've made me so hard, *zolotse*. It's only fair that you feel it."

"You don't seem the type to ask for permission," she said, her thoughtful tone demanding his attention, almost as handily as the way she circled on him like a lap dancer. "D-do you like women who tell you what to do?"

A pulse point he hadn't been aware of flared to life deep in his stomach, his knees dipping under the onslaught of anticipation. Sex for him had been a means to an end for so long, he'd built a dam. That had to be why he felt something give way and break at the idea of being told what to do. *By Polly.* His blood raced at the idea of it. Austin didn't have time to answer—what in bloody hell would he say?—before she curled her fingers in the hem of his T-shirt and tugged the material up his chest.

"I want to see you."

The look on her face intoxicated him. He worked hard to keep himself in peak physical condition—a con's appearance was his greatest asset—but seeing arousal color her cheeks almost sank him to the ground. The higher she lifted the shirt, the harder she breathed until his own breath raced past hers, wheezing from his lungs. When the material was lifted all the way to his neck, she blinked up at him, as if unsure. "Anything. Do it all," Austin said, without thinking.

She stuffed the T-shirt's hem into his mouth. Her eyes widened, as if surprised by her own actions, which turned him on even more, if such a thing were possible. It gave him the odd intuition that they were making the same discovery. With his chest completely bare, his cock pressing against the fly of his jeans for her inspection, he replaced his hands on the wall above her head, stayed still, and let her look.

This. She needs control.

Polly reached for his pecs with a featherlight touch, tracing them down to his navel with such sensual intention, he moaned around the T-shirt.

"Press yourself against me like this. Your skin…"

Austin dipped and fused their bodies together. The leather of her top felt incredible against his chest, her skirt brushing his belly. More. Need *more*. He needed them naked from the waist down, barriers of clothing torn away. With Polly wedged between him and the wall so tightly, the ownership he felt multiplied. Or maybe she owned him. Both possibilities were blinding in their perfection. He grasped the knee of her leg still wrapped around his waist, letting his fingers slide down to her hip where they could twist in her thong. She liked that...her breath shuddering out, body writhing. Giving her any form of pleasure made him feel exultant, so he twisted the lace again.

Her response was to rip the T-shirt from his mouth and demand a kiss with her eyes. Her undulating body. Austin was frantic to oblige her, stamping his lips down onto hers with a growl that only intensified when she moved her pussy in a whip-tight circle, rocking his world on its axis. The thong ripped in his hand, but he barely noticed because Polly's hands slid into the back of his jeans, tugging him closer into the endless temptation of her body. Christ. Jesus Christ.

"You going to spread your thighs for me against the wall, babe?" His tongue swept into her mouth, tasting, consuming. He breathed for the both of them, refusing to stop the kiss. Lost to it. Starbursts blinked behind his eyes, warning him he needed oxygen or he might have gone on devouring her, fucking her through the rough denim of his jeans forever. "Haven't been with anyone in a while. Is that right? Neither have I, because I've been waiting for this." His hand found her backside and kneaded the smooth flesh, lifting her off the floor and onto his cock, making them both moan. "You want to order me around? Tell me what to do with my cock, where to put it, how fast to pump it? God, babe, don't make me wait any longer."

When her body stilled, horror dawned. *Sod it.* He'd completely dropped character. Totally cracked. Impossible. Only it *wasn't* impossible, because Polly had filled his head, refusing to allow anything else in, including his goddamn conscience. Even now, he was praying she would be as taken by need as him and keep going. Let him give her pleasure.

God, he was an inexcusable bastard. Her eyes were half mast as she looked up at him, mouth still red from his kiss. Seconds from losing consciousness. *No.* He'd never justified his actions to anyone, but it was imperative at that moment. Unfortunately, she moved before he figured out what the hell to say.

Keeping her attention locked on him, she reached into his right pocket and pulled out the tea bag he'd placed there. "Motherfucker."

Austin caught her just before she could hit the floor. With her final expression of betrayal imprinting itself on his memory to haunt him for life, Austin tucked Polly gently into his side, bringing her feet off the ground as he slid through the emergency exit, lifting her into his arms with ease when they landed in the alley.

"I'm so sorry, sweet."

Chapter Four

Polly sat at her usual Denny's booth, palms flat on the table, staring down at the tea bag in front of her. The waitress had brought her a cup of hot water and left, but that had been half an hour ago, so steam no longer rose from the mug. She didn't remember her three-block walk to the diner, nothing really beyond waking up sprawled on her couch with the tea bag still clutched in her fist.

This. *This* was what stark humiliation felt like. After what she'd seen her fathers go through at the hands of Charles Reitman, she'd sworn never to be had. Never to be conned or have her decisions dictated by another person. Having that person be Austin Shaw was the stuff of nightmares. Worse…she really hadn't thought he'd had it in him. Sure, they bantered back and forth. Sure, there was no love lost between them. But underneath the layers of contempt, a modicum of respect must have been reserved with his name on it, because she still couldn't *believe* he'd drugged her.

She hated that it hurt. He'd divested her of the ability to function physically or mentally, and a smart man like him knew what a hard pill that would be for her to swallow. Said pill was currently stuck in her throat like a prickly pinecone. Because as pissed as she was at Austin, she was angrier with herself for letting her guard down, two consecutive nights.

And that fact was still a distant second to her having enjoyed those stolen moments on the dark dance floor.

Enjoyed. Ha.

Polly's mouth became so parched, she couldn't swallow. With shaking fingers, she reached for the tea bag and dunked it into the lukewarm water. She cast a glance around the half-empty diner, positive everyone could see residual lust coming off her body like steam. Until now, she'd hidden inside the excuse that shunning the physical attraction between her and Austin was necessary so he wouldn't *win*. She'd prided herself on being able to resist him when he was accustomed to getting everything he wanted so easily, with a few practiced lines and a smile. Apparently she'd been lying to herself, because even with his incredible looks neatly disguised, she'd been scored by fire the moment he touched her.

There had been a moment that morning while piecing the previous night's events together where she'd placed the blame for her enthusiastic participation in their dance-floor make-out session on the sedative. But as her head cleared beneath the shower spray, she'd felt it. Desire climbing up her thighs and setting up shop in her stomach, tickling out like a fistful of feathers. Even now, recalling the way he'd planted his hands above her and let her *look*, biceps flexing against the backdrop of the writhing dance floor. The way he'd groaned at her exploring touch. His...his stiff, protruding erection.

Yeah. Austin might have been playing a part—for what reason, she intended to find out—but there'd been no pretense on either of their parts during the kissing.

You want to order me around?

Polly took a long sip of cold tea, a paltry attempt to cool herself down. That question, posed with such gruff desperation, haunted her. Made her insides vibrate like a tuning fork. What would it be like to wield control over a man like Austin? She'd never attempted to impose her will in bed, except for a few rare occasions when she'd dipped her toe in and been greeted with laughter. There was no shaking the bone-deep intuition that Austin would respond the way she'd once fantasized about a man doing, but had never experienced. The way his eyes had slid closed when she shoved the T-shirt into his mouth...the memory had Polly crossing her legs together and swallowing a groan.

What. A bastard. For taking a chunk out of her pride. For making her want him even more. For knowing exactly the buttons to push. How? How had he known what would make him infinitely more irresistible to her?

She meant to give Austin straight-up hell as soon as she shook the heavy cloak of humiliation. Other than the shame living in her gut just knowing that he'd bested her, the only thing keeping her from tracking Austin down right this moment—before the sun had even completely risen—was the fact that she'd been fully clothed upon waking. If he'd removed so much as one high heel, it would be lodged in the side of his neck by now.

That satisfying image popped like a bubble when Erin fell into the booth across the table, lifted her hands like she'd just won an Olympic race, and shouted, "*Pancakes!*"

"Good morning to you, too." Polly lifted her mug of tea for another sip, but grimaced and set it back down. "You know, they hate us in here. Between you setting napkins on fire and me having a staring contest with the wall, we're bound to be voted off the Denny's island sooner or later."

"Listen to me very carefully." Erin leaned forward. "Is the wall talking back yet? I can coach you through this."

Polly considered saying yes, just so Erin could distract her with imaginary wall communication instructions, but she shook her head. "So far, it's giving me the silent treatment."

"Consider yourself lucky."

The waitress approached the table and refilled Polly's tea mug with steaming water. Polly gave a grateful nod and refocused on Erin, who was silently mouthing *pancakes* at the server. "What are you doing out of bed this early?"

Erin shrugged. "I heard you leaving and wanted a short stack. Slipped out without waking up Connor." Grinning, she rubbed her hands together. "He's going to hate that."

Polly lifted an eyebrow. "And that makes you gleeful?"

"No, I just like the reminder that I've still got it."

"I don't think your ability to escape undetected was ever in question," Polly said, wishing she had another tea bag. Just another reason to want to punch Austin in the nut sack at the first opportunity. "Although I'm sure Connor wishes you were slightly less adept at sneaking out."

"He understands. Most of the time." The blonde's forehead wrinkled. "Plus, when I give him the slip, he knows I'll let him tie me up later to make up for it."

"You know, that was far more information than I needed."

Erin craned her neck to look at the kitchen, obviously searching for her pancakes. "You probably already hacked into his bank account and saw the multiple trips to Home Depot." She produced a lighter from her pocket and flicked on the flame. "*J'accuse.*"

"Are we speaking French now?" Polly hid her laugh with a cough. "I suppose anything is better than Russian."

The waitress set a plate full of pancakes in front of Erin, eyeballing the still-lit lighter as she did so. "Anything else?"

"Yes, please. A Lumberjack Slam to go. For my man." Erin looked smug as she reached for the syrup. "Coincidentally, 'lumberjack slam' is the name of what he's got planned for later, so don't come a' knockin'."

"I'll do my best to resist."

They sat in silence while Erin took her first few bites of pancakes, until the blonde finally spoke, gesturing toward Polly with her syrupy fork. "You're still wearing your fake eyelashes from last night."

Polly didn't so much as flinch. "Last night?"

Erin chuckled. "Okay, if that's how you want to play it." Another bite of pancake. Another long chew-filled pause. "I heard two sets of footsteps in the hallway last night and saw Austin carrying you inside. That's the real reason I'm here so early. I was…worried. Not a good look for me, Banks."

Every once in a while, Polly was reminded that Erin was far more astute than she allowed the world to believe. Usually, when Erin decided to drop that knowledge on someone, it amused Polly. Or gave her an odd sense of pride. But being on the receiving end of that perception sucked. It also made her wonder what else Erin knew. "Did you talk to him?"

A slim hesitation, before Erin started to sing under her breath. "Not last night, but the night before…twenty-four robbers came knocking at my door…"

"Erin, stop evading."

She stabbed her fork into the pancakes, leaving it standing upright as she fell back against the leather booth. "This is why friendship is bullshit. I wish I'd never met you."

"Fair enough. Just tell me what you know."

"I didn't mean that. It was the syrup talking." Erin flipped the lighter over in her hand. "Austin made me set off your smoke alarm the other night. I don't know why, so don't quiz me. He said you were in trouble, so I did it. And it was fun, if you want to know the truth."

Polly's molars ground together until pain shot through her jaw. God, the embarrassment just kept on giving. After last night, how the hell hadn't she put Austin at the scene of an unconscious Slim? Polly was bombarded with realizations, flying toward her from all corners. He'd been following her longer than one night. Did he really think she was in danger? How could he when no one was privy to Polly's plans but herself? "What did he promise you in exchange?"

"A Ruger." Erin pouted. "And thanks to my new, inconvenient conscience, I won't be able to accept it. So *thanks.*"

"Forgive my lack of guilt." Polly stuck her pinkie into the mug of tea, wishing it were hot enough to burn. "Next time you see an unknown man carrying my passed-out body down the hallway, alert the cavalry, will you?"

"It wasn't an unknown man. It was Austin."

"How did you know it was Austin? He was wearing a disguise."

Erin ran her tongue across the front of her teeth. "The way he looked at you."

Polly's hand crept up to her throat before she forced it down into her lap. "How is tha— Never mind. I don't want to know."

"Yes, you do." Erin squished her lips together and wiggled them like a fish. "Remember prison?"

Discomfort invaded, but she squashed it back into her mental filing cabinet. "It's hard to forget."

"*Iknowright?*" Erin made a humming noise. "You know those days when other prisoners would get paroled? Everyone else has to stand in the yard and watch them get loaded onto the bus…on their way to freedom."

"Yeah, I remember those days."

Erin nodded as the waitress dropped off her to-go order. "That's how Austin looks at you. Like maybe *you* are the freedom and he's still stuck in the prison yard."

Polly looked away quickly before Erin could see the alarm she felt transforming her features. She wished she could crack open her skull and remove that inconvenient information. She didn't want to *know.* How could she ever feel him watching her again and not replay those words? They couldn't be true, anyway. This was one of those times where Erin's perceptiveness had failed and the crazy had crept in. "I'm no one's freedom, except my own. From now on…" She reached over and took a forkful of Erin's pancakes. "Please don't aid Austin in ruining my plans."

Erin's expression was grave. "What *are* your plans? Why do they require those eyelashes? Are you moonlighting as a Liza Minnelli impersonator?" She ran a single finger over her own black lashes. "If so, it's more serious than I thought."

Polly was saved having to lie or even worse—spill the truth—when Connor blew into Denny's like a category five hurricane. He grumbled something to the hostess and advanced on their table. Erin's lips lifted into a smile, even though she hadn't seen him, being that her back was to the entrance. "Saved by the SEAL."

Connor stopped at the end of their table. "A note next time, Erin. I'm only asking for a note."

"I left a lipstick kiss on the mirror."

The surly ex-street enforcer was not impressed by his girlfriend's statement. He crooked a slow finger at her. "We're going."

"Home Depot isn't open this early, baby," Erin complained, but contentment and pleasure were evident in every line of her body. She handed Connor the to-go bag and launched herself onto his back, giving Polly a thumbs-up on the way out of the restaurant. "Go with God, Liza."

Polly waited for Connor and Erin to leave the restaurant before she blew out the breath she'd been holding, peeling off the false eyelashes. The conversation with Erin had given her a lot to think about, filled her with restless energy. First order of business? Track down a certain elusive Brit and obtain a satisfying explanation for his underhanded actions. And make damn sure no other satisfaction was garnered in the process. She'd faced fiercer obstacles than Austin Shaw.

When Polly realized her fingers were pressed to her lips, the lips that had been moving in a frantic coupling with Austin's just hours before, she curled them into a tight fist.

Oh, yes. It was high time to regain the upper hand. Starting this morning.

Chapter Five

Austin unlocked the fifth and final lock of his one-bedroom flat in Lincoln Park and pushed open the door with a weary hand. Exhaustion weighed on his shoulders, so heavy that if he had the energy to turn his head, he would probably find them decorated with lead parrots. He'd gone far longer than one night without sleep in the past, but it appeared his gluttony for punishment knew no bounds at this particular juncture of his life.

It had been a terrible idea, going to see his daughter after what had taken place with Polly. *Any* day of the week, he had zero business being anywhere in the vicinity of three-year-old Gemma Klausky, red-headed ballerina dancer… and illegitimate offspring of an international grifter. The product of a con gone terribly wrong. His greatest shame, while simultaneously being his foremost pride. Pride he had no goddamn right to feel, since he'd played no part in her upbringing. He merely caught glimpses of her from behind newspapers or through shop windows, when he felt the need to punish himself for his unforgivable lapse in judgment one night in São Paulo. A night not so long ago, but one that felt ten years in the past, probably because finding out he'd created a child with his then-mark had thrown his guilt-free existence into a tailspin. What had followed with his partner, Charles, the betrayal...well, he hadn't quite recaptured his ability to give zero fucks since then, and it wasn't for lack of trying.

Yes, guilt was a cruel mistress he wished would shove off, right enough. The old bat had put quite a damper on his lifestyle, hadn't she? Furthermore, he'd let her. After São Paulo, his cons had grown steadily less organized. More spontaneous, almost as if he'd wanted to get caught. And he had. By one Captain Derek Tyler.

Austin's being in Chicago hadn't been a coincidence. A hired investigator had passed on Gemma and her mother's whereabouts to him, a moment still crystallized in his mind. He'd met the investigator at a public park in New York City, could still remember the manila folder being handed over. The feel of it in his hand, accompanied by the knowledge that once he opened it, he couldn't go back. As he'd flipped open the file and seen pictures of his daughter for the first time, the irony of a group of nearby children playing hide-and-seek hadn't been lost on him.

It had taken him over a year to leave New York and venture to Chicago, but he'd wasted no time writing bad checks. Putting a target on his back. His actions hadn't been conscious at the time, but looking back with twenty-twenty vision, Austin knew what he'd been about. Getting caught meant he wouldn't be able to leave Chicago. He'd be forced to remain and face his mistakes. If that wasn't pathetic and twisted, he didn't know what was.

He'd met Derek on the afternoon of his arrest in an interrogation room with abysmal lighting and the stench of decaying cold cuts. It had been impossible to lump the captain in with his gray surroundings, however. With the opening line of, "You're too good to write a shit check. What gives?" Derek had earned his respect. Not only because his staunch observation had been so damn true—he *was* good— Derek had been smart enough to stroke his ego without them exchanging a single word. *Not bad.* He'd signed on for the undercover squad that same day, giving him proximity to his estranged daughter and the chance to assuage his damnable guilt.

Little did he know he would walk into their first meeting and find Polly, a temptress with brains to complete the gorgeous package. Rosy of lip and porcelain of cheek. Wide brown eyes and a backside that she appeared to be *presenting*, no matter her position. Sitting, leaning, bending. An arse that begged to be dealt with. Rather surprisingly, however, since last night, he'd made the switch from dealing with Polly to…Polly dealing with *him*.

He knew his brilliant mind well enough to know the score. Getting between pretty Polly's legs had been his objective since day one, and last night, she'd handed him the necessary means to get there. Control. Really, it should have occurred to him before now that Polly wasn't a submissive woman. What surprised him was his response to her preferences. He…liked the idea when it came to her. Quite a lot.

Austin realized he'd been standing poised in his entryway for several long minutes and cursed. After locking all five dead bolts, he unbuttoned his black overcoat, shrugged it off, and hung it on the back of the door. Despite his exhaustion, thoughts of a demanding Polly dressed in an abbreviated Snow White costume had roused his cock, and it needed tending. On his way to the bathroom, Austin unzipped his jeans, unable to wait for that first, blessed stroke.

"God, yes," Austin grated, closing his eyes to welcome his newest recurring fantasy. One that had plagued him since last night. Polly standing above where he knelt, her fingers snagged in his hair.

"Would you like to touch me, Austin?"

"Yes." Even in his own fantasy, he sounded winded. Starved. *"Yes, I want to touch every goddamn inch."*

"Good." She rewarded him with a simple brush of her thumb across his forehead, but somehow her approval made his cock thicken. More. He had to have more. "Tell me where you'd like to touch."

He leaned closer, let his breath drift over her silky white panties. She was bare underneath, he could tell thanks to the tight, sheer material guarding her pussy. Her sweet, smooth pussy. "Between your legs."

Her grip tightened in his hair until he winced. "What's the magic word?"

"Please. I need to satisfy you."

Austin groaned as he walked into the dark bathroom, not bothering to turn on the light. A few more jerks of his cock and he'd be able to think, figure out what the hell to do about real-life Polly and the clusterfuck he'd created last night. Ah God, she was letting him lick her delicious flesh now, yanking his head away periodically to torture him, forcing him to look and not taste —

The smell of lemonade had Austin's hand pausing in its movements. His eyes flew open to find Polly perched on his bathroom sink, her fingers wrapped around a red Beretta. "For the love of God, control yourself, Shaw."

When presented with an intruder holding a gun, he didn't stop to ask questions. Nor did he care about the identity of said weapon wielder. He'd never classified Polly as a threat before, but having experienced the sting of betrayal in the past, his nature had him lunging for the gun. Her gasp told him that response was unexpected, but she recovered quickly, fighting him for a grip.

"Drop the gun." He issued the order through clenched teeth. "I find the idea of hurting you distasteful."

She twisted her body, an attempt to regain control of the Beretta. "I can't believe you don't have the decency to put your dick away before charging at me."

Call him sick, call him whatever you liked, he loved Polly talking about his dick in any capacity. *Look at it. Want it.* "I'm the furthest thing from decent."

"No shit." They were breathing heavily, inches from each other's mouths. And hell if the swollen bastard between his thighs didn't react favorably to having her close, even though she *might* have come there to murder him in cold blood. Pity, his cock didn't deal in semantics.

"One last chance, Banks. Drop the gun or I'll take it away from you."

She pretended to think about it. "See, I'm not really in the mood to cry uncle."

"Are you in the mood to cry Austin? Now *that* could be interesting." She attempted to jerk the Beretta away again, giving him no choice but to dig his thumb into the pressure point on her wrist, releasing her grip automatically. "There now." Keeping his attention trained on Polly, he placed the gun out of her reach on an overhead shelf. "That wasn't so difficult, was—"

Her freed fist drilled him in the stomach. A grunt burst past his lips, but masculine pride kept him standing upright. Well, masculine pride and another fist flying in his direction, this time at his head. He shot a hand out to intercept the punch, using the grip to drag Polly off the sink and twist her arm behind her back.

"Aiming for this moneymaker face, sweet?" He clucked his tongue. "Now that's just cruel."

"Let me go," she demanded, her voice vibrating with anger. Although he detected more embarrassment than anything else. He'd never seen her anything but confident. Ready for a challenge. It didn't sit well that he'd scored her pride, so he let go of her arm. He had questions that needed answering, though, so as soon as he refastened his pants—not an easy feat when his cock still stood at attention—Austin pressed her body back against the sink, blocking both avenues of escape with his arms.

"How did you find my address? I've made it impossible."

Some of her confidence returned in the form of a chin lift. Jesus, he would've liked to see that chin pointed toward the ceiling as she wailed for more tongue. "You should know by now that nothing is impossible for me." Intelligence glimmered in her eyes. "I know you asked Derek to pay you by money order. I tracked the last several serial numbers to four different check-cashing places in the neighborhood." Her shrug appeared grudging. "That was smart, not using the same place consistently. But I was able to pinpoint your general location down to a three-block radius, nonetheless. This building is the only one not run by a professional management company, and the most likely to rent without a proper credit check and accept cash deposits."

It took an effort, but Austin managed to hide the chest-expanding awe she'd inspired. "And my apartment number? How did you manage to glean that information, my hot little sleuth?"

"I'm not *your* anything, Shaw." She narrowed her gaze. "And your buzzer has the name I.M. The Tits on it."

One corner of his mouth lifted. "Thank you for saying so."

Polly flattened her palms on his chest and pushed, but he refused to budge. Austin knew what was coming next, and they were having this conversation face-to-face, where he could witness her reactions. And fuck the nonsense, he loved being pressed up against her, loved being close enough to see the pulse dancing at the base of her neck, loved inhaling the comforting smell of lemonade. When she left, how long would the scent linger?

Austin frowned, not wanting to think about her departing just yet. Odd, when he'd never brought anyone to his apartment before. Not in Chicago. Not anywhere. He should be worried about making sure his location was secure after her breaching it, but instead, he only wanted to hash out what was sure to be an explosive discussion. Good thing he'd stowed his manhood securely away in preparation for battle.

She pushed up on her toes, and even though she was still at a ten-inch height disadvantage, her fury was formidable.

"What do *you* have to frown about? Did someone drug and take advantage of *you* last night?"

Remorse swarmed in his rib cage like bees. His first time kissing Polly and she believed it had been the drug's influence that caused her to wrap around him like ivy. Brilliant. Once he cleared up her misconception, they could continue. Austin leaned in and watched her pulse go wonky. "It was only meant to be a dance. Not even a full song. But you're too stubborn to pass out when you're bloody well supposed to." His attention fell to her parted lips. "Us making a meal of each other was independent of my mission."

Fireworks lit up her eyes like New Year's Eve. "I apologize for not adjusting to your plan. Mind telling me what it was?" Polly's tits heaved at her neckline, but Austin valued his hide, so he didn't give them more than a swift, appreciative glance. Okay, two appreciative glances. One for each sweet little globe. "Notice I referred to your plan in the past tense. Your interference is not welcome."

"You're getting it nonetheless, I'm afraid."

"*Why?*"

He blew out a breath, ruffling her hair. "You won't like the answer."

"It's safe to say you're right," she said on a burst of laughter. "Tell me anyway."

His balls had grown tight at the sound of her laughter, so he took a moment to center himself. Polly didn't laugh at his jokes, but he'd heard her laugh with Erin on occasion. The sound was musical, so at odds with her no-nonsense personality, it always caught him off guard. It aroused him while giving him an odd, incomplete feeling in his chest because *he* never brought it out of her. Not the happy kind, anyway. And today would be no different. "Whatever crusade you've chosen here, you're well out of your league, Banks." He cursed when she flinched. "If one of those men found you in *their* bathroom with a weapon, there wouldn't be a subsequent conversation."

"You're such a saint," she whispered, her lips barely moving.

"I'm well aware I'm much closer to Satan." He rolled his right shoulder. "Just not close enough to stand by while you get pulled into something you don't understand and can't control."

"Maybe it's worth the risk."

Frustration walloped him between the shoulder blades. "The risk being your *life*, Polly? Are you mad?"

"I came to Chicago to achieve something. Am I risking my life? Could I lose my spot on the team and gain one in the prison yard? Yes and yes. It doesn't change my mind."

They squared off a moment, wherein Austin reeled from her casual revelation that she would risk her very well-being for some cause.

"How do you know Slim?" she finally asked.

"*Who?*" Austin shouted.

An impatient noise sounded in her throat. "The man you dropped at the diner the night before last. Do you leave a lot of men unconscious on the floors of public restrooms?"

"It's been an age." When Polly sputtered, he laid a finger over her mouth, satisfied when her luscious body stilled against him, softened a few degrees. *Yes.* She wasn't immune to him, much as she tried to portray it. It would have been *perfect* to kiss her then, but if he used her attraction to his advantage before, what came next? It might be the last time she allowed his mouth in the same room with hers, let alone allowed him to gain more access to it. "Did Erin tell you I took the bollocks out of commission or was that a lucky guess?"

"Erin."

"Damn." He smiled to hide the stab of disappointment. "And here I thought I'd duped at least one person in Chicago into thinking me more than an unredeemable opportunist."

Polly peered up at him, as if she could read his thoughts. "If it makes you feel any better, I don't think she wanted to tell me."

Did he care? Discomfort blinked on the horizon, so Austin cleared his throat and moved on. "That man's name isn't Slim. I know *of* him. I also know *of* the man you tracked to the club last night, and you don't want to tangle with the likes of them. They're deadly, Polly. They protect their interests at all costs."

He watched the half truth sink in with a mixture of dread and resignation. Dread that would multiply if she ever found out the truth about his partnership with Charles. Resignation because he had no choice but to lie by omission. If he had a hope in hell of keeping Polly alive, she needed to trust him, just a speck.

"I..."

She shifted against him, her throat working in a way that told Austin she was suppressing her emotions. Lord, he wished she wouldn't. Wished she would lay it all on him so he could sort through.

"I don't like you, Austin, but I didn't think you ran in the same circle as murderers. I'm kind of disappointed in myself for not assuming."

He opened his mouth to tell her he'd never murdered a soul, but he stopped before the words could emerge. Polly would see right through him, and he'd lose whatever minuscule ground he'd gained by watching her back. "Listen, Polly. Whatever I've done in the past...I only want to help you now." Good God, he sounded like a man who presented women with stuffed animals and the like. "And obviously, my help is very valuable. You'd do well to accept it."

The look she blasted him with was pure...seduction? At once, his body went rigid with want, testosterone flooding his bloodstream. Ready to please, ready to *get* pleased in return. It occurred to him on some distant level that Polly was about to play him—that she'd only been acting wounded over his revelation, pretending to be shocked at his former associations...and he didn't give a single goddamn. He dampened his lips and brought their hips together. *Go on, sweet. Play me, so I can fuck you against the sink.*

"Your help is valuable, Austin?"

The husky quality of her voice made him growl. "Yes. My help, among other, more satisfying things. Say the word and you'll have the benefit of both."

Polly let her hands roam up his chest, the sides of his neck, and higher, where they tangled in his hair. "That man at the bar..."

"Yes, sweet."

"Tell me how to kill him."

Chapter Six

Polly had never said the words out loud before. *Tell me how to kill him.* And the moment they were out in the open, blinking like a trashy neon sign, she wanted to gobble them back up. That had to be a typical reaction, though. Didn't it? Revealing your intention to take an eye for an eye to another soul surely created room for doubt. Although she and Austin worked in close quarters, they'd managed to maintain an emotional distance. With the utterance of her dark request, she'd jumped feet first into…more. Infinitely more.

A mixture of impatience and nerves swept Polly head to toe as Austin stared down at her. Even with those sharp eyes scrutinizing her, his face was a blank canvas, making it impossible to tell what he was thinking. Would he agree to help or tell her she was crazy? Hell, maybe she *was* crazy. Maybe the grief of what had happened all those years ago had turned her into the type of woman who casually discussed extinguishing another human being. She didn't *want* to be that woman, but the injustice couldn't *stand*. Reitman couldn't just get away with tearing lives apart, tearing down something so *good* and going on his merry way.

Despite what she'd said to Austin, she was well aware what the Brit was capable of. He wasn't the only one in the dark bathroom adept at reading people. Finding out he knew Reitman, though. Now *that* had come as a shock. That connection between Austin and Reitman could provide her with valuable information. Maybe even get her in the same room with Reitman where she could demand recompense for the wrong done to her family.

"What do you have against Reitman?" Austin said, finally. "If you want my help, I need to know the particulars."

"I didn't say I wanted your help," Polly rushed to say. She had no intention of becoming a con, stooping to Reitman's level. Wouldn't that defeat the entire purpose? "I asked you to teach me. Tell me his weaknesses. Anything I can use."

Austin's laughter was hollow. "Use me and cut me out. That's your intention."

"Nailed it."

He tilted his head, let his gaze run down the side of her neck. "And is it also your intention to seduce information out of me, sweet?"

An invisible belt cinched around Polly's middle. Having this discussion while pressed together was ill-advised. His erection lay trapped between their bodies, reminding her how he'd looked upon walking into the bathroom, before he'd seen her. Not the polished, controlled con she'd come to know. No, he'd been a…beast. Jaw clenched, grunting as he pumped his own flesh. The sight of him performing such a personal act with such base lust on his handsome features wouldn't leave her. Each time the moving image arose, she grew damper between her clenched thighs.

Is it also your intention to seduce information out of me?

Could she? Could she exchange her body for valuable insight into the life of her nemesis? This was a dirty, dog-eat-dog world she'd insinuated herself into…perhaps it had only been a matter of time before her most personal morals were compromised.

"I ought to acquaint your pretty arse with my palm for considering it, Polly," Austin grated. She reddened at his angry statement, started to answer, but gasped instead when his teeth closed around her neck in a light bite, then licked a path down to her collarbone. "You should know better than to offer such a tempting exchange to the likes of me." He boosted her onto the sink in one fluid movement, without removing his mouth from her body. "My scruples are in short supply."

Polly couldn't get a decent breath. God, his mouth…the way he bumped and dragged against her as he spoke. She was falling victim to his trappings, and with each passing second, she turned more willing. "How do I know you'll keep your word and help me?" Her voice was thready, unstable. "I need a guarantee, before—"

Austin's hands gripped her knees, squeezing. She was still reeling from the effect of his intimate touch when her legs were wrenched wide. He ran his forehead across her cleavage and she could feel his attention stray to the vee between her thighs. "If I made you a guarantee"—his tone had dipped, turned rich and glossy—"would you believe me?"

"No," she whispered.

His head came up, his heavy-lidded eyes focusing on her. "We are at an impasse, then. A dreadful place to be, when I'd like to be bending you forward over the sink and taking advantage of all that wetness I've inspired." He regarded her like a meal, looking for an ideal place to dig in. "Are you a screamer, Polly? I wager you try to keep the sound trapped, but those lips were made to be accommodating." Masculine fingers caged her jaw. "You'd open them nice and wide for me, wouldn't you, sweet?"

Polly jerked her jaw from his grip, simultaneously pissed off and—dammit—*turned on* like never before. When he gave an imperceptible nod, almost in deference to her outrage, she realized he'd been goading her.

He removed his touch from her knees. She pretended not to see his hands curl into shaking fists before they were shoved in his front pockets. "I never negotiate in the bathroom. It's bad luck." He retrieved the gun from above her head with a censorious look and stepped backward toward the door. "The kitchen will suit well enough."

When Austin turned and strode from the room, Polly's mouth fell open. Remembering Austin's taunt, however, she snapped it closed immediately. What had just happened here? He hadn't exactly turned down the offer of sex in exchange for information, but his actions dictated that he'd done just that. There had to be a catch, and she could admit to being curious. And grudgingly impressed that he'd walked away when she'd been able to feel his need, straining between them.

She covered her face with clammy hands and breathed deeply. If the last twenty minutes had proven anything, it was the imperativeness of keeping her head around Austin. She'd thought him lost to the same chemical reaction she was experiencing, when all along he'd been searching for cracks in her exterior, advantages. His instant transformation back into smug con had proved that.

Polly slid off the sink onto wobbly legs and went to join Austin. Just outside the bathroom, a locked door distracted her. She'd noticed it on the way in, but hadn't wanted to waste time attempting to pick the lock. What was on the other side? She turned to find Austin watching her from the kitchen, a teakettle in one hand. "I wouldn't attempt to enter that room if I were you. It leads to a terrifying parallel universe."

"Funny, I thought I was trapped inside one already."

With a twist of his wrist, he turned on the flame beneath the kettle. "Because I turned down your martyr's proposition of sex, you mean."

The kitchen was absent of anywhere to sit, empty save a toaster and frozen clock, so Polly leaned back against the wall. "I guess you could say that."

"Good news, then." He removed two white mugs from the cabinet. "As I'm not a complete idiot, Polly, I didn't turn it down."

She despised the lust that tickled her belly. "I don't understand."

He paced halfway across the kitchen in her direction, crossing his arms as he considered her. "I have no problem admitting that I value pleasure. Or that I choose pleasure over supposed happiness. When you're experiencing pleasure, you know it. Happiness is too vague a notion and a fleeting one, if you manage to experience it."

She didn't know how to respond to such rare honesty from Austin, so she stayed silent and waited for him to explain his point.

"Pleasure is what I want from you...from your body," Austin continued in a gruff tone. "But for some elusive reason, I will also derive pleasure from your safety. So I will find a way to accomplish both. Are we on the same page?"

"Yes," Polly answered slowly. "But I'm not sure I want to be."

His smile was pure, lethal charm. "That's why we're negotiating, sweet."

God, he was dangerous. "I'll take what's behind door number three."

"Door number three could lead to you being harmed, so I've put a padlock on it. Choose again."

Polly traced a circle on the floor with the toe of her boot. "The only reason you've been following me is to...keep me safe? No other reason?"

His facade shifted, but quickly snapped back into place when he shrugged. "Keep your friends close."

"And your enemies closer?"

Austin's response was to sip his tea, narrowing his eyes at her over the rim.

• • •

Rather unfortunate timing, being interrupted before he could finish himself. Austin swallowed a scalding sip of tea, praying the pain would prevent him from tossing Polly over his shoulder and hauling her into his bedroom. Her upturned nipples were outlined by the thin T-shirt she wore, all but screaming, *suck me, Austin*. And if she rubbed her damp palms against the outside of her thighs one more time, telling him her hormones were still singing as loudly as his own, he would give in with a heartfelt curse and complete his orgasm while she watched. Right in the kitchen, like a horny choirboy. Honestly, he'd never been hard up for sex in his life, and it was goddamn inconvenient when he needed to keep a sharp mind.

He watched Polly purse her plump lips, blowing on the surface of her tea in slow motion, giving him no choice but to adjust his groin, lest he reveal his desperation. Under no circumstances could he let Polly know how little control he possessed when it came to her. In a million years, he never would have anticipated her considering an exchange of sex for information. A rare miscalculation on his part. He'd managed to tear himself away before making a severe misstep, but if she so much as sighed against his skin just then, he would be on her like an animal.

"Shouldn't a negotiation take place at a table?"

Austin shrugged. "I've never been in one place long enough to procure furniture."

"Not even a—"

"Bed? Yes." He held her eyes. "I have one of those."

She smirked. "I was going to say laundry basket."

"Sure you were." Austin clasped his hands around the mug, welcoming the sting of heat. "I'd like to know what you have against the man you intend to ruin."

A beat of silence passed. "Don't you know his name?"

"He goes by more than one. I'd hazard a guess he has over thirty identities, and that's a modest estimation."

Her gaze dropped from his, perusing the kitchen. "I'm

not telling you anything until you explain what exactly we're negotiating."

"I want an active role in helping you." His gut tightened when her attention snapped back to his. "My nature doesn't allow me to remain in the background, feeding you helpful tidbits and leaving the outcome to chance. Not where you're concerned."

"My nature doesn't allow me to involve someone like you in my private business. This is my show and I don't need a costar."

He zeroed in on the most troublesome part of her statement, although he didn't know why he should be surprised at her disdain. She'd never made a secret of it. Perhaps the fact that he'd had his tongue in her mouth on two separate occasions within twenty-four hours played a part. "Someone like me?"

"Yes." She crossed the kitchen to look out the window, although the view was only a brick wall. "You're too much of a variable, Austin. Always working an angle, looking for a way to manipulate a situation to your advantage. Manipulate *me*. How do I know you won't decide to join forces with…with this former acquaintance of yours, and play me instead?"

"I never said he was an acquaintance. I said I knew of him." Her jerky shoulder roll told him she'd been trying to catch him in a lie. Good. He would expect nothing less. "I assure you, my assistance will leave no doubt as to where my loyalties lie. If you feel different at any point, you can cut me out."

"Generous of you," she murmured, drumming her fingers against the side of her thigh. "You have to know accepting help from you won't be easy for me."

"Oh, I've thought of that." He spread his hands. "I think of everything, you see. Give me the barest detail of your vendetta against this man and I'll share how I plan to reward you for trusting me."

"Reward me?" She threw one of those amazing laughs at the ceiling. "God, I'm going to regret this, but I'm too curious to pass up that undoubted gem."

A smile threatened at the corners of his mouth, but he contained it. "I'm waiting."

Polly paced silently a moment. "The man at the club last night." She brushed her hair back with a trembling hand. "He took away someone very important to me."

The onslaught of rage took Austin off guard. He didn't do rage. His keel stayed even, steady, through good times and shit times. But somehow knowing Polly had been wronged by his ex-partner in a truly despicable way made him want to bury his fists into the Sheetrock walls of his flat. Although he suspected it wouldn't help a whit. Austin took a long, slow breath through his nose, attempting to find purchase before speaking. "Who did he take away? How?"

She shook her head. "You said the barest detail."

Austin ground his teeth together. "Fine." He probably shouldn't go near her while white-hot ire infused his blood—he'd never experienced the feeling before, but suspected it would make him prone to mistakes. Or revealing too much. Even that hint of her pain, however, had brought vulnerability rising to her surface, and it magnetized him. Made him long to ease whatever jagged edges had been left behind by the evil man he'd spent so many years learning from. See if his own rough edges corresponded with hers. *They did.* He knew they did. "Would you like to hear about your reward now?"

Even his voice sounded unnatural. If her sharp intake of breath was any indication, she'd noticed. Noticed the change he felt taking place in himself. Before he registered the movements of his own feet, Austin was across the kitchen, stopping less than a foot from Polly, soaking in her body heat with greediness he didn't bother to conceal.

"Y-yes." She attempted sarcasm, but he didn't buy it. The awareness in her gaze as it strayed to his mouth gave her away. "I'm dying to hear what you could give me that I'd consider a *reward*."

Fuck it all, too many secrets fought for precedence in his brain. Untruths. This one thing, this bloody attraction to her—he couldn't hold it back anymore. Slow seduction hadn't worked. She was too headstrong. Too stubborn and cemented in her convictions. Which is why his casting aside of pride momentarily—in the name of greater glory—had to be done. She needed to call the shots? He would let her. Hell, his body had given him every indication that he would even enjoy it immensely.

The only one who saw right through him was Polly. She didn't let him get away with his transgressions. Didn't give in to his charm. There was something deliciously tempting about baring his guilt over the past to Polly without admitting it out loud. She felt the need to punish. And he needed to be called to the floor for his actions. Exhilaration followed on the heels of admitting it to himself.

Austin breathed deeply of her citrus scent and closed his eyes. "I'm aware that taking assistance from me will be a hardship for you. Until now, we've had an even balance of power, but I tipped the scales in my favor last night by inserting myself into your operation without consent." He reached out and gripped her right hip, brushing his thumb across the exposed swath of skin above her waistband. When her quickened breathing told Austin she wouldn't pull away, he tightened his hold and yanked her body against his. "My intent is to balance the scales once again by having a physical relationship with you, Polly." He sucked his bottom lip through his teeth. "Which is a weak description for wanting to ring your tight, sexy bell so loud they'll hear it in Russia."

She didn't manage to contain a whimper, and he memorized the sound like a covetous bastard. "I don't...I don't see how that balances the scales."

The moment of truth had arrived, and he couldn't let the opportunity pass now that he'd glimpsed a sliver of clarity. Focusing on her brown eyes a moment, he ignored the innate urge to hide anything that could be considered a flaw—an urge he'd been indulging so damn long—and laid his cards down on the table.

"You'll have control over what we do together."

Polly swayed toward him, appearing dumbstruck by what he'd offered. No taking it back now. For someone who orchestrated the outcome of every situation, handing over the reins to another wasn't easy, but seeing her pupils dilate, feel her pulse kick with excitement, told him this was right. It was right to want what she needed. And damn, nothing compared to having her parted lips so close, her tits grazing his chest. Austin massaged her waist in slow circles, slipping closer toward her navel with each lap.

"Every encounter. On your terms. I want to be...directed by you. I want you to *demand* I satisfy your body, in any and *every* way you decide."

As he spoke, passion glazed Polly's eyes, but it was tempered by uncertainty. "Are you making fun of me, because of last night…what I did…"

"What you did," Austin repeated, his thumb dipping into her belly button and sliding down, where his fingers toyed with the button of her pants. "Shoving my shirt into my mouth and perusing my body like it was for sale?" The already-scorching heat between them turned blistering. He'd never seen her eyelids flutter before, and the involuntary show of want had Austin dropping a bit more of his armor. "I…liked that treatment from you. I want more of it."

"Oh," she whispered, her breath hitching as he unsnapped the button of her jeans. "More. More…now?"

Austin gave a single nod, noting the color climbing her neck, wondering if she turned red elsewhere. Impatient to find out. Watching her closely for a reaction, he let his index finger trace the elastic of her underwear, but when he tried to breach the silk barrier, she gripped his wrist to stay him. Time suspended itself as they breathed into each other's space. "Do you need me to humble myself further, Polly?"

Her swallow was audible. "It wouldn't hurt."

"Very well." He clutched her panties in a turned fist and leaned down to speak just above her ear. "This is a rare instance where I'm not 100 percent sure what I'm doing. It might even be the first time in my life. I only know that when I think of you mistreating me, then making up for it rather vigorously, my cock gets stiff in a way that demands we fuck until our bodies give out. Is it still unclear what I'm asking?"

"No." He could hear the creak of denim as she squeezed her thighs together. "I'm accepting help from a man I don't trust. And in exchange I—" She broke off with a head shake. "How did…how *do* you know I even want to mistreat you?"

"Don't you, sweet? I saw *you* last night." He trailed his lips down her neck and back up. "You'll have free rein to neglect me. Strap me to a chair and give me a naughty striptease until I'm begging. Give me a hand job beneath the table in a restaurant and leave me on the verge of coming. Make me crazy. Make me pay for everything I've done. Everything you hate." He nipped at her earlobe. "Or simply prop your sweet arse up in the air and ask for a rough bang. I'll peel those little low-rider panties down to your ankles and orgasm you until you can't go anymore. I'll keep myself hard until you've finished on me—again and again—and I'm dripping with the evidence."

"*Stop*. Stop talking." Polly's belly shuddered almost violently against his palm. "Jesus. I have to think. I can't think when you're—"

For once in his life, Austin didn't think. He shot forward and cut Polly off with his mouth. Not kissing her, but keeping their lips interlocked. One joint breath. Two. If she needed a push, he'd give her one. "You sound like a coward."

She slapped him across the face. The bite of her palm echoed below his belt, making his erection bulge against his fly. *Goddamn.* The disapproval in her expression was fleeting before it transformed into shock, but something in him had already been germinated. His cheek throbbed in time with a telltale erotic pulse.

Polly looked down at her hand and started to back away, but Austin followed. "Don't. In *this one thing*, Polly, we're not playing a game. Look what you do to me."

She pressed a fist to her mouth, closing her eyes for a

beat. Then he let her hand drop and took a deep breath. "You'll give me anything I need?"

"Yes."

"Show me what's in the locked room."

Chapter Seven

Growing up, Polly had been an indoor kid. Once she'd been introduced to computers, her fathers hadn't been able to tear her away. Still, like every high school student in America, she'd been forced to endure physical education class. Justin O'Malley had been a grade higher than her, but forced to retake the class due to numerous suspensions. He'd fixated on her from day one, needling her with derogatory nicknames, poking her in the ribs when the instructor's back was turned. By the middle of the semester, his treatment had gotten so bad, Polly would get physically ill in the bathroom before class started.

Common sense dictated she alert an administrator. She'd needed to. But that semester had been right on the heels of Charles Reitman divesting her fathers of their life savings. Adding to their already sky-high stress level had been out of the question. So she'd endured well past her breaking point, which had come during a game of capture the flag. He'd called her "pudding." Polly still didn't know why that nickname in particular caused her to see red, but it had, especially combined with him pinching her waist every time they passed on the field.

As soon as she'd made the decision to put Justin in his place, calmness had settled over her like a woolen blanket. Having been given up for adoption as a young child by a mother she couldn't remember, her own destiny never felt within her grasp. Until that moment, standing beneath an overcast sky in ratty gym shorts and tube socks. She'd waited for the perfect opportunity, right in the middle of a down, the football on the opposite side of the field distracting the instructor. Then she'd gone up behind him, grabbed Justin's balls in a death grip, and twisted. As he'd writhed around on the ground in pain, she'd experienced a sense of exhilaration. There'd been nothing sexual about her triumph at the time, but her show of assertion had woken something up. Feelings that multiplied as she'd gotten older.

Now, with her palm tingling from the force of the slap, with liberation pirouetting in her stomach, Polly acknowledged the truth. *Her* truth. She liked harnessing control. Austin's glassy eyes and harsh breathing left no doubt he liked giving that control up to her, and months of attraction, months of trying to explain an unshakable connection, became all too easy to decipher.

And she was petrified down to her bones. Austin Shaw was the last person on earth she wanted to feel an affinity toward. She didn't want to feel anything but resentment and loathing for him. His chosen career. Unlike her, Austin didn't work by a code, stealing only from those who'd earned the loss by being cheats or liars. Oh no. It had taken her all of ten minutes to hack into Chicago PD's database and read his case file. With the exception of one encrypted file to which she was still working on gaining access, she'd read his record front to back, same as she'd done for all her squad mates. Austin's was the worst by far, in the sense that his crimes lacked a conscience. He hadn't been a victim of shitty circumstances like Bowen, Erin, or Connor. Hadn't been bankrupted and poor like her. He'd created his own corrupt lifestyle and lived it to the fullest.

Yet as he stood in front of her, hands curling into fists as if he wanted to reach out in her direction, she was tempted. More than tempted to explore the side of her he'd successfully goaded to life a moment ago. A moment she couldn't snatch back. Was the chance to delve deeper into her secret desires worth working on the same side as Austin? A man who represented everything she'd spent years bringing down? For all intents and purposes, Austin was another Charles Reitman.

Wasn't he?

There it was, a hairline fracture in her foundation. A moment ago, she'd wanted Austin to go on touching her forever, wanted to embrace the new self-awareness she sensed on the horizon, but she forced herself to step back. It was so much to take in and happening all too fast. She needed to breathe.

Polly realized her pants were still unbuttoned and quickly did them up. The jerky action caused the seam of her jeans to shift against her center, which had grown damp and needy. The gasp that fell from her lips had Austin stepping forward into her personal space. "*Let. Me.*"

"No." She staved him off with a trembling hand. "I

meant what I said before. I need to think. Spontaneity isn't really my jam."

"There's nothing spontaneous about six months of wanting to fuck, Polly."

God, he was right. All roads had been leading to here; she just had to decide whether a U-turn was in order. "Show me what's in the room."

A muscle jumped in his jaw. "I'd rather not."

"There can't be secret rooms or parallel universes." She swallowed hard, a little shocked that she was toeing the line that had always been so defined between them. "Not if you want the trust required to work together."

Austin's expression didn't waver, but the air changed around them. "You're actually thinking about it." He breathed a curse and dug a key from his pocket, tightening the jeans over his full erection with a wince. "We'll see if that's still the case in a few minutes."

His dire tone bred discomfort, but didn't detract from her curiosity. When Austin turned on a heel and strode to the locked room, Polly followed, meeting his eyes briefly when the lock clicked open. With a stiff nod, he pushed open the door and stepped back to allow her entry. Polly bit back her nerves and passed over the threshold…and stopped, allowing her surroundings to register.

Racks of clothes lined all four walls of the room, some of them in plastic, all of them spaced the precise amount of distance apart. Polly floated toward them in a trance, not sure if she should be relieved or twice as alarmed by what the room contained. Feeling intrusive, despite Austin's permission, she went through the hanging garments. A police officer's formal dress attire, a pilot's uniform, complete with wing pin, a business suit that looked as though it cost a fortune. She stopped at the familiar black T-shirt and designer jeans, the outfit worn by her Russian from the previous evening. Recalling how the shirt had molded to Austin's chest, biceps, and stomach, lust spiked in her belly.

Feeling Austin's attention resting on her back, she quickly moved on, turning in a slow circle. A large table in the center of the floor, stacked with containers that looked to be fishing tackle boxes. Polly moved forward, running a finger over the nearest container and lifting an eyebrow at Austin, who stood like a statue just outside the room.

"Go on, then." His voice was stiff. "You've come this far. Might as well open it."

Just then, she wanted to turn back. Leave the room, the apartment. Forget the whole morning had ever happened. She could figure out a way to shake Austin and go back to flying solo, just like she'd always done. This...this felt too personal. Like rummaging through the contents of someone's porn stash. It would be a sign of weakness, however, if she didn't open the box now, and she'd already been called a coward once today. Putting some steel in her spine, Polly unhooked the plastic latch and flipped open the lid.

Tattoos—fake ones—of all sizes, colors, and description. Various country flags, Chinese symbols, barbed wire, representations of each American military branch. Naked women, sports team logos, and individual letters in a multitude of fonts.

Polly closed the box and moved on to the next one. Facial hair. Goatees, mustaches, sideburns, laid neatly in thin plastic wrapping. There was a tiny glue kit nestled alongside the packages, with a comb and mirror.

She'd seen Austin in various disguises—they worked undercover so his talent had come in handy several times. He'd posed as a loud, outspoken Texas millionaire. An IT worker with thick-rimmed glasses and a slight Slavic accent. Once he'd shown up to a squad meeting dressed as Derek, proceeding to mimic his voice and movements with eerie perfection until the real captain arrived and put the kibosh on the sideshow. Yes, she'd been well aware of Austin's best asset—becoming someone else—but she'd never pictured the process. Never thought of him, all alone in his apartment, transforming himself in silence. The moving image rolled now, flashing like an old-time projector, until it started to bother her.

Polly shut the movie off with a quick headshake. "Who is your favorite person to be?" She gestured to the walls of identities. "Out of all these."

His rigid demeanor remained, but she could see he'd been thrown by the question. "That's like asking me to pick my favorite child," he said, his humor sounding forced. "I don't have a preference. My favorite is whoever's currently getting the job done. Although the Russian clubber may hold a slight advantage as of last night."

"You should probably stop bringing up last night."

A wolfish smile spread across his too-handsome face. "You can't prevent me from thinking about it. The way your leg felt gripping my hip, the way you tipped your ass up as I squeezed it." He growled low in his throat. "How you kiss like you're about to come in your panties." His smile dropped like a shattered vase. "I'm bored with this room, sweet. The bedroom is far more exciting, I promise you. Shall we? If you get on your back for me, I'll be whomever you wish."

"S-stop." Polly lassoed her runaway libido and dragged it back, kicking and screaming. God, her resolve was growing shakier by the moment. She needed to get out of there before he obliterated it. Standing in the doorway, Austin was larger than life. A sexually charged man in peak physical condition, confident in his ability to please scores of women. A man who'd asked her to control him, be the one who made the rules. What would it be like, having a man like Austin conceding to her demands?

Spectacular.

And he was right. Knowing she'd decide when and how they explored the attraction boiling over between them would make up for the pride she'd lose in accepting help from a con. She suspected it wasn't easy for Austin, either, watching her snoop around in his secret room, going through the private tools of his trade. But he wanted her enough that he'd made the difficult concession. Whatever conflict had always been between them, his actions were what spoke loudest at that very moment. *Please don't let me regret this.*

Before she could stop herself, Polly spoke, allowing words she'd never spoken aloud to tumble free. "That man from the bar...I know him as Charles Reitman." Austin had gone still, didn't even appear to be breathing, and she pushed on before the silence could unnerve her. "My fathers adopted me when I was seven. When no one wanted me, Kevin and Drake took me in. They gave me a bedroom. Yellow walls with fluffy white curtains. We were *happy*." She lifted a hand to her throat, rubbing to relieve the stiffness. "They had a clothing design business they were taking to the next level. They had been content before me, but they wanted to give their new daughter more. Me. They thought *I* needed more. But Reitman vamoosed with their life savings, leaving them with nothing."

"I'm sorry."

She went on as if Austin hadn't issued her his first-ever apology. "Kevin…he was the stronger one. Or we thought he was. He was the one who tried to make the motel room look like home. The one who made a game out of ordering from the ninety-nine-cent menu. We thought he was handling the loss. He was the one who kept insisting our family would come back better and stronger."

Austin took a step in her direction, his brow furrowed. "Polly—"

"And then one day, Kevin left us. By his own hand." She released a slow, shaky breath. "I've been supporting Drake with what I do…or *did*, rather. He still lives just outside Fort Wayne, in Roanoke. He set my room up again, exactly as it was with the white curtains, waiting for me to come visit. But I can't go back. Not until I can hand him what Reitman took away and tell him Kevin didn't die in vain."

Silence stretched for a full minute before Austin spoke. "You have my word that we'll see this accomplished."

By fair means or foul was the subtext to his statement, but having gone into the mission touting the same motto, it didn't dissuade her. "What is the word of a con man worth?"

"I wouldn't know." His response was automatic. "I've never given mine."

Oddly, Polly believed him. Not that she would ever admit it out loud. Something about the way he'd hung on her story, as if absorbing every detail. The fact that he'd allowed her into this room full of damning evidence in the first place. She realized they'd been having a staring contest, when he finally broke eye contact to rake her head to toe with a heated look. *Ah right, this is about more than a simple mission. So much more.*

Austin reached up and gripped the door's frame in his hands, stretching his all-too-enticing, muscular body for her inspection. "When shall I come to you, Polly?"

His smooth, aged-whiskey tone filtered into her stomach like blue fog. In his current position, his hands appeared bound above his head. A pulse began to drum between Polly's legs, repeating in her head like a loud refrain. Was he doing it on purpose? Yes. He knew. A corner of his mouth lifted lazily, telling her so.

"Come to me?" she asked in a daze, partially repeating his question.

He licked his bottom lip, back and forth. "Was that an order, sweet?"

"No," she all but wheezed. Lord have mercy. What would she do if his hands really were shackled above his head? *Suck him off,* a devilish voice whispered at the back of her head. Unzip his jeans, stroke him, take him to the brink with her mouth and stop, only to do it again. And again. Until his words stopped making sense. "Tonight."

Oh. Okay. So she'd said *that* out loud.

"Very well." Austin's hands fell from the doorframe. "You text me where and when." He flexed his fingers, making them crack. "It will be your show to run. I only have one mandate."

"Which is?"

The teasing had bled from his expression, leaving only starvation. "Your orgasms belong to me. Whatever torture your cunning little mind has planned, it won't involve me being deprived of milking come from your body. Whether it be my fingers, mouth, or cock that accomplishes your pleasure, it will be *me.*" His look was meaningful, but her senses were reeling too dramatically to interpret the actual meaning. "If you take that honor away from me, it will become *my* goddamn show. Are we quite clear?"

"Yes," Polly choked out, too turned on to address his arrogance. It alarmed her that he could turn her inside out with some well-delivered lines. Slipping. She was slipping. Acting on impulse, she turned to the garment rack and snatched up the plastic-covered business suit. "But you'll wear this."

"I see." His countenance turned to stone. "Shall I have an accent, too?"

"I-I don't know," she managed, sucking in breaths between words. He was so magnetic, preying on her desire one minute, her sympathies the next. Needing to get some breathing room, she moved past Austin out of the room. She ran two steps in the wrong direction, reversed and headed for the front entrance, feeling as though she were trapped in a maze while drunk on absinthe. Down the building's stairs and onto the street she went, hating herself for counting the hours until night fell, even as anticipation shrouded her in a consuming, pulsating, red fog.

Chapter Eight

Austin didn't really do "guy time." Sure, he'd been to numerous poker nights, always walking away the winner—especially when operating in a group as the shill, his easy wins thus giving the other players a false sense of security. The notion of "hanging out" made little sense to him. What was to be accomplished by sitting in a group, talking nonsense? The odd time he'd gone out for beers with the squad, he'd mostly gone to observe Polly and make sure single men within the establishment who glanced in her direction were quickly made to believe Austin was her boyfriend. Not that she'd been aware of his threatening glares at countless Coors Light–chugging wankers in Cubs hats. As if they could keep up with her.

No, shooting the breeze wasn't exactly in his repertoire. Today, unfortunately, he'd been in need of a distraction from the upcoming "date" with Polly and the relentless worry that she would cancel. A text had come in from Connor inviting him to watch a baseball game at the local cop bar they all got a laugh out of frequenting, since the undercover squad hated cops and the cops hated them right back. The captain's influence and reputation kept the officers' mouths shut, which riled them up even more. Truly, it was a thing of rare beauty.

Connor had never invited him anywhere before, and his grudging tone had come through clear as crystal in the text message, leading Austin to believe he'd been nudged a bit by Erin. No doubt the minx was feeling guilty over selling him out to Polly, and he intended to increase her guilt by bestowing the promised gun on her, anyway. She'd never be able to turn down something with such firepower, and it always paid to have someone feel beholden to him. Perhaps it would come in handy on a rainy day.

The ex-SEAL probably didn't expect him to show up at the bar, which would be packed full of off-duty officers on a Saturday afternoon. Why would he when Austin's relationship with every male member of the squad was contentious? Excellent question. But damn it all, he was desperate for a distraction today. If that distraction came in the form of talking nonsense with a couple of former Brooklynites, so be it. He'd endured far worse company, not that he would tell Bowen or Connor that. At the very least, he'd make the afternoon interesting.

Austin waltzed into the bar, saluting the closest group of officers. "Hullo, boys. Your wives send their regards."

One member of the group lunged in Austin's direction, but drew up short when one of his mates issued a reminder of Captain Derek Tyler's wrath. Austin felt a shot of disappointment. A good row might have provided just the type of distraction he was seeking.

"Jesus Christ, Shaw." Bowen Driscol's voice prodded him from the right. He tugged on his haphazard mess of hair, the likes of which gave Austin nightmares. "Still have your coat on and already breaking balls, huh? Let me finish my drink and I'll join you."

It was moments like this Austin *loathed* because they made him feel...part of something. A member of a team. He and Bowen might hold a patent dislike of each other, but if the choice was between Austin and a group of police officers, Bowen would throw his lot in with Austin every time. He refused to acknowledge the suspicion that he'd goaded the officers for that very reason. To feel some sense of camaraderie on a day where he felt raw, frayed at the edges over Polly. Over what he knew now about her association with Charles, how she'd suffered at his ex-partner's hands. And God, he hated the guilt that came along with not disclosing his association with Charles on the heels of her being so beautifully honest. It made him feel ten kinds the bastard, but he *needed* this chance with Polly. Wouldn't breathe properly until he got it. His guilt had increased tenfold since her confession, and it needed an outlet. Polly was the outlet—he knew it in his gut. How she would choose to utilize the power he'd handed over remained to be seen. The anticipation ticked in his stomach like a clock.

Remembering his current situation, Austin eyed the mottled-faced member of the Chicago PD. "Pass. They hardly seem like a challenge, do they?"

"Don't feel bad, man," Bowen said, addressing the other man. "There's not much I'd consider a challenge."

The man pointed a shaking finger at each of them. "Stay

on your side of the bar. I don't give a fuck who you are."

"Why, Driscol." Austin laid a hand on his chest. "He's a rhyming poet."

Connor came up between both of them. "Problem here?"

"Nah." Bowen turned his back on the group of officers, an outright slight he clearly enjoyed delivering. "Who's up next on the dartboard?"

"You are," Connor answered.

Bowen nodded. "Come on, Shaw. I'll practice my technique on your face."

And just like that, they were back to enemies. Thank *God*.

Austin ordered a pint of Boddingtons from the indifferent bartender before following Bowen and Connor to the dartboard toward the rear of the establishment. He leaned back against the far wall, giving himself the best view of the entrance. It didn't escape his notice that Connor did the same thing. Bowen, being the reckless one of the group, might as well have had a middle finger embroidered on the back of his leather jacket, facing it toward the door.

Austin sipped his ale, watching as Bowen threw a handful of darts. "A free afternoon, eh? What are the womenfolk getting up to without their bodyguards in tow?"

Connor sent him an annoyed look, shifting against the wall. "My mother took Erin and Sera shopping," he grumbled. "Something about a boot sale."

"You two would still rather be shopping than watching your beloved baseball. Wouldn't you?" Neither of the men answered, drawing a chuckle from Austin. For the first time, the two lovesick fools didn't seem quite so pathetic. Wouldn't he rather be in disguise, watching Polly's back? Christ, yes. "They'll probably come home with those tidy packs of men's briefs for you. Maybe some argyle socks…a sweater with room for your guts to expand. God help you both, you've been domesticated."

"You're goddamn right," Bowen said, taking a slug of his Budweiser. "Sera knows better than to bring home underwear for me, though. I like to make it as easy as possible for my wife to jump me, so I don't usually bother with them anymore."

"Jesus," Connor muttered. "We're clearly spending too much time together."

"Amen to that," Austin said, contradicting the fact that he was actually sort of enjoying himself, too much information notwithstanding. He opened his mouth to needle Bowen further, but a hush fell over the bar, distracting him. All three men turned their attention toward the entrance where their newest squad member, Henrik Vance, had just walked into a sea of stony disapproval.

"No heartwarming reunions today, apparently," Austin observed. Henrik's ex-coworkers had obviously lumped him in with their band of convicts, likely thinking he should be in jail instead of on the Chicago PD payroll. To Henrik's credit, he didn't look the least bit concerned by the death glares being sent his way from every corner of the cop-filled bar. His smile was unconcerned as he swaggered toward the dart section, hands in his trench coat pockets. When Henrik reached them, Austin arched an eyebrow. "Right. It would appear, by your lack of fuck-giving, that you might be more suitable for the dark side."

Henrik put his back up against the wall, his stance that

of a man who wanted to be prepared for anything. "Both sides are the dark side, man."

"Truer words…" Not for the first time, Austin pondered what the ex-cop had done to have his badge stripped. Now was the perfect opportunity to find out. Remaining in the dark about someone who worked closely with Polly was so far outside his wheelhouse, he could hardly glimpse it. Anyway, it had been far too long since he'd shown off. "What would you say, Henrik, if I told you I could have that group of cops buying us all drinks within ten minutes?"

"I'd say, great, I'm thirsty. But I want to know the catch up front."

Austin split a look between Connor and Bowen. "I don't detest him. Is that crazy? Tell me if I'm being crazy."

Both former Brooklynites shrugged.

"Simpletons, the pair of you." Austin straightened the collar of his shirt. "Fortunately, the same thing can be said about these particular cops. The Hoboken Bottle Cap bet should do quite nicely and it won't take much time."

Connor set his beer down with a *clunk*. "The Hoboken what?"

"Watch and learn, my not-so-eager pupils. This is your chance to observe a master at work. Or *play*, as it were." Austin scooped a bottle cap off a nearby table. "All I ask is that you don't dummy up the mark."

Henrik scratched the dark stubble on his chin. "I was led to believe the entire squad was fluent in English. What're *you* speaking?"

Austin strove to maintain his patience. "When you dummy up the mark, you tell a man—with or without words—that he's about to be taken. You won't be doing him any favors acting the hero, trust me. Humans detest the truth tellers over liars every day of the week. It's proven in every election."

"You have a point," Henrik said, eyes narrowed on the group of cops. "I still want to know the catch. If you succeed in getting me served by a bar full of men who want me behind bars, what am I giving up in return?"

"Ah, I think you know." The atmosphere surrounding the group of four men altered, turned gray. "Us cons deal in information. I'm sure Bowen and Connor have already badgered the captain for access to your rap sheet."

"Damn straight," Connor said.

Bowen threw a dart, looking disgusted. "He stonewalled us."

"It's not a rap sheet," Henrik drawled. "That implies there was more than one offense."

Austin smiled as a little more of the picture became clear. "So it was one major transgression, bad enough to lose your badge. Interesting."

Henrik's expression remained impassive. "I don't like you."

"Welcome to the club." Bowen snorted. "It's a big one."

"Yes. That *is* what the ladies say." Austin stepped back from the group. "Try not to die of boredom while I'm gone, gents."

The foursome of cops turned at Austin's approach, as if they could sense him. The leader who had lunged at Austin upon arrival rocked back on his heels with a cocky look on his face. Still, Austin saw his grip tighten on the Coors Light bottle, his face grow splotchy. He was intimidated. *Understandable.*

"Gentlemen, I do believe we got off on the wrong foot. I'd like to buy you a round of drinks to make up for my insensitive comment."

One of the background guys sucked his teeth. "You think we'd accept a drink from one of you assholes?"

Austin pretended to consider his question. "No, I suppose not. If we placed a friendly wager, however, and you *won* the round of drinks, it would ease the sting of accepting beer from an asshole such as myself. Would it not?"

Give him any group of four red-blooded American males in a sports bar, and—at the very least—one of them would find it impossible to turn down a wager. Every single time. As predicted, the leader felt compelled to step forward, although he was clearly wary. "What's the bet?"

Austin placed the bottle cap on the bar and nodded at the bartender. "A brandy snifter and an ashtray, if you please, good sir."

The bartender looked to the group for approval, doing what Austin asked only when he got the nod. Once the brandy snifter was set down beside the bottle cap, Austin turned the glass upside down, placing it on top of the bottle cap. To the right of the snifter, he positioned the dented metal ashtray.

"All you need to do is get the bottle cap into the ashtray, using only the snifter." Austin grinned. "Shouldn't be difficult for a man of constant action and daring such as yourself."

"I don't like this," one of the cops muttered, but Austin kept his focus on the glass as the cop took hold of the glass stem…and quickly twisted the snifter on it's side, attempting to scoop the bottle cap up. And failing. They *always* tried to scoop.

"Almost had it. I'll give you one more go." Austin sighed. "But if you fail this time and I succeed, you'll send my friends and I the round of drinks instead. Sound fair?"

The leader grunted. "That wasn't part of the deal."

"No?" Austin sent a perplexed look toward the dart section, where Henrik, Bowen, and Connor watched him with quiet amusement. "I suppose you're right. I'll take my bottle cap back, then." He held out his palm for a shake. "You gave it the college try, old chap."

"Now, just wait a minute," the leader said, right on cue. "I can get it in the damn ashtray this time. You'll be buying the drinks, asshole. Not us."

"You're probably right." Austin nodded toward the snifter. "You just needed a warm-up round. Now you've got it."

He tried to scoop it. Again.

All pretenses dropped, Austin inserted himself between the men and took hold of the glass stem, swirling it faster and faster in a circular motion. Centrifugal force had the bottle cap rising higher and higher in the glass as it spun. When the metal piece reached the highest point inside the snifter, Austin lifted the glass quickly and let the cap drop into the ashtray.

"We'll have two Budweisers, a Boddingtons…" Austin pointed at Henrik, lifting his voice to be heard above the cops' irritated grumbling. "Henrik, what's your poison?"

"Scotch. Top shelf."

"Huh. I would have said whiskey." Austin patted the disgruntled leader on the shoulder. "Much obliged, mate. Send them over when they're ready." Before the man could respond, Austin took his victory and sauntered back toward

Bowen, Connor, and Henrik, who greeted him with a slow clap. "No autographs, please."

"I can't believe we've been paying for drinks this whole time," Bowen said, flipping a dart over in his hand.

"Now." Austin inclined his head. "Aren't you glad your Erin talked you into inviting me?"

Connor appeared surprised by his astuteness. "She can be persuasive."

Austin focused his attention on Henrik, who no longer looked quite so at ease as when he'd entered the bar. "Drinks are on the way. Now it's your turn."

The ex-cop ran a hand over his shaved head, glancing away. "I never agreed to the catch, if you'll recall."

"Ah, Jesus," Bowen interjected. "That's a total cop move."

Austin cursed. "You know you're married to a cop, don't you, Driscol?"

"Fuck yeah, I am," Bowen murmured.

Henrik's jaw remained tight a moment, before his breath released in a long gust. "Destruction of evidence," he finally said, voice low, challenging. "And I'd do it again. What do you think of that?"

"Money is a powerful motivator," Connor spoke up. "Makes men do things they didn't think they were capable of."

Henrik shook his head. "I don't give a fuck about money."

Austin had the story now, the dips and edges defining themselves. "Ah. A woman. There was a woman involved."

The ex-cop turned his sharp gaze on Austin. "Keep the drink."

Henrik didn't look back as he left the bar.

As the door closed behind their new squad member, Austin picked up a dart and tossed it toward the dartboard, landing a quarter inch south of the bull's-eye. "That's how it's done, chaps."

Chapter Nine

Polly sat at the polished hotel bar she'd chosen as the meeting spot with Austin, her nerves too jumbled to drink the glass of sauvignon blanc untouched beside her right hand. She'd positioned herself strategically, across from a mirror that gave her an uninterrupted view of the hotel's revolving door. Any minute now, Austin would walk in, dressed to kill in a dapper business suit. She really should have picked the cop uniform for him to wear. Maybe having him dressed as her least favorite profession would have turned her raging river of lust into a koi pond.

Yeah, right. He could dress as a clown and she'd be itching to get him naked.

On second thought. She picked up the wineglass and drained the contents, giving the bartender a thumbs-up when he lifted the bottle up. *More?*

Yes. Oh, yes, there was going to be more tonight. With a man she'd despised on sight. After the last forty-eight hours, however, she'd begun to question that dislike, wondering if it stemmed from the stirring he inspired beneath her belly button and between her thighs. The way he challenged her mind at every turn. The way he seemed to crave her challenging him back.

Thinking past tonight wasn't an option. She'd made that decision on the seemingly endless walk home from Austin's apartment. Already she was overwhelmed by the role she'd taken on in their relationship. Total control. She felt the power all the way down to her fingertips where they brushed back and forth over the smooth bar. Perhaps it was unwise to approach tonight without an exit strategy. What if she enjoyed what took place between her and Austin so much that she couldn't stop? They worked together. And as of this morning, he was helping her with Reitman. A sexual relationship could jeopardize both of those situations, and *nothing* could get in the way of getting justice for Kevin. Justice had driven her since childhood, had dictated every decision that had brought her to the present, and she wouldn't let the importance of her mission fade one iota.

Polly got lost in the clear liquid sloshing into her wineglass, courtesy of the chatty bartender. She was only half listening, nodding during the brief pauses, as seemed appropriate. But she ceased all movement, inside *and* out, when Austin walked into the hotel. Sounds grew heavy in the bar, the lights seeming to dim. Immediately, she knew he'd been watching her, maybe from across the street or just outside the window. His gaze was locked on her before he was fully inside the lobby. He wore the suit, but no prosthetics on his face, a fact she found herself relieved about, but didn't care to explore why. He'd paired the suit with a fedora, pulled low over his forehead.

His mannerisms and walk were different. Polly found herself marveling at his skill in becoming an entirely different person, but as he approached, her thoughts fled, replaced with the image of him, hands braced on the doorframe as they'd been that morning. Waiting. *Was that an order, sweet?*

She took a gulp of her wine, the cool, crisp liquid getting caught in her throat when Austin sat at the opposite end of the bar, hanging his hat on the stool's wooden back. When he ordered a gin and tonic from the bartender, Polly heard his American accent and narrowed her eyes. Taunting her? But when he thanked the bartender, she heard notes of the South. And even though she knew it wasn't authentic, the smoky tone of his voice enlivened the desire left over from that morning. No, it had never gone away; it had only quieted in his absence, hadn't it? Why was he sitting on the other side of the bar?

Austin regarded her steadily, his attention unwavering as his fingers drummed in a hypnotic rhythm on the bar. *Drum, drum, drum.* Impatience had Polly squirming in her seat, but her attention refused to stray from his compelling masculinity. And after a moment, she realized her heartbeat had begun to match the drumming of his fingers. Her breathing followed shortly after. In, out, in, out. The volume in the bar lifted in pitch...or was that all in her mind? She couldn't decide. The sounds his fingers made and her body's corresponding reactions only got louder to compete with the music. The tip of his tongue skated along the inside of his top lip, slowly, so slowly, from one end to the other, and Polly's thighs shot together.

"The gentleman sends you a drink," said the bartender, jolting Polly out of her stupor. *Look alive, Banks.* She hadn't even heard the girl approach. "Would you like to accept it?"

"Um. Yes," Polly answered, cupping the back of her neck with a hand, hoping to cool her temperature enough to function like a normal human being. When she glanced back across the bar, Austin had stood, heading toward her with unhurried steps, that golden gaze still fastened on her, far hungrier this time, wreaking the worst kind of destruction on her concentration.

Austin stopped beside her, entirely too close for the stranger he was pretending to be. So close, his slow exhale moved the hair covering her ear. "Beg pardon." He spoke just above a whisper, but his tone was laced with concrete. "But I'd like to know just what you're looking at, ma'am."

His bluntness piqued her temper, somehow elevating her awareness of him right along with it. "*Excuse* me?"

His hand gripped the chair supporting her back, making it creak. "I came in for a quiet drink and you're staring. Is there something you want?"

It was a dare. An *Austin-style* dare. *Are you going to back out, Banks?* She could practically read his thoughts, knew damn well she was being goaded. And didn't care. His challenge was working right when she needed to be pushed. Her middle was twisted in knots, *had* been for six months, and she wouldn't let this opportunity to lessen her suffering slip away. Nor could she pass up the chance to learn more about herself. "Yes, there is something I want."

She sensed his relief even though he didn't move a muscle. "I'm going to need specifics, ma'am. I'm not terribly gifted in mind reading," he drawled.

"What *are* you gifted in?"

Polly couldn't believe the purr that had emerged from

her throat, but once it was liberated into the dim bar, the moment changed, became shinier and more manageable. Her nerves calmed little by little, until it felt entirely natural to turn her head and meet Austin's intensity head-on. It pulled her under like a swirling eddy, but her legs kicked, allowing her to tread water.

"I'm waiting for an answer. What *are* you gifted in?"

Austin dropped his attention to her lap where Polly knew a healthy amount of her thighs were exposed beneath a short, fitted gray skirt. "I'm gifted in ways that matter," he murmured, that Southern accent staying perfectly in place. "But we won't find that out for sure sitting here, will we?" His smooth index finger found the inside of her thigh, traced higher and higher, slipping beneath the hem of her skirt. "I can get you started, though, if you've a mind to finish that drink."

Even as Polly breathed a denial, she struggled not to slide her legs wide on the leather seat. The thudding beat between her thighs hadn't ceased since this morning, and having his finger there, touching and rubbing, would be divine. Could she allow it? Just for a moment? Before any poor decisions could be made, a loud couple blew into the bar, arms slung around each other's shoulders, shattering the illusion of privacy within the establishment.

Austin didn't pay them the slightest attention, his gaze roaming over her breasts, that maddening finger still stroking the skin of her upper thigh. "Where does that smell of lemonade come from? Lotion or a perfume bottle?"

She rolled her lips inward to moisten them. "Lotion."

A noise vibrated in his throat. "You're the kind of lemonade with lots of sugar stirred in, aren't you?" His single finger traced higher on her thigh, tucking beneath the edge of her panties. He pushed his mouth up against her ear and groaned, his knuckle dipping between the lips of her dampening flesh. "I love sugar. Can't get enough of the stuff. Why would anyone want to eat anything else?"

"I, um. I don't know." Oh Lord, if he touched her clit—so much as grazed it—she would put the orgasm scene from *When Harry Met Sally* to shame. *Not here.* Her toes were beginning to curl inside her turquoise pumps, a sure sign she would go off like Mount Saint Helens if he touched the right spot. And all signs pointed to Austin not only finding the right spot, but tenaciously exploiting it, too. Polly saw the bartender approaching in her peripheral vision and grabbed his flexing wrist, drawing it from between her legs. "I have a room upstairs."

His cocky mouth moved into a smile where it lay buried in her hair. The hand he'd been using to drive her insane disappeared into his pocket, pulling out a stack of bills. He laid two twenty-dollar bills on the bar and eased her off the seat, into the cradle of his hard body. "By all means, lead the way."

The walk to the elevator and subsequent ride to the twelfth floor would forever be remembered as the longest three minutes in her lifetime. Austin didn't touch her, but she felt him *everywhere*. Felt every breath he took, her body heating underneath his rapt regard. He positioned himself in the corner of the elevator, tapping his fingers against the wood-paneled interior, until just like in the bar, her heartbeat started to keep time with his taps. His intensity sucked her in, made her feel naked in the small, moving space. She could hear her own pulse, oxygen sweeping in and out of her lungs...and she didn't care. The time for hiding her weaknesses from this enigmatic man could resume again tomorrow, when her life didn't depend on sweet relief.

His body heat was volcanic at Polly's back as she slid the key card into the door lock and turned the burnished gold handle. Once inside, she didn't bother flipping on the light. Wouldn't have been able to find the focus if she wanted to. Because when Austin sauntered toward the king-size bed and climbed onto the firm mattress, removing his jacket and stripping his dress shirt down his arms as he went, Polly forgot to think, or breathe, or reason. She only recalled his words from that morning. *It will be your show to run.* At Polly's sides, her hands twitched. She felt light on the balls of her feet as she circled behind Austin, wanting to see the magnificence of him from all possible angles. Standing on his knees in the bed's center, bare-chested, his usual arrogance was tempered with vulnerability he couldn't totally hide. Something was odd about his stillness…was he breathing? No. His tension-filled muscles were strained and unmoving, hands in fists at his sides as he waited. Waited for *her* to direct him. A tingling began at the top of her scalp and shimmered down, down, to her calves, leaving her aglow on the inside with feverish sense of purpose.

Resolving not to question her inclinations, Polly reached out and smoothed a hand over Austin's taut backside, watched mesmerized as his erection rose against the fly of his dress pants, his ripped abdomen shuddering above that impressive, lengthening flesh. "No touching yourself," she said softly, gratified beyond comprehension when he gave a jerky nod in response.

Loath as she was to lose sight of his chiseled-from-granite chest, Polly continued her journey around the bed, dragging her fingertips along his ass as she went, noting the way his breathing grew more labored with each of her measured steps. When she stood directly behind him, her progress halted. Even in the muted light of the hotel room, clusters of red marks were visible on his back, out of place set against his unflawed physique.

Polly's hand hovered above one group of marks. "What are these from?"

He didn't answer right away, but finally cast her a wary look over his shoulder. "Fingernails." He faced forward again with an indifferent shrug he didn't quite pull off. "Always digging in. You know how it goes."

Jealousy rocked her, but Polly held fast against its green-eyed potency. She brushed the pad of her right thumb over a trio of angry moon-shaped scars. "All from the same woman?"

"No." He crossed his arms over his chest and hardened his jaw, the move striking her as…self-conscious? *Austin?* "Do they bother you?"

Yes. *Yes.* But not for the reason they should. The scars had almost certainly been put there by women he'd been playing, *conning*…and yet her anger didn't stem from that knowledge. It bothered her that he bore any reminders of other encounters or other places in time, when this moment was *theirs.* The sexually inexperienced part of her wanted to call it off, but it was overruled by an unbreakable will she'd never been aware of deep within her bones. So he had marks from other women? Those women weren't here now. She was. And unlike the others, she had the distinct advantage of being in the know.

No games.

Polly lifted her knee onto the bed and knelt behind Austin, not understanding the compulsion to kiss his back, but following through in the spirit of not holding back. Being incapable of it in the face of such freedom to explore. His hot skin shuddered beneath her lips, muscles going whip-tight. She aligned their bodies, molding herself to the curve of his ass, feeling her way around to his front with both hands. The fingers of both hands met at his belt buckle, pausing in their actions when he heaved a masculine moan.

"*No*. Dammit, don't stop." His head fell back on his shoulders. "I could come just knowing you're about to unzip my pants."

The raw desperation and honesty in his voice, despite the Southern accent he'd just managed to maintain, was inebriating. Her limbs turned limber and heavy at the same time, excitement rising like dense steam to cloud her thoughts. "I'm going to do more than unzip your pants." She tugged the leather of his belt through the pant loops, letting it fall to the bed. "Can you handle it?"

"Try me," Austin grated. "Try me *hard*."

Holy God. Wet heat gathered between her thighs, but instead of pressing her legs together to ease the sensual pressure, she positioned them wider, allowing herself a moment to writhe her hips against his bottom. Her fingers worked of their own power, unbuttoning Austin's pants and lowering the zipper. She was still unzipping when his erection pushed through the opening, obscenely long and… plump, a description she never would have expected to apply to any part of Austin. She'd caught a brief glimpse of his manhood that morning in his bathroom, but holding him was an entirely different experience. His aroused flesh weighed down her closed fist, seeming to grow heavier, thicker, as she massaged him from behind.

Again, it became apparent that Austin wasn't breathing, his body gone stock-still against her. Unable to push coherent words past her lips, Polly let them whisper over his neck, bathing the spot with her tongue. His body jerked on a rough intake of oxygen. "Y-you h-have to breathe," she forced out.

"I'm *trying*." His hips pumped into her grip. "It's just that it never felt...good before when someone else did it. I hated when they touched me."

Somewhere in her passion-clouded brain, everything clicked together. Later, she would rebel against the overwhelming sense of understanding, sympathy for a con man who'd mistreated women, but claimed he hadn't enjoyed doing it. Later, she would scoff at her moment of weakness and loss of reason, but not now. Now all she could do was whisper words of comfort into his hair, hold his erection tighter in her fist. Stroke him faster. *I make him feel good. Me. No one else.*

"Polly..." He broke off on a groan. "If you want me hard for your pussy, you have to stop jacking me. Otherwise, I'm going to paint the fucking wall."

That was what she'd been working toward, wasn't it? Somehow his loss of composure had become the most important aspect of her existence, transcending all else. But she couldn't allow her eagerness to see him shatter end this so soon. Biting her lip until pain bloomed, Polly released his arousal and...picked up the belt. She stared down at the expensive leather object, her calculating mind colliding with lust to formulate bad plans. Hot, naughty plans that should have seemed foreign, but perhaps had only been lurking in the background.

"Do it. Whatever you're thinking of doing with that belt, *do it*." Austin's body vibrated with unconcealed anticipation, all traces of the phony accent a thing of the past. *Everything* was a thing of the past. "I can take it. I *need* to take it." His gaze was penetrative when he delivered a blistering look over his shoulder. "We both know I deserve it. Are you going to show me the error of my ways, Mistress? Or not?"

Thunderclaps boomed in her ears, the belt's weight feeling like a live electrical current in her palm. With her free hand, Polly wrenched Austin's pants down to his knees, exposing his backside, which was as cocky and breathtaking as the rest of him. She knew what he expected. Now seemed a good time to let him know she'd never provide him with the predictable.

Polly walked on her knees around Austin to face him, blasted by the bridled intensity shooting from him like sparks. Ready to snap, but equally determined not to give in. The conflict was all there in his burning eyes. Amazing man. She let her focus drop to his erection, dense and capable of pulverizing where it strained against his belly.

"All yours. You've been its cruel keeper for months." He tilted his hips, presenting himself to her in a way that should have been crude, but on Austin, it was all animal grace. "At any time at all, you could have demanded me. Sent me to my knees to lick you off with one word. Grabbed my cock through my pants in front of everyone and told them who it belonged to." His eyelids drooped as if the scenario was an aphrodisiac. "Please yourself with me, Polly. My body. My cock. Own it all."

"I will," she whispered, shaken by his speech. Emboldened by it. Holding his gaze, she lifted the belt to his arousal and looped the leather around its ruddy base. A broken curse fell from his mouth, the muscles of his abdomen jerking. His big hands flew up, as if to grip her shoulders for balance, but they fisted and dropped back to his sides, where she told him with her inaction they must remain. Careful to keep the buckle from touching him, Polly tugged the leather to her right, watching the belt slither around his erection in a circular caress.

"Oh, fuck. Fuck. Fuck." He swayed on his knees. "More. *More.*"

Polly leaned close and ran her tongue along the seam of his lips, pulling away when he tried to capture her mouth in a kiss. "Only if it pleases me."

"Yes." His nod was disjointed, breathing uneven. "Only if it pleases you."

"It does." Faster than the first time, Polly pulled the belt left, whimpering at the sight of his aching flesh being squeezed by the leather strip, the precome that beaded at his tip. She repeated the action twice more, faster and with more surrounding pressure on his length each time. "How does it feel?

"Like nothing else," Austin groaned, neck muscles straining. "There's nothing else."

His declaration made her want to prove him wrong. Or maybe she needed a distraction to avoid feeling humbled. With the decision to stop thinking and *experience,* Polly grasped Austin's hand and dragged it up her skirt, between her thighs where his palm conformed to her shape without hesitation, ripping a moan from her throat. "Th-there *is* something else."

Austin's gaze turned intent, fixated on her face. "You need to fuck now, sweet?" There was nothing casual about his perusal of her body. It was predatory *filth* and it set Polly ablaze. His middle finger pushed at her entrance, through the barrier of her underwear. "Ah God, just set me loose with a yes. I will split the fucking headboard down the middle from bucking into this pussy."

Polly's legs and hands shook, almost making her drop the belt. A scream of *now* clawed at her throat. She wanted to fall back on the bed and allow Austin to follow through on his words. But the new, persistent desire to rule both of their actions won out. "Almost." She smoothed her fingers over his wrist and removed the secure grip he had on her wet center, moving sideways to put a foot of distance between them. "Almost."

Austin breathed a vile curse, falling forward and planting his fists on the mattress. His marred back lifted and plummeted in great, racking breaths. In the minimal light of the hotel room, his powerful body was majestic, not just for its superior form, but for all his many assets being tethered. By her.

Polly shook out the belt still tucked in her grip and ventured back behind Austin. Her new position tensed his shoulders, his thighs, and ceased his breathing once again. His need bled into the air surrounding them, beautiful and terrifying all at once. Above all, it was undeniable.

"Want," he said, voice unrecognizable. "*Need*."

Static currents zinging and multiplying in her veins, Polly lifted the belt and snapped it down onto the tight flesh of Austin's backside.

Chapter Ten

With the sting of the belt reverberating through Austin's body, a brief moment ensued where he felt nothing at all. To some, that might be an alarming feeling, to feel absolutely zero, apart from the bite left by leather. People were adept at numbing themselves, after all. Pretending the wealth of negative forces in their world existed only in movies and television, when in fact they were more real than their positive counterparts. For Austin, having the constant flow of cognizance cease for a sparkling handful of seconds was a thing of unattainable dreams. It had never happened before, the total and utter blanking of his mind. The unawareness of his surroundings and ideas and ways out and mind reading and tricks.

He'd found utopia.

There was only one single thread that lit up like spun gold in the empty space, and it connected directly to Polly. His too-fast moment of nothing passed and...*everything, dear God, everything,* blew in like a flash storm and flooded him in no time. Drowning whatever had been present before *her.* Or before *him.* Because he wasn't playing a part of hiding…for once, he'd been exposed. And she was still there.

"—stin." Polly's voice. She sounded anxious, which brought his head up. "*Austin.*"

"Present," he murmured. "Mostly."

Austin felt, rather than saw, her body deflate. "I thought…are you—"

"*Again,*" he interrupted, through clenched teeth. "If it pleases you."

A beat of silence ensued, shattered in seconds by the snapping of the belt. The quieting of his mind was more brief, but no less potent. Polly's golden thread glowed brighter this time, anchoring him to her. He could hear her tiny whimpers, shuddering intakes of breath as she doled out the sweetest torture he could have devised. It was amazing to feel pain after being invincible so long. To feel a physical representation of what he'd caused in others. *You deserve this…*

…but you'll never deserve her. The effect on him, wrought by each carefully spaced slap of leather, became secondary to how it made Polly feel. He turned his head to observe her over his shoulder, swallowing a growl when the belt greeted his flesh.

Her kneeling position had rucked her skirt high on her thighs, her rapturous expression leaving him no doubt that she was dripping wet in those panties. *Let me at her.* The shouting in his head roared back, louder and sharper than ever, making up for the silence she'd gifted him with. He welcomed it. Craved the clarity.

She noticed him watching her, whatever she regarded on his face making her hand go limp, releasing the belt and letting it land with a *thud* on the soft carpet. "I don't want to think anymore. Don't want to think about why it feels so good. Just don't let me thi—"

"*Done.*" Austin rose and twisted, circling Polly's waist with one arm and throwing her down on the bed, thanking Christ his pants were already down. His cock was the very essence of pain, full to the point of leaking onto the bedspread. The friction of a closed zipper would have masturbated him into coming by now, and that would have been a bloody crime against humanity, because Polly's legs were spread, her pussy begging for rough treatment from his stiff, angry dick. "You don't want to think, pretty Polly? Is that right?"

She thrashed her head side to side on the pillow. "*No. No more thinking.*"

Austin hummed a noise of sympathy as he reached beneath her skirt, whipping a pair of black lace panties down her legs. Wishing to immortalize the moment, he palmed Polly's knees and slowly pushed them wide, revealing her naked pussy to himself for the first time. Her legs twitched in his grip, as if uncomfortable with being so blatantly exposed, but he only shoved them wider, drawing a cry from her teeth-abused lips. "Oh, you *will* be indulging me now, sweet. I've been mad to get a look at what you've denied me." He groaned at the slickness coating her pink flesh. "Skirts, so many skirts," Austin muttered, bending down to swipe his tongue from her puckered back entrance, all the way to her clit, where he sucked until she screamed his name. "I could've been pumping you full of hot come since day one, you cruel little girl."

"Do it now." She struggled to free her knees, fingers stabbing into her hair and pulling. "Do it *now*."

In a reversal of what she'd done to him at the club, Austin lifted her blouse and stuffed the hem into her sobbing mouth. His groan rent the air as he fisted his cock and dragged it through her pussy, working his head into her tightness and predicting he'd have a tough time fitting through. Good. *Good.* He wanted nothing more than to make the same fucking impression she'd made on him. An impression he was too far gone with lust to attempt analyzing.

Austin made a grab for his pants to extricate a condom and roll it down his cock, dipping his head for rough sucks of her pointed red nipples all the while. Clamping his lips down on her pebbled peaks, he drove himself to the back of her pussy.

Austin's ears went temporarily deaf, time slowing around him. No…them. *Them.* They were so securely joined, he couldn't shift an inch without her moving with him. Having a profound reaction. He knew Polly screamed around the material in her mouth, saw her head thrown back, felt her thighs band his waist, but he couldn't hear it over the incomprehensible silence in his head. His mind groped for a handhold on the golden thread leading to Polly, twisting it in an unyielding grip. Calm pervaded immediately, the volume of reality lifting to greet his ears.

She was lifting her hips and whimpering his name, begging for movement. God, he needed to move, but self-preservation had kicked in, warning him that finding release in Polly would *end* him. Ruin him forever.

Fuck it. I don't care. Don't care. I'm ruined without this.

A need to provide pleasure struck him deep in the chest, like a molten arrow. Austin braced his hands on the headboard, reared his hips back and pounded into Polly's hot, contracting pussy, stopping to growl in disbelief that one thrust had been enough to make her come. She arched on the bed beneath him, hands fisted and twisting in the bedclothes.

Yes. Mine to satisfy.

The headboard creaked in his fists as he slid partially from her body and fucked back in with a twist of his hips. "Legs back up." When she jerked her limbs back up to his waist, he gave her a series of wet, slapping drives, allowing pressure to increase in his balls until it became unbearable, forcing him to slow with a moan of her name. By all that was unholy, she was a tight, liquid vise around him, but the wicked squeeze of her pussy was only half responsible for putting him on the verge of combustion. She was sin and beauty, her body undulating in time with his thrusts. Her chin was tilted toward the ceiling, as he'd pictured it that morning, eyes blind as she whispered *yes, yes, yes*. If he died tomorrow, it would be with that image on his mind, and he'd go with a smile.

There'd been women. So many women. Names, faces, voices that probably cursed his name to this very day. At the best of times, none of those hazy faces had ever made him want to smile. None of them had ever inspired a sense of privilege. An irresistible call to duty. *Fuck her. Gratify her.* What she'd given him with the belt compared to nothing in his memory. For so long, he'd craved the opportunity to use every trick at his disposal to satisfy Polly. And he wouldn't waste a second addicting her to his body. It was selfish. She would hate needing him. *So be it.* He couldn't give up the brilliant woman who brought the silence.

Austin loosened his spine, so his hips were pressing down onto Polly's, but his back was still at an angle, his hands still clutching the headboard. He used his thighs to push her legs wide as possible, her knees touching the bed in a provocative split, and ground the base of his cock against her clit. His movements were slow, but *hard*, giving her no way to escape them. Oh, and she tried. The heels of her hands found his shoulders, pushing him away while she wailed at him to keep going.

"*Too much*," she cried out. "Oh God, don't ever stop. *Don't stop.*"

"Yes, ma'am." High on Polly's approval, Austin turned his head and kissed the fingers curling into his shoulder, licked each individual one, increasing the pace of his grinds as he did so. He closed his eyes and focused on the little bud being rubbed by his heavy cock, his aching flesh so in need of relief. *No. Can't let it end. Make her need more. Make her always need more.* Austin let go of the headboard, meshing their bodies together and—*oh Christ*—she reacted like a wildcat to the new position, all his body weight concentrated on her precious clit. *Bump, grind, bump, grind.*

"*Austin.* Jesus…I'm g-going to…"

He slowed his ministrations just a fraction, rasping the scruff of his evening beard against the side of her neck. Words flowed from him. Words he could pretend were being spoken because she needed to hear them to feel fulfilled, but it would have been a lie. Somewhere amid the storm, her approval had become a requirement for him. "Am I a good boy, Polly? Tell me. Tell me I was a good boy for your belt, so

I can finish getting you off. All I want to do is get you off. "

She drew her knees higher, tweaking her hips beneath him, visibly overcome with the need to release. "Yes. You were...*are*. You're a g-good b—"

Austin bore down, shouting a curse when her fingernails landed on his back. A familiar sensation. But with Polly, it wasn't unpleasant. "Go ahead." They locked eyes. "Dig in. You know you want to."

A stricken look transformed her features for a beat before her expression returned to where he wanted it. All-out lust. "No." She cupped the back of his neck, drawing him close to her mouth. "I want this more."

Their tongues met first, licking together, apart, back together. An act so intimate, he became more aware of his cock than he'd ever been in his life. It felt like lead, every inch buried in her, wrapped in tightness. Incapable of making her wait any longer for what he would deliver, Austin groaned and fell into a wet kiss, giving her clit quick side-to-side strokes with the root of his dick. As she started to spasm, the climax traveling through her body in a way Austin could feel, their kiss turned voracious. Neither of them would break for air, mouths slanting, sucking, and biting, lips sliding, sinking back in together. He was lost. Fucking *lost*. Could have drained every last ounce of his passion into her shaking body from the kiss alone. They weren't done yet, though. She still had too much fight left in her.

Austin broke their kiss with a curse. Polly threw her head back on the pillow and echoed his sentiment on a release of breath. Her whisper turned into a scream when he sat up in an abrupt move, positioning himself on his knees and yanking her hips onto his lap, without ever leaving the heat of her body. "That one was for your clit." He ran his thumb over the rosy spot in question and made a savoring sound in his throat. "Look how pretty."

Polly gasped, twisting on the bed. "Austin—"

"Shh." He reached beneath her body, took her delectable ass in two firm hands. "This good boy is going to bang you until pleasure drips down these cheeks. Unless it pleases you to take a break and use the belt on me again." He lifted Polly's hips and jerked her up and down his erection, biting his lip to contain a growl at the way her tits bounced. "Which do you prefer?"

Her gorgeous eyes were wild with heat, fogged over yet remaining sharp in true Polly fashion. "*Again.* Please do that again."

Without a single hesitation, he tightened his hold on her sweet backside, slid her up his slick length and brought her back down hard, thrusting up into her simultaneously. *Sweet fucking hell*, she was slippery and responsive, little aftershocks from her earlier orgasm pulsating around him. "Tell me which part of my cock is hitting your G-spot." He moved faster. *Faster, faster, faster.* "I want to know how to move my middle finger the first time I finger-bang you beneath one of those short skirts."

"All of it is touching…" Her heels locked together behind him, her sex-goddess body pumping in rhythm with his drives, tight little bottom flexing in his hands. "I don't know. All of it. All…"

"Come on. Feel harder." Goddamn, he loved that he'd robbed her of speech. *That's right, sweet. That's what Austin does.* "Show me with your hand where I'm rubbing you so good."

With a throaty moan, she slapped a shaking hand down, four inches below her belly button, pushing down with the heel. "Here. *Here.*"

A curse tripped past his lips when he felt the corresponding push against the head of his erection. "Keep your hand there," he ordered, adjusting his angle slightly to exploit the spot he'd discovered with her help. "Push your tits toward the ceiling and feel me hit it. Ahhh…there we are. Gorgeous fucking girl."

An invisible claw dug into the base of Austin's spine, telling him holding out wouldn't be an option much longer. He'd never reached a climax so fast, with such force. Spending himself in a woman was always a necessary function, one that had increasingly been accompanied by guilt. Not with Polly. No, everything was out in the open. All his faults. All his transgressions. He was fucking her as himself, no one else. *Just a little more…need more.* Austin released one cheek of Polly's backside and circled the base of his cock, using his thumb and index finger. Pausing in his drives, he gritted his teeth and squeezed, allowing the building orgasm to subside.

"Austin, I'm so close…oh my *God…*"

"Jesus, I'm close, too. I'm never close. I never even *want* it." He bent forward and licked a path from her belly to the soft skin between her tits, giving a few hesitant bucks of his hips, cursing when his balls drew up tight again. *Too tight. Fuck.* He found her exposed clit, worrying the bud with his thumb. Refusing to neglect the spot he'd found inside her, he used his remaining grip on her ass to work her down onto his dick, a savage smile spreading across his face when she moaned loud enough to be heard in the hallway. "Tell me there will be a *next* time, Polly."

Austin heard the vulnerable note in his voice and swallowed hard. This was about addicting Polly, giving her everything she needed. Not opening himself up for a knife in the side if she denied him. No. *No.* There would be no denying today.

"I—"

"*Yes.*" His pronouncement interrupted her, the pace of his touch on her clit turning punishing. "You want this. You want it every fucking day. Don't you?" His upward thrusts moved like an accelerating machine. "I want to be commanded by you. I want to be your fuck. As soon as I empty myself, I'm going to fill right back up and wait for another chance at your pussy. Tell me you want that. Tell me you want me on goddamn speed dial to be *your fuck*, Polly. *Say it.*"

Her answering orgasm was so violent in its potency, Austin fell forward on a strangled shout of her name, catching his weight on one elbow, still managing to pump his hips. Not for long, though, the sound, feel, knowledge of her pleasure making him a slave to his own. Austin's seed left him in earth-shaking waves, indescribable bliss blanketing him in a silence that somehow connected him to Polly by virtue of its association with her. Their damp bodies were pressed together so tightly, he could feel her heartbeat knocking in time with his.

"Say there'll be a next time," he said, easing off Polly to collapse chest-down on the bed beside her. Not relaxing, however. Not until she answered.

Polly's chest shuddered up and down. "There—"

Her hand flew to her mouth as she caught sight of something behind him. Denial speared him that a threat could be in her vicinity, but a glance toward the door eviscerated that fear. Nothing there. They were alone. *Thank God.* "What is it?"

"Your back." She reached out a hand, then drew it back. "I didn't know I was doing that. I...God, I made you bleed."

"Polly." He shook his head, wishing she'd laid that hand on him. Wanting to be touched after sex. Who knew? "It's fine. It means you enjoyed me."

Nothing about his statement appeared to comfort her. She sat up without bothering to shield her nude body, and Austin's anatomy stirred, forcing him to adjust the weight pressing down on his length. Polly must have misinterpreted his wince, believing it had to do with her nail marks, because she made a small noise, her gaze running down his back, his ass. "Does it hurt where I used the belt?"

If he said no, would the moment be over? Having this tenuous bond broken so soon made him anxious. The cool, dark air of the hotel room enfolded them, somehow making them as close as they'd been with their bodies joined. Normal people held each other after sex, but they weren't normal people. They weren't afterglow people. Still, old habits died hard, and Austin's gut told him how to achieve what he wanted. And what he wanted was Polly touching him, in any way.

"It doesn't *not* hurt," he murmured. "I suppose."

A handful of silent seconds slipped by while Austin held his breath. As if in a trance, she ran gentle fingers over his backside, tracing lines he imagined the belt had left behind. His eyelids fell like stones when she began to knead the sore flesh...*caring* for him. Austin was so overcome with the unfamiliar sensation of contentment, he didn't realize she'd moved closer until he felt her applying pressure to the wounds on his back with soft fabric. Pressing, pulling away, pressing. When her lips replaced the fabric, Austin's eyes flew back open, the organ in his chest attempting to smash free of his rib cage. He didn't dare move as she kissed each and every scar on his back, still massaging him beneath the small of his back. Her breath drifted over the trail her kisses left behind, making his stomach muscles seize. God, he wanted to rock his hips, wanted to drag his cock up and down on the bed, but what if she stopped? He'd die if she stopped because of something he did.

"How can I hate these marks so much when I left the same ones?" Polly's soft voice cut through the darkness, a single finger trailing down the center of his ass, forcing Austin to stifle a groan. "And how can I see these red lines and want to put them there again tomorrow?"

Someone up there loves me. Austin lifted his upper half off the bed, twisting to face her. The uncertainty arranging her features made him want to reach out, cup the back of her neck. Something he pictured a lover doing. He opened his mouth to reassure her, then realized for once he had no answers. "I asked you for it, Polly. We both needed something and took it. That's a sentiment we both recognize, isn't it?" He waited for her slow nod. "In this room, let's forget what happens outside and do only what we understand."

Holy motherfuck, he was really putting himself out there, wasn't he? Not something he typically did unless the outcome was a sure thing. Polly was the opposite of a sure thing. A gamble. One he really wanted to win, although he hadn't a goddamn clue what he'd do with his prize. *One day at a time.* Or night, as it were. Perhaps if he wanted her to agree to see him again, he should behave in the manner that befitted a...suitor.

Good God. When had his brilliance turned to shambles?

For once in his life, Austin didn't think. He reached for Polly and laid her down lengthways among the rumpled comforter, attempting to situate her in a comfortable manner, no idea if his actions were strange or necessary. It just seemed to him that since he wanted her to stay and be comfortable, he should see to it. When he was satisfied that she wasn't going to launch herself from the bed, he took his place across the pillows. Going on impulse, he reached behind her and drew his fingers up and down her spine, striving for nonchalance when she sighed with enjoyment.

"Okay," she husked. "Just in this room."

Austin blew out a slow breath and attempted to ease closer without her noticing. "Don't think for a while," he said.

She yawned. "You either." Oh, he'd thought Polly in a skirt was his kryptonite? Sleepy, sated Polly had just taken the motherfucking lead. "We'll talk about everything when we wake up," she murmured.

Austin made a sound of agreement, already knowing he wouldn't let the conversation happen.

Chapter Eleven

Polly tried to appear her usual unruffled self as she scrolled through old emails on her department-issued phone. She saw none of what appeared on the screen, but it beat the hell out of watching the door, waiting for Austin to arrive at their scheduled squad meeting. He'd been gone when she woke up sometime in the middle of last night, disoriented and alarmed by the total darkness. Usually the screen saver from her laptop served as an adult version of a night-light, and the pitch black had catapulted her into a panic. Then she'd remembered. And her panic had been replaced with an even more unacceptable emotion. Hurt.

Austin's postcoital vamoose had resulted in today feeling like the world's longest walk of shame, although her rational brain told her it was ridiculous. She'd been the one holding the belt, after all.

She sat up a little straighter in the fold-up plastic chair, swallowing a gasp when her core pressed against the hard seat. Sensitive. *So* sensitive. It almost embarrassed her how much one fleeting memory of Austin's treatment of her body could provoke such delicious swelling between her legs. His knowledge of the female body and how it reached the peak of pleasure should have turned her off. But alas. It did not. Recalling his rapt interest in every shiver of her body, every moan and clench, the way he'd attacked those weaknesses at the slightest show of enjoyment…nothing worked to subdue the craving for more. Again. *More.*

Yeah. Not *even* happening. She'd let him glimpse her weaknesses, begged in front of him, and even *slept* beside him. The ultimate show of trust. And he'd bailed, delivering a serious blow to her feminine pride. He'd even left a single teabag on his pillow, in lieu of his big, dumb, gorgeous head. A taunt? She didn't know. Worse, even when he finally deigned to grace them with his presence at the meeting, she probably wouldn't have a damn clue what his leaving without a word meant. Last night had been a fluke. Today, he would be hiding everything behind a smug mask once again.

The one not-so-minor detail preventing her from feeling totally played? She hadn't been the only one to let her guard down in that hotel room. Not only his guard, his…will. He'd handed it to her on a gilded platter. Polly wasn't so seduced by Austin that she couldn't see his agenda. He'd gotten her into bed by utilizing what he knew. It was how he operated, whether his decisions were conscious or not—and she'd dropped her armor that night in the club long enough for him to see her desire to be in charge. As long as she was aware of his con, she wasn't being conned. Right?

Only, the con had been absent in the hotel room. His need for atonement had shone through in his words, his actions and reactions.

Whatever you're thinking of doing with that belt, do it.

If it pleases you.

Yes, ma'am.

Polly gulped down the remainder of her tea. What would she do now that he'd unlocked that part of her? It had only been lingering in the shadows until last night. A suspicion, not an actuality. Now a demand blazed like a comet from one end of her belly to the other, burning brighter with each trip.

"Polly," Erin prompted from across the room. When had she gotten there? The blonde sat perched on Connor's lap, waving out a lit match. "I ate pancakes alone this morning. What gives?" Connor grunted words meant only for Erin, making her laugh. "Hey, I might have done a run-out, but I went back and paid."

"Only because I made you," Connor said, battling exasperation. "And I don't think they found it funny when you tried to pay with Monopoly money."

"Ah, they did, too."

Erin waved off Connor's lecture just as Bowen and Sera entered the room, followed after a moment by Henrik. Still no Austin. Polly forced her hands to remain still in her lap, but they longed to fidget some more with her phone.

"Damn. Does the captain ever show up on time anymore?" Bowen paced in a circle, hands on hips. "I'm starting to feel a little slighted, if you want to know the truth."

Henrik gestured toward Bowen with the paper coffee cup in his hand. "What is that on your knuckles?"

Bowen scratched the back of his neck. "Paint. What of

it?"

"Nothing. I just had no idea you were an artist."

"He is," Sera broke in. "An amazing one."

Henrik's amusement over the couple's defensiveness had made him even more striking, in a rugged, worldly manner that would usually appeal to Polly over, say, a flawless man who could grace the cover of European fashion magazines if he so chose. Henrik was an ex-fighter, a nice tidbit she'd learned via a little internet research this morning upon returning home. He came straight for a person, while Austin launched sneak attacks.

Checking her phone and realizing Mr. Sneak Attack was now three minutes late, Polly felt her own defensive move coming down the pike and did nothing to prevent its arrival. She smiled at Henrik and indicated the empty seat beside her. The one Austin usually fell into with the carelessness of an alley cat just in from a night of prowling the streets.

The ex-cop gave her a truly knowing look, reminding Polly he'd been placed on this squad for a reason, but took the seat anyway. God, Henrik was massive. From a distance he'd been tall, but up close his shoulders looked better suited to an NFL linebacker. The police force had lost a valuable asset in kicking out Henrik.

One of his dark eyebrows dipped, a conspiratorial move. "I think we're interested in pissing off the same guy."

She gave him a prim look. "I have no idea what you're talking about."

He gave her a slow wink. "Message received, sweetheart."

Polly decided Henrik was good people, criminal record and all. Heck, his misdeeds might have even tipped the scales in his *favor.* She wondered if he would be upset knowing that—in dire need of a distraction—she'd hacked into his personal bank account this morning, the historical transactions of which had interested her enough to peruse his file on the department's crime database.

To this day, Mr. Henrik Vance refused to admit why he'd destroyed police evidence that would have implicated local Irish mob boss Caine O'Kelly. But if Polly were a betting woman, she would have laid every last cent on that destroyed evidence implicating the beautiful, rarely pictured redhead who had the misfortune of being born with the O'Kelly last name. Ailish O'Kelly, the mob boss's daughter, who—coincidentally—had been in custody around the time Henrik committed his crime.

Brisk, purposeful steps interrupted her thoughts, sending the heat comet ricocheting around her belly. Unless you'd been studying Austin for months as closely as she had, you would have missed the slight pause in his step, the tightening of his arrogant smile, as he joined everyone in the room.

Henrik didn't even turn to look at the new addition, merely giving Polly a nudge in the side with his elbow. "Nailed it."

Polly couldn't prevent her smile, even though it trembled just a little, not unlike the insides of her thighs. A product of having the cocky Brit nearby after the orgasm festival he'd treated her to last night. She lifted the ice-cold cup of tea to her lips and watched Austin over her shoulder, as casually as she could manage. His answering look from just inside the entry was blistering, singeing her skin like a thousand tiny torches. As his attention shifted between her and Henrik, his reaction didn't stop at anger. No, it promised retribution so powerful it swiped the oxygen out of her lungs.

Then his smug countenance was back in place, like it had always been there. In a movement brimming with male grace, he reached into the inside pocket of his trench coat and removed a package, handing it to Erin.

"What the fuck is that?" Connor thundered.

"Repayment for a favor," Austin replied, voice even more brisk than usual. "Fat lot of good it did me."

Erin stared down at the brown paper bag in her lap, chewing on her bottom lip and looking miserable. "Why are you doing this to me? You know I didn't hold up my end." With an unhappy sound, she snatched up the bag and removed a Ruger, pointing it at Austin. "I feel guilty now. Why do you people insist on making me feel feelings?"

Polly realized she'd shot to her feet with a shouted denial of *no* when all six sets of eyes landed on her. Making sense of her reaction was too difficult with adrenaline sweeping through her veins; she only knew she didn't like that gun pointed at Austin. In fact, she found herself swallowing a shout at Erin, her feet itching to move in their direction. What the hell would she do when she got there?

Her gaze was drawn to Austin, who watched her through narrowed eyes, that same unnerving but arousing way he'd done last night. "It's not loaded, sweet."

"Too bad," every other male in the room muttered.

Feeling the beginnings of a red flush climb her neck, Polly spun back toward the front of the meeting room and dropped down into her chair, ignoring Henrik's pitying headshake. Austin's footsteps were the only sound in the room as he came closer, circling in front of her and Henrik, the way a hawk circles field mice. She refused to look up when he stopped, although his regard made her want to squirm, much the way he'd made her do on the hotel bed.

A steaming cup appeared in her line of sight, a string dangling from the side attached to a familiar square of pink paper. Her verbena mint tea. She risked a glance at Austin as she accepted the drink in his hand…and felt it down to the soles of her feet. Rage danced behind his calm exterior, making it so much more effective for the control he displayed.

Her stomach muscles seized as Austin leaned down and spoke for her ears alone. "If this is a newly devised brand of punishment, sweet, know that I prefer your other methods far more. As do you."

Oh God. Oh God. She crossed her legs out of absolute necessity when moisture gathered in a desperate plea for Austin. Having him inside her. Hearing him beg with such urgency for the delivery of pain.

An unsteady breath shifted her hair. *Gathering himself.* "Be very aware that I'm considering murdering him for sitting beside you."

With that icy statement hanging in the air, he straightened and went to lean against the wall to her left, leaving her feeling polarized and wickedly aroused at the same time. There was a sense of accomplishment she didn't want to feel, but had no choice but to embrace. He'd left her, and she'd punished him in return. His discontent was more extreme than she'd imagined, but it bred anticipation. The things he would do to please her…

I barely know myself anymore. New Polly feels… buoyant. Sexy.

Derek entered the room and went to stand at the dented metal desk, but Polly barely registered him among the chaos lighting up her head. That is, until he dropped a heavy file onto the desk, the loud sound sending her heart leaping into her throat.

"This file belongs to a man I want out of Chicago."

Henrik leaned forward, elbows on knees. The picture of eagerness and relief, perhaps at the promise of a distraction. A place to center his displaced energy. "A big fish."

Derek nodded. "He's wanted internationally, not to mention seven states. But only for questioning, because law enforcement doesn't have one solid goddamn shred of concrete evidence on him. He has operated under over thirty known aliases. And I say *known*, because he's gone off the radar for months at a time. An embedded officer on an unrelated case has reliable information that he's in Chicago." Derek paused, letting the information sink in. "We believe his real name is Charles Reitman. And since he's decided to show up on my watch, this big fish is about to get fried."

• • •

"Listen, Shaw. You walk into any goddamn place, be it a dive bar or the White House, someone is being fed bullshit. Lies are told everywhere. Someone is always getting played." Charles Reitman tossed his cigarette over the railing of the Atlantic City boardwalk onto the deserted beach, creating a red arc. *"When you walk into a room, look around. If you don't see someone getting played, odds are* you're *the sucker."*

"Be the liar, not the lied-to." Austin propped his elbows on the worn wood, riddled with carved initials, and stared out at the black ocean. *"Is that to be the evening's lesson, then?"*

"Close enough for today." Charles tipped his hat to a trio

*of passing women, earning himself series of muffled laughs.
"Like any skill, lying gets better with practice. The trick is to
believe your own lies. Who the hell's to say what truth means
anyway? Maybe we make our own."*

*"Make your own truth," Austin murmured, thinking back
to earlier that evening at the poker tables, he and Charles soft-
playing, whipsawing, and signaling their way to five grand in
under three hours. It had been too easy, sharking tourists out
of their entertainment money, all while becoming their best
friend. They'd probably never realize they'd been had. "What
happens when you start to forget the actual truth?" Austin
sent Charles a sideline glance. "What then?"*

*His partner's face split into a wide grin. "When you can
con yourself, you can con the world."*

Austin drifted back into himself. To the present. Back
to the meeting room, surrounded by faces that didn't look
quite so familiar anymore.

*Look around. If you don't see someone getting played,
odds are you're the sucker.* It wasn't mere coincidence that
his ex-partner's name and presence in Chicago had been
shoved in his face not once, but twice in a matter of forty-
eight hours. Someone in the room was working an angle,
and it appeared Austin was the mark. There was no other
explanation for Charles being targeted in a city that boasted
no shortage of criminals, was there? No. He'd never believed
in coincidences, even when he'd been green, but his efforts
to keep his aliases disconnected from Charles's had been
stellar. No one should have put them together as partners.
Or even acquaintances.

Except Polly. Had she brought the captain in on this?
Had he not moved fast enough to help her and she'd grown

impatient?

If she only knew how he'd spent his morning. After Austin's usual trip to Gemma's school to watch her walk safely into the single-story brick building that housed her exclusive day-care center, he'd begun tapping associates for information, formulating a way to achieve Polly's end game doing what he did best. Conning. Waking up with her beautiful face inches from his own had been the oddest and most awe-inspiring moment of his life. She'd...trusted him. Even when he'd given her every reason not to, she'd slumbered beside him, allowing her mind to go blank around a man whose lies came easier than his truths. Even more miraculous, he'd done the same. He'd slept with Polly.

After allowing himself to experience her body heat among the sheets for the better part of an hour, a sense of urgency had penetrated his dense, satiated fog. She'd asked for his help, and so far, all he'd done was fuck her into next bloody week. Which wasn't to say the mind-blowing fucking they'd done hadn't been helpful, because he certainly felt in top form. Polly had better feel the same, or he'd lost his touch.

Self-disgust followed on the heels of that thought. She wasn't someone on whom he'd used his *touch*. Once you knew how to please a woman, you couldn't simply turn off the knowledge, but there had been more to what they'd done. Infinitely more. Hadn't there? The girl had turned him inside fucking out.

Unless Charles had been right all those months ago... and Austin had been the sucker being played in the hotel room.

Afraid at what he might find, Austin dropped his gaze

to the girl who'd supplied him with a heaping dose of brutal jealousy only moments ago, and prayed he wouldn't find deception on her exquisite face. Her hands were clenched around the tea he'd brought her, attention focused straight ahead. So pale, he envisioned rubbing his hands together and laying them on her cheeks to give them color. She looked as shell-shocked as he felt. Was it guilt? Or was the captain's newest case actually a coincidence?

No. He didn't believe in those.

Austin felt the captain's sharp gaze transfer to him and did his best to appear bemused. He had no choice but to act surprised by the news until more information could be obtained. "A fellow con, is he? He must have felt the draw of my unparalleled talent and wanted to get a glimpse of me in the flesh." He crossed one ankle over the other. "He'll be sorry to learn I'm not passing on my secrets."

Derek's dark look said he wasn't entertained. "Have you crossed paths with Reitman?"

Here lies a crossroads. If he lied to Derek, he would lose this squad job if it ever came out in the wash, which could spell prison time if he didn't get out of town fast enough. Eventually, he'd have to make his way out of the country, never to lay eyes on his daughter again. Probably a good thing for all parties involved, but it would be...unpleasant. Never seeing her again. His other option was to be honest—the horror—which would fuck him over with Polly if she didn't already suspect he had more than a passing knowledge of Reitman's activities. All these thoughts occurred to Austin within a split second, as did the subtle headshake from Polly caught at the edge of his peripheral vision. And a flash of them tangled together in the darkness without the bitter taste of deception between them.

"I've crossed paths with no Charles Reitman, although I might have met him by another name." Austin nodded toward the file. "Have you a picture handy?"

It took Derek a moment to act, reaching behind him to scoop up the heavy file, settle it on his lap, and remove a five-by-seven snapshot. All without his focus wavering from Austin. *Interesting.* When it became obvious that the captain didn't plan on getting up any time soon, Austin sauntered over and accepted the glossy picture. Keeping his features schooled, he took a moment to scrutinize the shot, although he recognized his ex-partner instantly. It must have been relatively new, because Charles had aged around the eyes, hair gone silver at the temples. Being that they'd only gone their separate ways almost four years ago, he wondered if Charles's usual wells had run dry. Karma could be a bitch, as Austin was sure he'd find out for himself someday soon enough.

"Not familiar." He handed the picture back to Derek and swore he could feel Polly's energy calm to his right. Where she still sat beside the motherfucker who'd taken his seat. God, he couldn't wait to get her alone. Screw waiting until tonight. His smile was more unnatural than he would have liked as Derek circulated Charles's snapshot. "What has brought this poor imitation of yours truly to the windy city?"

Derek finally turned away to include the rest of the room. "Reitman's MO is fairly straightforward. Cozy up to new money and involve them in a nonexistent investment scheme. He plays the long con, and his patience makes him good at it."

Austin realized he was still standing in front of the room

and went to take his position once more against the wall, casting a discreet look toward Polly as he went. She was still white as a sheet drying in the wind, attention trained on Derek. Perhaps it was a good thing they weren't sitting beside each other or he might have yanked her up against his side by now, shaken some red back into her lips.

Sera's voice made the image blur. "Does Reitman already have a mark? Do we have a starting point?"

"It appears he does." Derek sifted through the file. "She's nothing like his usual victim. Well-moneyed, cultured, established in the upper echelon of wealthy society, not just in Chicago, but international circles. In the past, he's been more apt to target up-and-coming businesspeople with little experience making investments. But he appears to have switched gears." The captain took the photograph back from Sera, tossing it faceup onto the desk's surface. "Reitman arrived in Chicago with the young woman, although they're not living together, nor do we have any idea how long they've been acquainted. But they're frequently seen together at parties, dinners, and what have you. It's possible he's going for one final score, getting this woman and several of her peers to invest in a fabricated idea. That's what we need to find out."

Austin's sixth sense began to ping. Derek was right; this wasn't Charles's racket. It was too big. Too risky. And to Austin's knowledge, Reitman didn't mix women with business, although he certainly indulged that particular vice off the clock. Handling the women had been Austin's end of the bargain and the reason Reitman had taken him on as a partner in the first place. His ability to charm the fairer sex had been his way into the life. Not to mention, the reason he'd wanted out after years of using his body to make money. He'd been nothing short of a prostitute.

Something was afoot here, and the acid boiling in Austin's gut told him it was bad. *Very* bad. But when Derek opened the folder again and Austin caught a peek at a woman's photograph, Austin realized he'd had no idea the level of fucked-up that had been achieved. Reitman's mark was the last woman Austin had ever conned. Isobel Klausky. Sitting on the woman's knee was his illegitimate daughter in her ballet costume, red hair in pigtails tied up with ridiculous white bows.

"No," Austin whispered, the room crumbling around him.

The captain was looking at him again. "If you have something to say, Austin, speak up."

Years of training gave Austin the outward appearance of composure, even though razor blades made mincemeat of his organs. "I said, *no*. A leopard doesn't change its spots." *Find out as much as possible. Find out what Derek knows.* Austin had a feeling it was more than he was letting on. "There must be a personal connection between them. Something that gave him an inroad to which he wouldn't typically have access."

"Such as?"

Derek didn't have the answer yet. It was there in the frustrated set of his jaw. But Austin reckoned he only had a matter of days before the captain was in the know. He hadn't underestimated Derek on day one, and he wouldn't make that mistake now. Nothing happened in this city without their leader being fully informed. Austin ran a hand through his hair, turning it into a stretch. "I can't work miracles, old boy. Give me some time."

The captain inclined his head. "Had a feeling you might finally decide to be useful on this case."

There was his answer. The captain was just as all-knowing as Austin had suspected. A silent communication passed between them, and Austin hated the gratefulness he felt as a result. Instead of outing him in front of the squad, Derek was giving him a chance to do what he did best, alone. But he wasn't working alone, was he?

Derek handed him a packet from within the folder, likely a broken-down version of Reitman's record. God, he hoped it didn't contain a copy of his daughter's picture. At the same time, he hoped it did. His head was going up in flames, just knowing what Reitman was capable of doing. He might never speak a word to the child he'd fathered, but knowing a single hair on her head was harmed in retaliation for what had taken place between him and Charles? Unacceptable. He couldn't let it happen. Damn it all, he wanted to be back in the dark hotel room listening to Polly breathe. Feeling his way along the bumps of her spine. He wanted to go back to those stolen hours and never leave.

It couldn't be a reality now, though. His past had come back to smother him and thus, Polly. Once she knew the kind of monster she'd allowed to touch her, she'd never look at him with anything less than loathing ever again.

"I'll be checking in via phone for the next few days. Once Austin has something solid, we'll meet and discuss our next move," the captain said, before giving Austin a meaningful look. "That shouldn't be longer than two days." Chairs scraped back around the room, assaulting Austin's ears like otherworldly shrieks. Dismissed. How easily they'd dismissed his potential tragedy without even realizing it.

His gaze found Polly where she still sat frozen in her seat. He wanted to touch her in some way. Any way. Ask her what she knew. What she *wanted* to know. Instead, he tucked the file under his arm and strode from the room.

Chapter Twelve

Polly's chest felt hollow as she moved down the hotel corridor, the walls on either side close enough to cave in and smother her. Austin had vanished into thin air after the meeting, and she hadn't questioned herself about coming here, to the place they'd been together only hours before. She simply knew he'd be there waiting, on the other side of the door. So why did fear attempt to slow down her legs? Without a conscious decision, she stayed close to the left wall as she walked, poised to turn around and run back the way she'd come. Why?

Because although she knew Austin would be inside that room, she had no idea which *side* of Austin would greet her. The cocky bastard for whom she'd spent months building a patent dislike. The lover who'd stolen her will and mastered her body in the dark. Or the man who'd finally let his exterior crack back in the squad room. Had anyone else noticed? Polly hadn't been able to tear her eyes away from Austin to make a judgment. The fractures in his veneer had been subtle, but on Austin, who never exhibited signs of anxiety, the tiniest difference was like a boulder dropping into a still lake.

She needed to know what that boulder represented. He'd agreed to help her. She'd confided in him. And she wasn't about to let him hang her out to dry. Or use the information she gave him to bring down Reitman on the squad's behalf. This was *her* mission. She hadn't come this far to watch it go down in navy-blue flames in the hands of the police.

Polly stopped in front of the door and felt a punch of unwanted excitement dance through her middle, knowing she and Austin would come face-to-face in mere seconds. Who would he be? What would he do? The enigma of Austin used to increase her distrust, reinforce her hatred for his chosen profession. It still *should*. She needed to remember that. Needed to remember that despite what happened on the other side of the hotel room door, they would always have the potential to become opposition once they walked out.

She lifted her hand, noticed it was trembling, and took a deep breath, pleased when her knock sounded firm. Assertive. Not ready for any bullshit.

The heavy oak door opened approximately two feet and came to an abrupt stop, revealing the hotel room, bright and sunlit this time. Polly's muscles tensed when a beat of heavy expectancy passed, opened her mouth to call out —

A blur of white shirtsleeve snaked out through the opening, strong fingers binding her wrist and dragging her inside. A decisive *click* signaled the door's being closed, the breath propelled from her lungs when she was backed up against it. By Austin. Which Austin? Which one? Her mind tried to cloud over, an effect of his sudden presence, but she fought clear.

He caged her in with forearms laid flat on either side of her head, golden eyes flecked with silver taking her measure. Shrewd and sexual. Predatory. So alive with intelligence that her nerve endings tingled in response.

"Did you come to play, pretty Polly?" He laid a hand on her neck, making her pulse jump. His thumb brushed back and forth in the hollow of her throat, once, twice. "We're going to have a little talk first, you and I."

Oh, he had nerve, making demands after pulling a disappearing act and sending her running across town. "Why do you think I came here?"

Without breaking eye contact, his thumb detoured to the skin beneath her cotton T-shirt. "I can think of a few reasons. They all end in you begging and sobbing with your legs spread." He touched his tongue to the corner of his mouth. "Flexible girl, aren't you? Gives me a lot of options how to accomplish that."

"Stop." She breathed through her nose, unable to calm the desire that sprang to life. He was backlit by the almost-blinding sunlight, his face shadowed in contrasting darkness. It should have multiplied her unease, but not being able to fully make out his features only presented an excuse to give in to the need he inspired. *Withstand it. He's doing it on purpose.* "What happened back in the meeting?"

"Indeed, I have the same question." Polly had no time to prepare before Austin whirled her around, pressing her forward until her cheek met the smooth door. A strangled cry spilled from her mouth, purse dropping to the ground.

Bracing her hands against the door, she pushed herself backward, but only met Austin's hard body. Mouth open against her neck, he walked them both forward, flattening Polly between him and the door. "I can't hold a fucking conversation while looking at your lips. They still have your teeth marks on them from last night."

A tickle moved upward, starting from the insides of Polly's knees and spreading, spreading to encompass everything. Lord, how could he conduct her body like a symphony? It wasn't fair. Breathing deeply, Polly closed her eyes, commanding herself to remember why she'd come there. "I'm waiting for an answer. You lost it back there."

"Did I?" Austin murmured, the fingers of his right hand curling in the hem of her skirt, scant inches beneath the flesh he'd become too well acquainted with in that very room. "Maybe you're just more attuned to me than most." The tight material was drawn slowly up her thighs, where he left it gathered just below her hips. Polly's mouth fell open in a silent moan when one skilled male finger dragged down the underside of her panties, stopping to tap in a slow rhythm against that ultrasensitive spot. "You knew just how much I could take yesterday, didn't you? Knew just how to give it to me."

"I-I didn't come here to…talk about that."

"Did you come here to admit you went to Derek behind my back?"

"*What?*" Polly stiffened, immobilized by outrage. "Why would I do that? You think I want the cops on this? Cops make deals, cops destroy evidence and fumble around with red tape we don't have. I *wouldn't.*"

Austin continued as if she hadn't spoken, but Polly

sensed him filing away her statement in some internal hard drive. Sensed that she'd somehow convinced him with her honesty that she hadn't played him. "I didn't lose it back in that room to anyone but you." His mouth found her ear, tongue tracing the entire curve in one long, groaning lick. "And I don't care if it's sick, I love it. What would you have done if we were alone and you saw me breaking, sweet?" His easy touch turned rough, his big hand clutching her core and holding tight, tighter, until Polly cried out, knees bumping the door. "Would you have slapped some sense into me?"

"Yes." The word released on an unsteady exhale, surprising even Polly. As did the rush of control the revelation allowed to sweep in. "Maybe I'll just do it now."

"If it pleases you," he enunciated just above her head. "Although I feel my slap in the face already came in the form of the green-eyed monster. You made me jealous, Polly, and I *didn't like it*." His grip increased in power, ripping a gasp from her throat. "Your pleasure comes from me. Any hint to the contrary is unwelcome. I thought we had an understanding."

"You *left*." Oh God, the mortification. Polly wanted to slam her head against the door at having disclosed such a typical insecurity, but now that the reason for her initial irritation this morning had set itself free, it ran rampant. "I woke up and you'd left me a tea bag. What am I supposed to *do* with that?" Her jaw felt like it might shatter from grinding her teeth. "And you want to talk about jealousy? Do you, really? After leaving me without a note or…or even a-a text…you show up with a gift for someone else."

She struggled against his hold, twisting to get away, but he only shoved her back up against the door. "You made me jealous with Henrik because I left." He sounded like a man trying to solve a riddle, which should have brought on the century's biggest eye roll, but his touch had turned soothing between her legs, petting over her lace-covered flesh the way one might stroke a kitten. "I spent the morning tracking down an old contact, Polly. A Chicago man who could give us a lead on Reitman." His voice turned to a gruff whisper, mouth laying a lingering kiss on the back of her neck. "I thought information would please you more than breakfast in bed. A rare misjudgment on my part, it would appear."

"No." Stupid. So stupid for her heart to be beating so damn fast. They'd agreed he would help her. He'd taken steps to keep his word. That was *all*. She desperately needed to corral her hormones. "What did you find out?"

"In a minute, sweet. This might be the last time you allow me to touch." Austin's breath moved the hair at her nape, his capable middle finger hooking around the crotch of her panties and tugging them aside for his index finger to explore. "Wouldn't that be a shame when I haven't yet had the honor of screwing you with my tongue? That little spot we discovered yesterday wouldn't be too difficult to reach. We'd hook those knees beneath your arms and pray you could keep them up." Without warning, the panties were jerked high against her center and tugged, creating unexpected and devastating friction. Back and forth. Back and forth. "Could you keep your knees up, Polly? Or would you clamp your thighs around my head? I need you to let me find out."

Already she could feel the approaching climax, felt the inner walls of her core convulsing, searching for his absent fingers, begging for the erection she could feel against her bottom. But the urgent edge to his words forced her to concentrate. No, it was more than that. His behavior back at the meeting. Something was wrong, and they couldn't go any further until they turned the page and found each other. "Why might this be the last time, Austin?"

He almost managed to disguise his sigh of frustration, but she heard it. Or maybe she felt it. *Connected to him.* His touch was suddenly absent between her legs, both hands pressing to the door in front of her face. When his hips began to circle in slow, seductive thrusts against her backside, lace and a zipper all that separated them from guaranteed ecstasy, she almost gave in and let him seduce her into what, according to him, could be the final time their bodies were joined together. Why? *No. Don't want that, despite everything.* Following instincts she'd only just begun to recognize, Polly reached up with her own hands and laid them on top of Austin's bigger ones.

Behind her, Austin stilled. The sudden lack of sexual movement almost bred regret inside Polly, until his forehead dropped to her shoulder. It stayed there while they caught their breath and then lifted. "Polly, listen to me. I—" He broke off, his hands turning over in a lightning move to clasp her fingers. "What's happened to your nails?"

She'd forgotten. Really, it had been a decision made during such raging internal conflict after leaving the hotel this morning, it had gotten lost in the current of anger, confusion, and lust. Upon walking into her apartment, she'd gone straight to her bathroom with the intention of taking a shower, but she'd flung open the medicine cabinet instead and snatched up the fingernail clippers. She hadn't simply trimmed her nails; she'd kind of demolished them. The skin beneath was red and angry, her nails shorn to the point that she wouldn't be scratching any itches for weeks.

"Polly?" Austin brought them back over her shoulder to his mouth and kissed each individual one, a frantic use of lips. "Ah, sweet. What have you done?"

The nickname, usually employed with sensual intention, used instead as an endearment untied some vital knot inside her. "You don't like those marks on your back, and I won't contribute to them again." She turned to meet his eyes, chaotic in the shadows. "I'm sorry that I did."

Austin looked like a man who'd just glimpsed tragedy, which made no sense. He kissed her damaged fingers one final time and replaced her hand on the door with a gentleness that made her throat close up, the picture of a man on the way to his own execution. With the utmost care, he tugged her skirt back into place. When he finally stepped back, she felt the few feet of distance in her bones. "I'm the one who's sorry."

• • •

How unfitting that Polly should be bathed in pure white sunlight when bitter darkness fought to get free of him. She turned to face Austin, appearing almost angelic but for the caution in every gorgeous feminine line of her body. That wariness was a testament to her intelligence, and he appreciated it, while wanting to melt it away with his touch. If he hadn't seen the abused tips of her fingers, he'd have her in bed now, halfway to her second orgasm. But he had. He'd seen the evidence that she'd felt...regret over hurting him. And double damn if heavy responsibility hadn't come with that knowledge. It pressed down on his sternum, making it hard to inhale. She'd done something to prevent him pain. Affording her the same respect was his only option, even if it meant placing her out of his reach.

Life had been so much easier as a selfish prick.

Seeing that her T-shirt was untucked, Polly did an adorable double take that made his heart lurch, smoothing the fabric back under her waistband. "Why are you sorry, Austin?"

Needing to buy himself a little more time with her in the sun, Austin crossed to the mini-fridge, opened it and plucked out two small bottles of Jameson. Unbelievable. His hands could barely function well enough to twist off the metal caps, clumsy under the mere prospect of truth-telling. "I'm sorry…that I haven't told you yet about this morning's endeavor and what it yielded."

Polly said nothing behind him, but Austin could hear her bullshit detector going off. She accepted the glass tumbler containing two fingers of whiskey and perched herself atop the polished desk. It didn't escape his notice that she was as far from the bed as possible. Very likely, Polly's proximity to a bed would never be far from his consciousness.

"Darren Burnbaum," Austin started. "That's the name of the man who found himself unconscious on the bathroom floor three nights ago."

"Found himself." Polly took a swallow of whiskey and grimaced. "That's one way of putting it."

"Honestly, taking a woman of your caliber to a diner was reason enough to shut his lights out, sweet. But I digress." Austin undid the top two buttons of his shirt, only half aware of his actions until Polly's gaze dipped to his exposed throat, those teeth-marked lips parting in awareness. *Turn it off.* Why couldn't he just turn it off? He cleared his throat and made a silent vow to keep a safe distance from Polly until the whole picture was revealed. "Darren's brother used to grift with the best of them, until he went straight. Now he's working a six-figure job behind a desk downtown. Has a wife, kids, and a dog. The whole messy business."

"I never thought to look into siblings," Polly said, her voice quiet. "You have something damning on the brother?"

"Very good." His right eye ticked. "Unfortunately, so does Reitman."

"I see."

The battle waging inside Polly was quite apparent to Austin. She hated the casual manner in which he spoke about ruining men, understandable considering what Reitman had done to her fathers. But the steady rise and fall of her chest, the constant rewetting of her lips, told Austin she had an appreciation for the game. Fuck, her legs looked extra spreadable in the sunlight. That same light would make her nipples shine like rubies if he sucked them. It would be so easy to distract them both with sex, postpone the inevitable just a little while longer.

You owe her more than that. Deep breath.

"What do you have on him?" Polly asked, dragging him back to the present.

"You don't want to know, sweet. You don't *need* to."

Austin set down his already-empty glass, more than a little shaken by the protectiveness unfurling within him. There was more at stake here than ruining his chance at being with Polly again. He didn't want her sullied by the knowledge of how his world worked. The things he'd done were vile. They had no goddamn business touching Polly or making a home inside her remarkable mind. But he'd come this far, and she wouldn't let him skate if he backed off now.

"Reitman used Darren's brother's connections to gain entry into the large-scale investment community," he said. "And with the threat hanging over his head, the brother had no choice but to make introductions. It wasn't long until Reitman found his mark."

Austin swallowed the cement coating his throat, felt the weight drop into his stomach. "His mark is Isobel Pierce, the woman Derek spoke about this morning in the meeting. Her last name is different from when I…knew her. It used to be Klausky, but she's divorced now, you see."

Some of the color drained from Polly's face, the transition made all the more drastic by the luminous sunlight. "You know her?"

"I *knew* her." Austin paced to the bed and dropped down onto the edge, running stiff fingers through his hair. "Polly, this is one fucked-up story. I'd rather you go on thinking I'm simply a cheat with an unforgivable ego. I'd rather you think of me that way than know for certain I'm a monster."

The silence that fell was ear piercing, but she ended it mercifully after a minute. "I don't want to be like everyone else, looking at you and seeing whatever illusion you choose to project. Tell me."

Already knowing the outcome would be Polly walking out on him, Austin's courage was pathetically low, but he held on to it with an iron grip. "I started off in Brighton, making suckers out of tourists with a basic shell game. That's all it was ever supposed to be. Supplementing my allowance while alleviating the boredom that plagues most sixteen-year-olds." He clasped his hands together between his knees. "A man approached me one afternoon and asked for a game. I don't know what it was about him, but I refused to give him a go. He would have taken my winnings, I was sure of it."

Restless at the memory, wishing he could go back in time and warn his past self of what lay on the horizon, Austin stood and blew out a breath. "He convinced me to pack it in for the night and we talked. He showed me monte and some other easy moneymakers." Finding the right words was hard, having never explained what drew him to the life. "Until then, every day was the same. Gray skies. School uniform. The same conversations each night at dinner. And then there was this person, telling me I could make it on my own. See everything. That I had the right disposition and aptitude to be a self-made man. A...con."

Austin watched as Polly replenished her drink, crossing to his empty glass and filling it, too. As she closed the distance between them to hand him the whiskey, Austin's blood turned heavy in his veins, pumping with scorching need. He took the drink in one hand, grabbing her wrist with the other. "You know I could stop talking right now and use my mouth for something far more interesting." His thumb pressed down on her fluttering pulse, inhaling her lemonade scent like a junkie. "I know you wore that lace for me. Want to watch me use my teeth to get through it to what's beneath? I'll rip it off your pussy little by little until your sweetness is fair game for my tongue. All you have to do is take your skirt off, lie down, and call me your good boy."

She pitched to the side before righting herself and stepping back from him as if he'd already torn off the mask and revealed what lay beneath. Perhaps he had. Being censured for his past sins had never felt more vital than it did right now. Polly was the only one who could do that for him. Would she?

"Just keep talking," she breathed, taking her post once again on the other side of the room. "I'll be the judge of what's more interesting."

He raised an eyebrow, attempting to disguise his discomfort at having her so far away. Touching was his greatest ally, and she'd handily divested him of it. "If it pleases you." He took a moment to memorize the blush that climbed her neck before continuing. "That man was my partner up until about four years ago. We didn't always work the same mark. Sometimes months passed where he and I didn't even see each other, going off on our own. But we called each other in when necessary. I—" Hell, if he'd only detailed the cons out loud years ago, maybe the way it made his soul flinch would've been enough warning to stop. "We were in São Paulo and my partner told me about an American woman on vacation. Rich, spoiled, spending money like water…newly married."

Austin winced on the inside when Polly drained her whiskey.

"Her husband had gone back to the States for business and left her there for a month. She wasted no time telling me the marriage was rocky, the husband is a philanderer, which is what they all say as justification, before we—"

"I don't think I need those details."

Any other time, the underlying jealousy in her tone— although she'd tried to hide it—would've had him rejoicing, but celebrating in the face of his oncoming defeat proved empty. "My partner set it up. It was a simple investment scheme, much like the one your fathers likely encountered." The look he gave her was packed full of sympathy, but it didn't make her look any less numb. "I'm sorry."

She dropped into a seat at the square table, eyeing the police file he'd brought with him, but not touching it. "Are you really sorry? I don't know if a person can go from feeling nothing, caring for no one, to feeling regret. It's like a prisoner turning to religion. Buying because there's nothing else for sale."

"I can't convince you I'm genuine with words, Polly, only deeds. And I *will*, goddammit." He waited for her attention before resuming the story. A story that felt as though it had happened to someone else. Or a fictional character in some tragic play. "For the most part my associate stayed out of the picture, stepping in as the shill on two occasions, playing the success story who invested money with me." Scenes filtered through his mind. The smell of suntan lotion. The lapping of waves against the side of a boat. "With the way she spent money, we were surprised when she didn't bite right away. It was nearly a month before she decided to transfer the funds. And right after…right after she did, she told me she was pregnant."

Polly was an ice sculpture across the room. God, *God*, he felt sick to his stomach. He wanted to kneel in front of her and wrap his arms around her waist. Get in her face and demand she shout at him, just so she would push him away. At least there would be contact. *Never again. She'll never touch you again.* That knowledge was a deep, piercing wound, but not being able to protect her from Charles would be the death blow. So that had to be his goal here. Lose the fragile relationship they had, but still be allowed to protect her.

"I'm always so *careful*, Polly. Looking back, I think it was purposeful. A way to get back at her husband for leaving her alone. For the affairs." He laid his hands on his knees. "As soon as I found out, I reversed the transfer. I'm a thief, you understand. But I wouldn't steal from my own...my own..." A bracing inhale. Another one. "My partner reversed it back and took off with the money before I'd wrapped my mind around what had happened. I was...nearly catatonic after I found out about the pregnancy, or I would've stopped him." Austin stood on lethargic legs and commanded them to take him toward Polly, so very aware of her silence with each step he took. When he reached the table, he opened the file and removed the photograph that he'd stared at in a near-daze on the train ride to the hotel. "This is Gemma Klausky. My...daughter."

Polly's hand flew to her mouth, dropped away, and went right back to muffle a sound of disbelief. "Oh my God, Austin." Quizzical eyes scanned the photo, probably noting the similarities in her features and Austin's. "Is she why you came to Chicago?"

His chin jerked up. "Yes. Although, we've never spoken and I have no idea what I thought my presence would accomplish," he murmured, shocked that even Polly had landed on the reason for his arrival in Chicago in such short order. She didn't believe in coincidences, either, it would seem. "It appears Gemma is the reason Charles Reitman is in Chicago, too."

"Reitman? What's the connection..." Polly stiffened, no longer meeting his eyes. This was it. This was when she bolted for the door, cursing him to hell. The masochist she'd stirred to life inside him shouted at her to *do it!* Just so it would be over and he wouldn't feel the awful anticipation of watching her disappear down the hotel corridor. "Don't say it out loud," she whispered. "I know what the connection is, but don't say it out loud."

"All right," Austin said, not understanding her reasoning, but trusting it. And Christ, he was too relieved at her remaining within his reach to question a bloody damn thing. "But there's more, Polly. I retaliated." Austin removed the single surveillance photograph of Reitman, wherein he appeared to be looking straight at the camera. Straight at Austin. Reminding Austin of exactly *how* he'd retaliated, violating one of the oldest rules in any book. He'd involved the man's family, something he couldn't explain to Polly yet. Not when they were on such shaky ground already. "Suffice it to say, I didn't let Reitman get away with what he did, and he obviously hasn't forgotten."

"*Dammit*, Austin." Polly pressed two fingers to her forehead. "If Derek hadn't brought this case to us this morning, would you ever have told me?"

"No."

She laughed without humor, before lapsing into silence. Thinking. Austin gave her the quiet, even though his nature argued that he keeping talking, pushing, convincing. "So, it's not just *me* chasing Reitman anymore," she finally said, her voice sounding dreamlike. Far off. She stood, close enough that his hands itched to reach out, pull her into his body to absorb the warmth she represented. "It's both of us."

Austin nodded, the beginnings of hope stirring in his chest. "You still want to work with me on this?" Not that he'd been about to give her a choice, but it would be much easier if she was aware of his presence on her side.

"I'd be stupid to turn down your help." She appeared at a loss for what to do with her hands, lining up the edges of the pictures and replacing them in the folder. Nervous. And why wouldn't she be after the story he'd told? The past he'd revealed? "Any way I can succeed in accomplishing why I came to Chicago, I'll do it. Reitman pays for what he did to my family—that's the end game. You have just as much at stake as I do now. Maybe more. So you stay in the picture."

If that was how she chose to reason it out, Austin would take it. He'd take whatever she gave him, if only she didn't shut him out. "Reitman will be at a charity dinner Saturday night." He grabbed hold of her momentary flash of pleasure at the news. "That gives us some time to plan."

Polly narrowed her eyes. "You already have a plan, don't you?"

"The beginnings of one," Austin admitted. "Charles—Reitman, that is, is likely playing the scorned investor with Isobel, both of them having been taken for a ride by yours truly. However he plans to lure her into another investment, we need to distract him with a better score."

"How does that get my father's money back?"

"I'm working on that bit. Magic isn't always instantaneous." He took a chance by stepping closer, giving her the half smile that usually had a woman's panties dropping to her ankles. "Sometimes it's slow and…thorough."

She barely spared him a glance, skirting him toward the door, obviously intent on leaving. "Call me when you have something. In the meantime, I'll be—"

Austin beat her to the door, wrapping an arm around her waist to tug her back against him. "Stay, Polly. You want to stay."

"No, I don't." Her tone resonated with frustration she'd obviously been trying to hide. "Working together is one thing, but I can't...be with you now. Not knowing what I know." Her breasts heaved just above his forearm. "*Jesus*, Austin. You spent years with the man who robbed my parents of their *life*."

He released a warm breath against the back of her neck, satisfied when goose bumps formed in its wake. "When we're in this room, we forget what happens outside and do only what we understand. That's what we decided yesterday."

"Then you shouldn't have told me you were...*his* ex-partner in this room."

"I told you in this room on purpose." He nudged aside her T-shirt with his lips and laid an openmouthed kiss on her shoulder. "This is where we're honest with each other. About everything."

He raked his teeth over her ear, earning him a shudder, but still her muscles remained stiff. She slapped a hand onto the door handle, but didn't turn it. "What you told me? It's all I'll think about now."

"No. I won't let you think." He flattened his palm against her belly, pressing down just enough to force a whimper out of her. "I brought you a gift this morning, too. I just didn't think you'd appreciate me giving it to you in front of everyone."

Austin knew beyond a shadow she hated asking, but her inquisitive nature got the better of her, thank God. "What is it?"

His knees almost dipping under the weight of victory, Austin removed the silk rope from his pocket and slipped it into her hand. "Make me suffer, sweet."

Chapter Thirteen

For such a light rope, it held the weight of a thousand doubts. Polly was still reeling from finding out Reitman—or *Charles,* as Austin had referred to the ruinous man—was Austin's ex-partner. Based on Austin's age, the quick math she'd done to determine if they'd been partners at the time her fathers were fleeced had been unnecessary. But oh how she wished Austin *had* been a participant in that crime, so she would have no choice but to leave the hotel room without a single backward glance. The rational half of her brain commanded she leave anyway. She *hated* feeling so damn conflicted.

So why wouldn't her feet move? One step and she'd be in the hallway, moving away from temptation. Austin's body heat behind her represented the flames of hell in one respect and the promise of all-out erotic bliss in another. She *wanted* to punish him. Wanted to make him suffer for deceiving her, deceiving others, making her want him to the point of desperation.

He'd known exactly what would keep her from bolting. Giving her a tool to get back at him for inspiring too many emotions to count. Jealousy, anger, desire, confusion... even gratefulness for getting information she couldn't get access to even from her beloved laptop. She'd never held a rope such as the one caressing her palm, but it already felt familiar. Necessary. Lifeblood. Upon handing it to her like an offering, Austin's breathing had grown choppy against her neck. The outline of his erection was prominent against the small of her back, his touch so sure. For good reason. If she gave in, used this room for what they'd intended, he would spin a web of sex around her and banish all else. A blessing and a curse.

Polly closed her fist around the rope. No. He wouldn't spin anything around her. She would spin around *him*. Control had been handed to her; she only had to embrace it. Memories from the previous evening filtered from her mind, traveling lower until they grew heavy in her loins. The rush of satisfaction she'd experienced holding the belt. Using it on Austin. Being in that place was far more favorable than how she felt now. Running on empty, throat hurting with the need to shout. Maybe she would hate herself tomorrow for channeling her frustration with one of the main sources of it, but the outlet proved too tempting to pass up.

"I want you to..."

Austin's breath ceased behind her. "Finish that thought, Polly."

She ran her thumb over the smooth, twisted silk. "I want you sitting in a chair."

"Done," he rasped, his hand sliding from her belly, brushing over the front of her skirt as it went. Polly waited until she heard him moving one of the armless chairs from the dining table, dragging it across the floor. She knew the slow drag was deliberate when she felt it low in her belly, when her eyelids drooped. As much lip service as he paid to Polly holding the reins, he couldn't help manipulating, pushing the situation in the direction of his choosing.

Maybe he needed to be cured of those inclinations.

Careful not to look at Austin where he now sat in the chair, Polly turned from the exit and crossed to the sliding glass door, drawing the curtain closed and bathing the room in black. The effect was extraordinary, symbolic, creating a "before and after" that Polly knew was lost on neither of them. She was grateful for the change of scenery, the falling of darkness, because it was an excuse to pretend everything in the light was from another life. The *outside* life.

It was that freedom that had Polly stripping clothes off as she walked toward Austin. Shirt lifted over her head, bra unfastened and dropped without breaking pace. When her skirt came off, the soft material hitting the floor was accompanied by a groan from Austin. Dressed only in lace panties, she unfurled the thin rope and let it trail along the ground beside her.

Austin moved restlessly in the chair, splitting his attention between the rope and her mostly naked body. "You're going to drive me out of my fucking head. Aren't you?" His knees fell open, giving her a tantalizing view of the bulge between his thighs. He moved his hips in a hot upward roll that shot Polly's pulse rocketing sky-high. "Seeing your pussy in lace has me halfway there."

The flesh in question dampened, the rough quality of his voice, the base sexuality of his words, making Polly hyperaware of every centimeter of her skin. Her nipples felt tight in the cool air-conditioning, eager to be touched. *Not yet.*

"Take your shirt off," she ordered in voice she wished held more command.

Austin's masculine hands working the buttons of his shirt was nothing short of artwork. He released each one with an almost inaudible *pop*, eyes trained on her like some kind of sleek pleasure-giving machine. Cocky, but visibly *starved* for her next direction. Transfixed by…*her.* The combination of arrogance and need was an assault on her senses, compelling her closer, but she remained still until his shirt drifted to the floor.

"Pants?"

"No," she answered, shaking her head. After taking a moment to savor the power of standing above Austin, she bent forward, sliding her hands up his strong thighs, and stopped just short of his distended fly. "I'll be taking care of you below the waist."

When she dropped to her knees between his legs, Austin growled a curse, his sculpted stomach shuddering. "I should warn you, I'm feeling more than a little possessive of your mouth this morning after seeing you smile at another man. You made me want to *kill*, Polly."

Unable to ignore the jolt of feminine pleasure his admission gave her—dark though it had been—she undid his belt, yanking the leather free of his pant loops with enough force to jerk his hips forward on the seat. "Is that supposed to serve as a warning?"

"Yes." The single word came out sounding strangled, his grip so tight on the chair's edges the wood creaked beneath it. "I suggest using that rope to keep my hands off. I'll be tempted to reclaim the mouth that did the smiling. And I doubt I'd be gentle about it."

A shiver of heat coasted down her back. The idea of Austin's hands tangled in her hair, urging her mouth down faster, wasn't unpleasant. Just the opposite, actually. It caused a breath-stealing clench between her legs. But what she had in mind appealed much more in that moment. She lowered his zipper at a leisurely pace, so at odds with her thundering pulse. "Do you need a reminder of who's holding the rope, Austin?"

A muscle jumped in his cheek. "*Yes*. Remind me."

Polly ran her fingers around the back of his loosened waistband, barely caging a moan when Austin lifted his hips without question so she could tug down his pants, leaving him clad only in a white pair of boxer briefs. She could see right through them, and there wasn't a single doubt in her mind that Austin knew it. Knew she could make out every ridge of the erection pointing toward his muscled abdomen. He was extraordinary, in every sense of the word. His growled plea from the previous night came back to her, carried on a dark cloud of lust. *Please yourself with me. My body. My cock. Own it all.*

Confidence amplified, Polly ran a finger down his hard stomach, circling the fat head of his arousal, before tucking it under the material of his briefs. "Who owns all of this?"

His harsh exhale was directed at the ceiling. "You know you do."

Polly scooted forward on her knees and kissed Austin's erection through the white briefs, smiling when it swelled beneath her mouth. She ignored the way he widened his knees and offered himself to her, performing the same maneuver she'd done with his pants to remove the briefs, leaving him naked. The room was silent, save Austin's breathing. Or maybe it was all she chose to hear, because it garnered all her attention. *In, out, in, in, out.* It sounded like a rainstorm to her ears. Second-guessing herself wasn't an option as she looped the silk rope around the base of his erection. Once, twice. Even when the rainstorm cut out.

Complete silence reigned as she ran the rope alongside the chair. She wound each side once around the front corresponding chair leg, and walked on her knees to the other side, behind Austin. The muscles in his broad back rippled with awareness, his head turning to the side as if to watch her, although in her current position, she wasn't visible to him. Polly retrieved one of two loose ends of the silk, using it to manacle Austin's left hand with a secure knot, then doing the same with his right. When Polly had completed her task, she stared, a little disbelieving of the treatment she'd devised, but incurably excited by what was to come. Any movement of Austin's hands—bound on either side of his hips—would cause the silk loops to tighten around his erection.

And she planned to make sure it moved. Thickened.

Polly stood, running her hands up Austin's back—

The rainstorm started again, loud gusts of breath battering the room's stillness. When she circled back around to the front of him, she saw that his eyes were glassy, the impressive flesh between his legs straining, made all the more prominent by the tight silk at his root.

"Don't touch me just yet. It's too much...having you look at me like that." His right wrist moved, creating a corresponding reaction from the rope. He gritted his teeth to contain a groan as moisture beaded on the tip of his arousal. "Fuck, that's good. You're going to make it hurt so bad, though, aren't you?" His eyelids lifted as though he'd been drugged, his gaze raking over her breasts, her lace-covered mound. "Every second of the day I'm not inside your body hurts. This is child's play compared to what I've woken up with between my legs for the last six months."

"You think so?" The question emerged sounding choked, a reaction to Austin's intensity. To learn that she hadn't been the only one waking up with an unmanageable yearning, far more prominent on days after she'd been in his presence. Empathy urged her to get back on her knees and make up for his end of the pain they'd both experienced. But a quick removal of his edge wasn't what either of them wanted. Or needed.

It wouldn't teach him the lesson she'd been tasked with delivering. She didn't know if the delicious responsibility was a product of Austin's guilt and her disapproval, only knew they would remain unfulfilled without her following through. And God, she didn't have a choice. Her blood pumped; her hands felt weighted. He sat before her looking like a scorching-hot sacrifice. All for her.

Polly floated to the space between his legs, twisting her body in a slow dance, running light fingertips down her rib cage. "I've been waking up with the same problem. All…wet and needing to be filled up." She pinched the sides of her lace panties and peeled them just below her damp center, gasping when Austin jerked in the chair. "You think we were touching ourselves at the same time?"

"I've thought about it." His chest rose and shuddered

back down. "I've thought about it all while abusing my dick to your image."

God. She let the panties fall to her ankles, nudging them aside with one foot, before planting her hands on Austin's shoulders and leaning in to speak inches from his mouth. "Be a good boy and tell me your favorite thing to think about."

His gaze was trained on her breasts, so close to his mouth. So close. Polly eased nearer, letting her nipples hover just within reach, but when he tried to close his mouth around her, she moved back. Austin followed, the action sending the silk coiling tighter around his erection, ripping a vile curse past his lips. "Fuck. *Fucking Christ.*" Sweat broke out along his upper lip. "M-my favorite is flipping you upside down in one of those skirts. Bathing your pussy with my tongue while you attempt to choke me down. Your hands are on my ass, pulling me closer...and when you come for my mouth, I feel the reaction in your throat. Then—"

Thighs clenched together, Polly couldn't get a proper breath, swaying on her feet under the impact of Austin's vivid description of his fantasy. "Then?"

"Coming in your mouth used to finish me. But there's more now that I know what you need. Now...you don't let me come. Until I turn you back over and fuck you again." His eyes squeezed shut on a groan, his arousal growing between them. "Again. And again. Hard. Slow. Doggy. Until I need to come so bad, I can't move without my tip dripping. Then you finally give me permission and it's so goddamn *good.*"

Polly didn't realize she'd started touching herself between her legs until Austin opened his eyes and started to shake his head, a frantic movement so unlike him.

"No. *No.*" His right hand reached for her, resulting in a shout of pain when the silk tightened at the root of his erection. It took him a moment to speak again, voice shaking when he managed it. "Your pleasure belongs to me. We *agreed.*"

"Did we?" Polly breathed, using her index and middle fingers to massage her sensitive nub with painstaking slowness. "I don't recall agreeing to that."

His gaze started to lose its glazed quality, sharpening now where her fingers worked. "Don't do this to me," he grated. "I'll beg. Is that what you want? *Please.* Please let me, Polly. Climb up on my shoulders and let me eat you. Anything you want."

She didn't want to be affected by the abject misery in his voice, but it wrapped around her throat in a stranglehold, even as her desire grew. Conflicting emotions that packed a power punch. Hearing him beg, while reaching the point where she felt the need to beg for him as well, started a vicious churning for relief. An insistent inner voice urged her to push, though. Just a little more. The payoff would be worth it for the both of them. She had no choice but to trust that intuition.

"Stop touching what's mine *immediately*, Polly." When she dipped her middle finger inside herself, Austin's gaze went wild. His neck and chest muscles stood out, biceps flexing as he pulled on the rope. "Give me my hands. Give them to me *now*."

"No." Polly draped her legs over his strong thighs, seating herself on his lap. The position caused each stroke of her hand to nudge his rampant erection, earning her a shouted denial from his mouth.

"It's all I have to offer you." His voice was raw, urgent.

"It's all I've got. *Please.*"

His pain slammed her in the chest. Breaking point. *This* was Austin. The real man she'd seen only in glimpses. She couldn't explain what propelled her forward, seeking his mouth with her own. Only knew that if she didn't have the anchor of his kiss, she'd implode with the sensations careering through her system, puncturing the fabric of her being. Austin made a gruff, broken noise, mouth returning the kiss with frantic brutality. Teeth dug into lips, tongues slipped together as nonsensical words transferred from one mouth to the other. Polly had no consciousness of when she stopped touching herself and clung to Austin, giving and receiving the kiss she never wanted to end.

Finally, he broke away, his forehead now shining with perspiration. "Hands. *Hands.*" Polly's nod was jerky, breath coming in staccato bursts as she fumbled with the knots at his wrists. "*Come on, come on, come on,*" he growled against her lips. "I'm going to fuck the life out of you, cruel girl. Sit beside another man? Deny me the privilege of being the one who makes you come? Your lesson was lost in my jealousy. Untie me so I can take it out on your pussy."

Austin's body went rigid as she uncoiled the silk rope from his hard length, so swollen with need, she felt a rush of sympathy. But it was obliterated by excitement when he rose in one abrupt movement, Polly's legs still wrapped in an unbreakable hold around his waist. He stooped down to retrieve a foil packet from his discarded pants before striding across the room, breath rasping in her ear. They entered the dark bathroom. Her backside hit the marble vanity mere seconds before his thickness impaled her, sliding her back on the hard surface, forcing a raw, echoing scream from her throat.

Demanding hands found her bottom, dragging her back for more, holding her still as Austin drove deep. Deep, deep, *deeper*. There was none of his usual finesse or calculation, just hot, ruthless fucking. The sweat she'd inspired dripped from his forehead to her belly and breasts, trickling down to where their bodies joined. Polly's hands scrambled for something to hold on to, but no sooner did she seek purchase than Austin shoved both hands behind her back, keeping them prisoner with one of his own.

"I'm not your good boy right now, am I?" He reared back and slammed into her, their damp skin striking together. Polly's knees dug into his sides, a quickening taking hold, intensifying with each repeated movement. "Or maybe I am. Getting sweeter with every push of my cock, aren't you?" His words were punctuated by quick pumps of his hips, effectively rolling Polly's eyes to the back of her head. "Tight, tight, tight, aren't we, pretty thing? Go on and soak me. I earned every drop."

It wasn't mere relief but salvation that overrode all semblance of thought, pulling muscles taut she'd never been aware of, racking her in shudders. She had a vague awareness of Austin lifting her ankles and grinding into her, his groans splitting the air around them. *Holy shit, holy shit*. She attempted to drag in oxygen to replenish her empty lungs, but screamed instead.

Austin caught her before she could fall back against the bathroom mirror, pulling her forward into the heat of his chest. He kissed her forehead with a tenderness that belied his unforgiving length, still wedged to the hilt inside her. "You think you could have done that with your fingers?"

The utter arrogance of the question was tempered by the catch of vulnerability in his tone, making her recall what he'd said while still bound by the rope. *It's all I have to offer you.*

Polly shook her head.

His eyes drifted closed a moment, before his eyelids lifted to reveal sexual intention so concentrated, Polly trembled in awe. And perhaps a small amount of fear that he could see everything. All of the chinks in her armor, strengths in her arsenal. The same way she saw all of *him* in that moment. Her heart started to thrum in the hopes that he would move inside her again—she craved more, *more*—but Austin withdrew from her body with a wince. He whipped her off the sink and for one terrified beat, she thought he would punish her for what happened in the chair by not finding his own release. Until he spun her around, pushed her forward onto the vanity and rammed his thick inches inside her, eliciting a loud sob of his name. It was so dark in the bathroom, she couldn't see his face, only the outline of him in the mirror. But she'd never felt more like she was looking directly at someone.

His chest meshed with her back, and the contact was electric. "That first time was for making me jealous, so I made it sting a little." He dragged her earlobe between his teeth before stopping to lay a kiss against her neck. "But this time is for cutting your fingernails and kissing me with your eyes closed so tight." She felt the column of his throat work against her shoulder. "Okay, Polly?"

"Yes," she whispered, shaken. Austin afforded her no time to overanalyze, trailing his hands down her hips and yanking her back. He didn't thrust, giving only smooth undulations of his body as he fucked her back onto his erection, giving her control of the angle at which he slanted into her. "Oh God…stay right there," she gasped. "Just like that."

"If it pleases you." His voice had become a dark scrape of sound, caressing her shoulders and neck. When she felt his gaze on her bottom, she put an extra twist in her movements, sparks of light blooming behind her eyelids at the resulting friction. "You're making it very hard not to hammer you into the fucking sink."

"Why don't you?" she moaned.

"I'll come, *goddammit*," he growled with a powerful buck of his hips, holding himself deep, his abdomen shuddering against her backside. "You have me ready to spill, you dirty little lap dancer. It's not supposed to happen this fast, but *you*. It's you. Feels too *good*." He withdrew and pushed back inside her with a guttural groan. "I've got so much here for you, it's going to fill this condom and drip down those fucking legs."

Polly's mouth fell open. He'd been waiting for permission, and she'd been unaware or gotten lost in the unbelievable way he made her feel. This unselfish man was not the Austin she'd known. Or *thought* she'd known. Right then, in the dark, he was only her lover, and she'd inflicted him with pain. "You have permiss—"

She broke off on a scream when he found her clit with two fingers, rubbing in maddening circles as he started to pound, each thrust of his hips accompanied by a frantic growl. *Slam, slam, slam.* The force of his pounds pushed her facedown on the sink, fingernails scraping at the hard surface. Her flesh was already sensitized from her first climax, and it took her no time for the wave of oblivion to crest over her, holding her entire body in a vibrating grip that was only extended when Austin's shout echoed in the dark. Words made beautiful by their honesty spoke of untold relief that called to something deep inside Polly. *His pleasure is mine.*

"Tightened up all around me like a sweet girl. You feel all that heat I'm pouring inside you? *Take* it." His mouth moved in her hair, laying frantic kisses. "Never want anything else. Nothing else. Just this. Between your legs where it feels right. I'll give you everything, just don't take yourself away."

Polly's vocal cords squeezed so tight, she could only nod. And although she didn't have words for what agreement was made between them, she suspected it was unbreakable.

Chapter Fourteen

Austin leaned against the side of newspaper dispenser, hat pulled low over his eyes as he pretended to read the sports section. Disguising himself hadn't been necessary for this particular trip, but Reitman's presence in town demanded caution. And damn it all if he didn't feel the need to cover up after his epic reveal this morning in the hotel room with Polly. *I'll give you everything, just don't take yourself away.*

He'd even taken himself off guard, demanding promises. Promises were long-term matters, and his life until now had been all about cutting and running at the first sign of routine.

Perhaps he hadn't expected her to agree, so he'd unburdened himself to her, the same way she'd unburdened his body. She'd made him more than someone who was kept around to provide satisfaction. An object. A whore who stole his payment. He'd been more than an illusionist for the first time in his life, because he'd *needed* to be more for Polly. There had been no damming the demand for promises, because with exhilaration flooding his body, his filter had slipped away in the current.

But then she'd nodded. She'd *nodded.*

Austin had been so stunned by her acquiescence, he'd found himself back in the freezing-cold hotel room without remembering leaving the bathroom. As if some manner of fight or flight instinct had kicked in, telling him he'd been made. His cover had been blown. In the way that mattered most, it bloody well had. To Polly. To himself. His pursuit of her had never been solely about sex—or providing a desirable woman with pleasure, rather, since sex had never yielded such gratification for him until now. No, he'd wanted more since their first goddamn argument after the initial squad meeting. Since then, he'd been lying to himself and believing it, the con's affliction that had been prophesized by Charles. He'd been unable to tell truth from fabrication. And the truth was, he'd been in love with Polly since they'd sat across from each other in that conference room at Chicago PD headquarters.

Austin turned the page of his *Chicago Tribune* too hard, ripping a corner free. The sound reminded him of how the delicate fabric of his and Polly's relationship had been torn down the middle by his actions this morning. As soon as his fucking head had gotten back in the game and he realized he'd abandoned Polly in the bathroom, he'd all but lunged for the dark doorway, intent on—what? Not a sodding clue. He hadn't been given the chance to find out what spontaneous action he might have taken when Polly emerged from the bathroom, chin lifted as if she were wearing a ball gown made of sewn-together diamonds instead of a towel.

Yes, it was safe to say he'd broken the spell they'd woven

together. She'd had her laptop and portable printer out in under thirty seconds, documents spitting out onto the table he'd planned to fuck her on during round two. Round two *so* hadn't happened, to the utter devastation of his cock, which seemed to require Polly around the clock, now that he'd gotten a glimpse of her brand of heaven.

Instead…they'd worked. Briefly. His sexy mastermind had worked the laptop like a master pianist, handily providing the missing piece of his plan, which as it turned out was Henrik. Austin's observation of the ex-cop had been spot on. It turned out the man was not only good with his fists, but an amateur boxer who might've had a career if he hadn't chosen the police force instead. Those fighting skills and their usefulness were what brought Austin to Arcadia Terrace, waiting for the squad's newest member, instead of giving head to Polly, where he'd *love* to be.

That, and the annoying knowledge that Derek had given him a two-day window to accomplish something on the Reitman front.

Austin's thoughts returned to Polly like a snapped rubber band. Pleasuring her out of her mind wasn't really an option at the moment, was it? As soon as she'd stacked the documents and placed them in his hand, she'd dressed and blown straight out of the hotel room like it was haunted by a three-headed rottweiler. He might have made a lucrative profession out of charming women until they waved good-bye to their common sense, but it appeared the biggest con of his life lay in convincing Polly he wasn't a worthless shit bag.

And of course, making her his…girlfriend.

"Girlfriend," Austin murmured, testing the word on his

lips. "Be my girlfriend. I'd *like* you to be my girlfriend. Keep your hands off my girlfriend. *Ah*." He liked that. If he and Polly were exclusive, he only had to state the fact out loud and she became off-limits. Like an invisible net that kept other dicks away.

Henrik turned the corner at the south end of the block, grabbing Austin's attention. *Speaking of other dicks.* That giant motherfucker would be the first to hear the news if Polly forgave his earlier panic attack and agreed to keep seeing him outside of work. As in, every single day and night, no questions asked. An eventuality he would be pulling out all stops to reach, preferably *before* Henrik attempted to sit beside her at another meeting and Austin lost his very sanity.

Austin lifted an eyebrow when Henrik paused outside the entrance to his building. He turned to scan the street under the guise of checking his cell phone, obviously sensing Austin's presence. Was Henrik simply a good cop? Or had Austin really had a layer ripped away that morning?

Austin rolled his shoulders in a restless movement. No sense in delaying what he'd come here to accomplish. He tipped his hat back with a quick finger flick and checked for oncoming traffic before crossing the street toward Henrik. The ex-cop turned to watch his approach with a mixture of irritation and curiosity.

"Afternoon, mate," Austin said, removing his hat completely in a sweeping gesture and executing a mocking bow.

"I'm not your mate."

No, he wasn't. And he'd be even less so by the time their visit ended. "I wouldn't suggest pushing your luck after this morning."

Henrik rubbed his chin, as if to ponder Austin's meaning. "This morning?"

Austin tilted his head, smiling through the urge to coldcock the other man. "Do they teach passive-aggressiveness at the police academy?"

"No." A muscle jumped in Henrik's cheek. "But they teach us how to spot a bullshit artist, and I was paying extra close attention that day."

"Bully for you." Austin nodded toward the entrance. "Are you going to invite me in? Or should we discuss Ailish O'Kelly out here on the curb?"

Henrik turned to stone. Something sharp and unpleasant made itself known in Austin's gut. *Imagine that.* For the first time in his illustrious career, he was feeling a definite pang of regret. He didn't like using another man's love interest to put him in a corner, but in this case, it was all he and Polly had to work with. On the train ride over, he'd consoled himself with the fact that the O'Kelly girl would never be affected by what took place. She would, however, guarantee Henrik's cooperation. If the disgraced cop had been willing to end his career to protect her, it stood to reason he wouldn't change his stripes now.

After a moment of debate, Henrik unlocked the entrance door and shoved it open with enough force for it to bang off the opposite wall. "This better not be about me sitting next to your girlfriend this morning," Henrik gritted out as Austin passed him on his way into the well-lit hallway.

Austin gestured for Henrik to precede him up the stairs. *That's right, I know which floor you live on.* "This isn't about you sitting beside Polly, but I suggest you drop it. My temper is long, but nasty." They stopped on the third-floor landing, where Henrik tossed an exasperated glance at him. Austin's answering smile was forced. "I'll admit I wanted to slit your throat during the meeting, but I'm feeling benevolent now that you've referred to her as my girlfriend."

"Bully for me." Henrik was doing a bang-up job of hiding his apprehension, but it was there in the tight lines around his eyes, his uncharacteristic lack of smoothness. When they entered the sparse one-bedroom apartment, Henrik dropped his keys onto the kitchen counter and propped his notoriously lethal fists on his hips. "What do you know about Ailish?"

Austin took a turn around the room, noting the stacked boxes in the corner. The lack of anything personal. Maybe they weren't so different, after all. "I know you destroyed evidence to keep her out of prison." He narrowed his eyes on the other man's back. "I know she disappeared during your brief incarceration." His words caused Henrik's shoulder muscles to bunch. "Didn't leave so much as a love note, did she? I know firsthand how cruel women can be."

"Do the world a favor. Shut the fuck up." Henrik prowled in a circle around the card table serving as a dining room. "Why are you coming to me with this? Just to show off?"

"I *am* a bit of a show-off," Austin admitted. "But in this case, my—Polly is owed the accolades." Pride worked its way past his defenses. Honestly, his defenses had all but deserted him, the cheeky fuckers. "We need your help, she and I. You're going to give it to us."

Henrik's laughter boomed. "If I were holding a hose and you were on fire, I'd point it in the opposite direction."

Granted. "What about Polly?"

"I liked her until a minute ago, when you so casually

mentioned she'd hacked into my private business and obviously plans to use it against me." Henrik crossed his arms over his chest, legs braced in a fighter's stance. "I'm waiting to hear how."

"Before you had your badge taken away, you won quite a lot of money for charity on the department's behalf inside the ring." Austin inclined his head. "You're a boxer. We can use that talent to our advantage."

"I was a boxer. I'm nothing now."

God, Austin was starting to feel shabby about this whole business. "I hope you still have your old gloves lying around, because you're going to need them."

"You need me to fight?" Henrik's expression was incredulous. "Why the hell would I do that?"

Austin took no pleasure in delivering the blow. "We know where Ailish O'Kelly is."

For the second time since Austin arrived, he watched Henrik turn into a mammoth-sized sculpture. Unmoving, but intimidating nonetheless. There was more, though, lurking under the hardened surface. So *much* that it made Austin a little uncomfortable to witness it. In Henrik's eyes lay bedlam. "*Talk.*"

With a nod, Austin turned one of the dining room chairs around and straddled it. "Until now, your fights were merely for fun. Charity bouts and the like." He shook his head. "That won't be the case this time."

Polly had slept with the enemy.

Austin had been her nemesis from day one, but there'd

been a certain amusement behind their constant ribbing. In a million years, she'd *never* expected him to reveal a connection to Reitman. She should feel like a lowly traitor, having slept with him after he'd revealed that information. So why didn't she? Instead, she was experiencing the reverse. A sense of camaraderie to be after the same man. Hope that they could accomplish something together.

She stared at the lines of code flashing across her laptop screen, wishing she hadn't cut off her nails, just so she could chew them. Oh, who was she kidding? She wanted them back as of that morning. If she'd still had her nails in the hotel room, maybe Austin wouldn't have taken one look — and despite the antagonism created in the meeting and the uneven footing they stood on, known he had her. Hook, line, and sinker. She'd paid for the slip in the form of being draped over the bathroom sink, dragging in wheezing breaths in an attempt to recover from the force of nature that was Austin.

If you refuse to think about it, it never happened.
Sure.

As she waited for the desired information to appear on the computer screen, she checked the clock at the bottom right-hand corner. Evening had fallen and the man in question still hadn't shown with his promised "plan" in tow. Hell, maybe he'd never show, choosing to handle Reitman on his own without alerting her. Their parting at the hotel had been awkward to say the least, Austin clearly wanting to go another round, but Polly too thrown by the first time to give in. When she stopped to think about it, his behavior had been so un-Austin. Starting a sentence, stopping. Reaching out, letting his hand drop. So unlike his usual confident self, sure of his skill in seducing a woman.

As always, Austin was proving to be the ultimate riddle, intriguing her relentlessly, despite her remaining reservations. She could never discern his thoughts or puzzle out his motivation. That had never been so true as it was now. Twice now, he'd turned her universe on its head and left her wondering if she'd imagined what had transferred between them. They traded trust and pushed toward understanding, only to step back and leave Polly staring at a riddle that had become more convoluted.

Did she want the riddle of Austin to remain convoluted? It was a strong possibility. Because the solution meant casting aside doubt and going all-in with a man who excelled at deception.

But you're not thinking about it. Remember?
Sure.

As if her desperation for a distraction had called it forth, Reitman's credit card statement popped up on screen. This was her twice-daily ritual: checking for activity, searching for a way into his world. Normally, if he made a rare purchase on credit, whatever goods or services he'd procured would serve to strengthen her thirst for retribution. She sorely needed the benefit of anger now when uncertainty over Austin overshadowed everything she'd worked toward.

A tuxedo rental showed at the very bottom of the list. For Saturday's party? Likely. It must have been an expensive one, because the fee was over a thousand dollars. Paid for with stolen money. Money Austin helped him steal?

A knock at Polly's front door brought her head up, kicked her adrenaline twenty-seven notches higher. Austin was going to be inside her apartment for the first time in mere seconds. The same way she'd done at his barren two-bedroom in Lincoln Park, he would take in every detail with one sweep of his gorgeous eyes and just like that, he would learn more about her. What would that something be?

Polly tucked the short ends of her hair behind one ear, turned the ancient dead bolts, and opened the door. Austin captured her attention first, because *hello*. One forearm was propped against the doorframe, drawing up the hem of his gray long-sleeved T-shirt, revealing crucial inches of his ridged stomach. It reminded her of how he'd looked in the chair, legs splayed. Naked. Had she really come that close to taking him in her mouth and resisted? His knowing gaze told her he was wondering the same damn thing. *Arrogant jerk*. Why did his unabashed cockiness suddenly make her want to laugh?

Beside Austin, Bowen made an impatient noise. "Do you two want to be alone?" He slung an arm around Sera, who appeared busy trying to hide a smile. "We've got better things to do than watch some freaky peep show."

"Oh yeah?" Austin lowered his arm from the doorframe. "Like what?"

"Finding out why we're here, for one," Sera said.

"Or pretty much anything else you can think of," Bowen responded, guiding Sera into Polly's apartment like she was made of glass. "Let's get this over with."

That left Austin standing in the doorway. His focus on her was as unnerving as it was arousing, starting a down-low pulse she now associated with him. Not willing to give her weakness for him away so soon after that morning, Polly stepped aside in one brisk move to let him in, but he grabbed her wrist and tugged her out into the hallway. "We'll only be a moment," he called to Bowen and Sera. "Name your future children or something."

"What are you doing?" Polly asked as the apartment door clicked shut. "What do Bowen and Sera have to do with our plan?"

He released a *shhh* against her mouth. Which should have triggered her knee slamming into his nuts, but sent a ribbon of lust twirling in her stomach instead. As if he could sense the exact location of her chemical reaction, his thumb pressed two inches below her belly button. "You need to relax."

"Excuse me?"

Austin made a humming noise. "When you answered the door, your shoulders were up near your ears, sweet. I don't like seeing you overwrought." He leaned back to run calculating eyes over her form, an invisible motor churning in his gorgeous head. Seeing everything.

When his thumb left her belly to grasp her hip, turning her toward the wall, Polly protested. "Come on. What—"

She broke off on a moan when his thumb found the small of her back, an inch to the right of her spine, massaging with pressure so perfect in its accuracy, it made her sway. Even his chuckle didn't score her pride enough to order him to stop. *Shit.* How had he known exactly where to touch? Stupid question. This was Austin. Her tension had grown throughout the day. Over him. Over Reitman. His thumb moved to the left side of her spine, giving the new area his singular brand of treatment. "There now. That's better."

"I h-hate you."

He made a sound of disappointment. "Here I am trying to make you well and you're taking shots at me." She could hear his audible swallow behind her. "Apologies don't come easy to me, but I'm harboring a fair bit of regret over this morning. You deserved…holding. There will be *holding* next time, Polly."

When his words struck their target, a target shaped suspiciously like a heart, she scrambled to compensate for the fear that realization instilled. He was admitting he made a mistake, and for Austin, that was tantamount to a moonlight serenade delivered on bended knee. Did she want him to feel enough for her that he would learn new tricks, such as apologies? "I never said I needed holding from you."

"I'm well aware. But the fact remains that holding is in your future. By me." His big palm dropped to her bottom, and Polly's frown eased into a smirk. Thank God. He'd made the moment sexual, so she could end it. Figure out what these inconvenient feelings meant later, when he wasn't there to overwhelm.

But then…oh *God*. His thumb dug into the flesh of her right cheek and endorphins rushed through her veins with the effect of a hallucinogen. "Oh Lord. What are you even doing to me?"

Another dark male chuckle, this one more strained than the last. "Your ass muscles are sore because they flex when I bang you." His breath fanned her neck, and she felt it everywhere. Her nipples. The insides of her thighs. "That little flex gives you the qualities of being adorable and fuck-hot at the same time. The adorable half made me feel goddamn lecherous when I took you from behind this morning. Why do you think I needed to come so fast?"

Polly pressed her forehead against the wall, chewing her bottom lip to trap the moan of his name dying to break free. "Is that why?" she managed instead.

"Yes. Although I suspect there will be a different reason each time." He transferred the massage to the opposite side. "Your ass is already so tight. I can't even contemplate what a few more weeks of fucking each other will do to it. You'll be illegal, Polly."

"You're pretty confident…in how the next few weeks will be spent."

"I can't imagine why that would be, sweet. I'm only massaging your bottom in a public hallway." His mouth traced down her neck, before it opened and…French-kissed the space below her ear. There was no other description for the passionate movement of his lips and tongue. He may as well have been performing the kiss between her legs because—*holy God*—wetness rushed and gathered with such swiftness, she couldn't find the wherewithal to draw breath. "When you opened the door," he murmured, his hand still working the flesh of her backside, "were you thinking of sucking my cock?"

"Yes," Polly gasped. "And you knew it. Happy?"

"Quite," he growled. His touch moved, wedging between her stomach and the wall, before dipping lower to capture the juncture of her thighs in a firm hold. "Any time you want it, all you have to do is bat your eyes at me. I'm a slave to you and this pussy. I don't know how to make it any clearer…" He shoved his mouth against her ear in an unexpected move that made her gasp. "*Mistress.*"

His mouth, his hands, his voice. They all deserted her at the same time, sending her pitching toward the wall. Another purposeful maneuver, she was sure. Before and after Austin. With and without Austin. If he'd wanted to remind her what their chemistry had been like in the dark and what it would be like to live without it now, he'd made his point. Now that he wasn't touching her, however, she continued to rewind to his promise of…holding. And she couldn't help but suspect that the sexual trappings that came after had been his way of disguising the importance of that promise. To avoid freaking her out?

Or himself?

"Go on in ahead of me," Austin said, giving her hip a nudge toward the door. "I can't walk in there just yet or I might poke someone's eye out."

Polly turned to find Austin bent forward, hands on his knees, performing what looked to be breathing exercises. A smile curved the corners of her mouth. "You need something gross to think about?"

"I can't think of anything but you, Polly."

Despite the immediate schooling of his features, Polly's toes curled in her shoes. "Oh. Um." She laid her hand on the doorknob. "Once when I was in police custody, I found a Band-Aid in my oatmeal. Does that help?"

"Thinking of you in police custody?" He straightened, but kept his eyes closed. "Yes, I believe that just might do the trick."

"I'll see you inside." She opened the door quickly and stepped into the apartment, before he could see the scarlet blazing up her neck. How could such blunt statements have the effect that romantic poetry or a dozen long-stemmed roses might?

Polly busied herself making coffee for everyone while they waited for Austin to rejoin them. For once, she was grateful that Bowen and Sera were too absorbed in each other to give two craps about what was going on around them. Bowen was content to turn the wedding ring on Sera's finger again and again, saying things into his wife's ear that gave her a blush almost rivaling Polly's. After two minutes, Austin rejoined them, his confidence causing a palpable difference in the atmosphere. He sent Polly a wink before focusing on the couple seated at her functional, Ikea-bought dining table.

"Right, then." Austin clapped his hands together once. "Driscol. You're wondering why you're here."

Bowen's leg bounced in a restless gesture. "You think?"

"Constantly." Austin hesitated, a rarity for him. "You're here because you're the closest thing to a con on the squad. Apart from me, obviously, but I have to work behind the scenes on this one. So. Sloppy seconds it is."

"Man." Bowen dropped a fist onto the table. "Just when I think I can't hate you any more, you up your game."

It had always been a source of amusement for Polly, how much everyone disliked Austin. She'd been one of them—maybe she still was and her better judgment had been buried under a landslide of lust. But right about now, she didn't think everyone's open animosity toward Austin was so funny. In fact, it put her back in the meeting room when Erin pointed the gun at him. If anyone pointed a gun at him or implied he was a shithead, it would be her, thank you very much. Furthermore, he was defending his daughter here, although she doubted he'd be imparting that bit of information anytime soon.

Before Austin could respond to Bowen's barb, Polly moved to stand at his side. "Just hear him out, okay?" She ignored the surprise Austin turned on her. She was too busy fielding her own. "You think he would ask for help if he didn't really need it?"

"No," Sera answered. "He looks like he's swallowing nails."

"Look." Bowen plowed a hand through his dark blond hair. "Ask for any favor you want. But unless I missed Captain Tyler on the way in, he's not the one issuing this assignment. Which means it's fucking shady. And any time there's a chance for Sera to be in danger, the answer is no."

"She won't be in danger, per se." Austin blew out at breath. "I—*we* need you to be your old self just for one night. A man out to make some cash with an easy score. There's a series of unsanctioned fights taking place late Saturday night—an underground operation—and through a connection of mine, I've managed to put Henrik's name on the lineup."

Bowen and Sera exchanged a perplexed look. "Henrik?"

Austin nodded. "You'll be posing as his manager, for lack of a better term. Sera will be safe as houses, but her role as your night's entertainment may require her to show a little cleavage."

When Bowen's chair scraped back, Polly and Sera both stepped in between the two men with their hands out. "Bowen. Wait," Polly said, her attention straying to the desktop computer where she spent so many hours, reading, filing away information. "You won't just be helping Austin. It's for me. And you owe me."

That brought the Bowen up short. "How's that?"

Sera's head tilted, her cop sense obviously alerted by the seriousness in Polly's tone. In her periphery, she saw Austin rock back on his heels, hands dipping into his pockets. As if he simply knew something important was coming, even based on the little information she'd revealed so far. *Connected.*

"The police department set up…alerts on our police files. Past bank accounts, credit reports, social media profiles—not that any of us have one—but these alerts were put in place to ping the department if anyone tried to locate us through our cyber presence." Polly walked backward until she could open her file cabinet, located to the right of her desk. "The safeguards were garbage, though. It took me two minutes to circumvent the firewall. So I set up my own alerts. We've all had hits. People digging. But Bowen…yours and Sera's are continuous."

Bowen's face lost all color as he pulled Sera into the protection of his side. "New York?"

Polly nodded. "We've all been advised by Derek not to open new bank accounts or apply for credit cards…" She put her chin up. "But I opened one in your name anyway and routinely place bogus charges on it. To make it look like you two are in Los Angeles."

"Oh my God." It was obvious Sera's mind was already racing with possibilities. "Do we need to leave Chicago?"

"No," Polly assured her. "You're just as safe here as anywhere."

Bowen was silent for long moments, but Polly could almost see him replaying the horrors from his past, one by one, behind his eyes. "Tell us what you need." He threw a hollow glance at Austin. "Just so we're clear, this isn't for you."

Austin inclined his head at the other man, but he was staring at Polly. His expression was difficult to read, or maybe it just made Polly uncomfortable to read the awe she saw there, because she had to look away.

"Noted," Austin murmured. "Let's get down to business, shall we?"

An hour later, the plan had been detailed. Polly felt sick. Not because the plan wasn't sound. It was. It would put her up close and personal with Reitman on Saturday night. If it went off without a hitch, she would finally be able to return the money the thief stole from her fathers. Austin's daughter would be removed from the presence of evil. And everything would go back to…normal.

But would "normal" hold the same meaning anymore?

In order to beat a con, she would have to *become* one. The very thing she'd always hated the most. Sitting in a beige Chicago kitchen, hatching an illegal plan. One that required lying, stealing…it felt as though her very identity hung in the balance. And she felt a desperate need to remember where she'd come from. Why Reitman's demise was so damn important to her. Her fathers. What they'd been through.

When Austin's steady focus prickled along her skin, Polly realized she'd been staring at Bowen's small set of car keys where they sat on the kitchen table. She quickly looked away.

Chapter Fifteen

Having an almost-girlfriend was a damnable business, anyway.

Austin adjusted his starched collar, nodding at an elderly woman as they crossed paths, reminding him why he'd stopped wearing the priest disguise in the first place. The blue-haired set seemed to gravitate toward him when he donned it, asking him questions about *religion* of all things. It was Polly's fault, really. He'd been in a rush to grab supplies, sensing his almost-girlfriend was about to elude him in some manner that he wouldn't appreciate.

As usual, his prediction had proven correct, but it was of little consolation. Because instead of being ensconced in their hotel room last night, he'd spent the wee hours of the morning following her to Roanoke, Indiana. In a stolen Lincoln. One that had been parked on his block in Chicago for months, amassing parking tickets left, right, and center. Honestly, the owner had been begging for it to be lifted, hadn't he?

That morning in Austin's apartment, Polly had confided her father, Drake, lived in Roanoke, although Austin had no address for the man. Something a certain hacker might have been able to help him with, ironically. He'd followed her to an apartment complex, but while he'd been waiting outside, she must have exited through the parking garage or back entrance because he'd just managed to catch sight of her leaving in the passenger side of a red Jeep. Her father's vehicle, presumably, since Polly drove a black hybrid. He'd had to guess as to her destination, hoping she would come to town for breakfast, shopping, or some such activity. Waiting outside the complex for her return was an option, he supposed, but it would mean waiting longer to see her. And *that*, he didn't like.

Her gradual withdrawal yesterday during the meeting at her apartment gave him some indication of why she'd felt the need to get out of Chicago. And if he was correct—as he usually *was*—Polly had driven three hours for…comfort. Which jump-started the dreadful ache in his chest cavity that never seemed to stop anymore.

Austin thought they'd hit a milestone of sorts in the hallway outside her apartment. He'd promised to hold her, and she'd seemed amenable. Hadn't she? Yes. *Quite* amenable. If memory served, she'd moaned his name when he touched her pussy. In his experience, that served as a *yes, please* for any outstanding suggestions.

"You're mental," he muttered under his breath. Polly wasn't like *anything* in his experience, a fact that had been solidified on countless occasions. Not the least of which was her display of quiet genius yesterday evening. Of *course* she'd been protecting her squad mates for months without breathing a word. The stark opposite of what he would have done, likely lording it over their heads in exchange for something advantageous. In the end, she had, and it had everything to do with his influence.

You're bad for her. You'd be bad for anyone.

A squeal of laughter caused a stutter in Austin's stride, his attention zeroing in on a park across the moderately busy avenue of downtown Roanoke. Children hung upside down from monkey bars, kicked up sand as they ran from one end of the playground to the next. They were of varying ages, but if he guessed any of them, he would probably be off by a matter of years. He knew nothing of children or parks or squeals of laughter. Gemma was only three, so she wouldn't be among those children just yet, would she? Someday.

One of the children let go of the monkey bars only to be caught by a man—presumably their father—and tossed up into the air. Gemma would never know her father. Austin held no delusions in that regard. But his final act in her life would be to make sure she never felt the negative effects of his past misdeeds. That was all he had to offer.

But what did he have to offer Polly?

A hot tingle at the back of his neck made him break stride again. Did the mere act of *thinking* Polly's name cause a physical reaction now?

It always has.

Right.

No, this time it was more. Half a block ahead, Polly walked arm in arm with a gray-haired man. In the opposite arm, she carried a small bouquet of pink tulips, and it was very suddenly all too much. Seeing her walking with someone else—father or not. A someone who'd probably been the one to buy her tulips. He would have gone for roses. Red ones to match the way she blushed. The color of her lips when the wind chapped them.

What the sodding hell was he doing in Roanoke? She had every right to visit her father without Austin tailing her movements. It was an invasion of her privacy, and yet if he'd stayed behind in Chicago, he would have been climbing the goddamn walls by now worrying for her safety. Wondering if she'd needed space to remind herself why he was a shit almost-boyfriend. Really, that wouldn't take much space at all, which is why he'd been planning on fucking her to distraction, giving new meaning to "the best-laid plans."

Maybe you're not quite the mastermind you thought you were.

With an effort, Austin smiled at yet another elderly lady—apparently this town was bloody well brimming with them—and she stopped, laying a hand on his arm. "Good morning, Father."

He swallowed the irony of anyone at all calling him "father" and smiled back, careful to keep an eye on Polly as she stopped outside a café. The gray-haired man rubbed a circle onto her back as they perused a sidewalk menu, presumably deciding whether or not to go inside. "Good morning." He hadn't used his Irish brogue in ages, but it was spot-on. It was a good thing he'd done his homework while waiting for Polly outside the complex, too. This disguise required him to hide in plain sight, as it were. Priests didn't lurk behind buildings, after all. They chatted and employed patience. Damn, but he hated that disguise. "Could you direct me to Saint Paul's? I'm visiting, you see. I fear I've gotten myself a bit turned around."

"Of course." The woman pointed in Polly's direction, where she and her father had been seated at a sidewalk table, taking advantage of the unseasonably warm weather. She was smiling. How could he love that smile and resent it at the same time, simply because it wasn't for him? Would *they* ever eat together in public, or had he doomed them already by suggesting their encounters remain within the confines of a hotel room? He'd hoped it would just be a stepping-stone, but perhaps he'd sold them short early, thinking he'd satisfy her physically and worry about the rest later.

All right. Time to face facts. He was a bloody idiot. Yes, he'd found what Polly needed in bed and made sure she received it, but she wasn't a mark he could overwhelm with sex and expect her trust to follow. Even if he could accomplish such a feat, he didn't want the kind of blind, gullible trust from Polly that he'd won from women in the past with so little effort. No. The idea of it made him queasy. Earning her trust was the key, and the opportunity to prove himself worthy lay just ahead. His final con.

The older lady stopped and resumed her direction-giving one more time, but Austin had been safe tuning her out considering he knew exactly where Saint Paul's was located.

"Father, if it's not too much trouble, would you mind if I walked with you a ways? My friend Jean is sitting in the park over yonder and she could use some counsel. She'll tell you she doesn't, but trust me. She's a damn wreck and I know I shouldn't swear in front of a man of God, but I—"

"Lead the way," Austin interrupted gently. "I'm on God's time. And God's time belongs to the people."

She pressed a hand to her bosom. "Thank you, Father.

Now, I'll just fill you in on the way over…"

Austin actually had to bite down on his tongue as they passed Polly where she placed a breakfast order, for fear he would shout at her for leaving Chicago without a word. Honestly. When had he become so irrational? Or he might have just shouted at her for looking so edible in a red-and-white polka-dot dress when he couldn't get his fucking hands on her. God, the things he would do to her right now. Probably best to hold off on images of tongue-fucking Polly while dressed as a priest, however. A hard-on might be a touch difficult to explain.

When he heard Polly placing her order, however, he couldn't resist reaching into his pocket and dropping the contents onto her table.

…

"It's the strangest thing," Polly's father said, drumming his fingers on the table as he perused the menu. "I can't find our Fullings' verbena mint tea anywhere now. It's like it up and disappeared off the face of the earth."

The waiter stood to Polly's left, pen scratching down their orders as her father sighed in disappointment that their tea wasn't listed. "Yeah. Something like that," she muttered, wishing little reminders of Austin—such as his epic tea-bag hoarding efforts—would stop popping up. "I'll have coffee instead, please."

"Me, too," Drake said, handing his menu back to the waiter.

Polly followed suit, smiling when they were alone again. "So. Have you forgiven me for surprising you?"

"You *know* I hate surprises. There's a reason people have phones and calendars and *phones*." Her father reached across the table and tapped her hand in reproof. "Would it have killed you to call ahead? The guest room hasn't been dusted in months."

"I'm not staying." She had to look away from his disappointment. "I *can't* stay. I have to get back to work tomorrow."

"On a Saturday?"

Well. She hadn't really thought that one through, had she? Not that many nuggets of wisdom had been forthcoming since she'd made the decision to break up with Chicago for the day. The farther she'd gotten from Chicago, the worse the drilling in her middle had become. A little crew of tinkers chipped away at her stomach lining with tiny pickaxes, singing merrily through her misery. It had taken her a few hours to clue in to the problem, but her humorless laughter had rung out inside the borrowed car when the reason for her anxious feelings became obvious.

These were withdrawals. She was addicted to Austin. And God, she wished it were just the sex. Because, by all things holy, the man was criminally talented. Putting on her underwear, showering, tying her shoelaces. All these actions had taken on new significance. Every action felt like preparation. Would he call her "mistress" next time? Or would he be too desperate to allow games?

What would it feel like when he held her?

She wanted the promised holding almost as much as the epic, leg-shaking orgasm that would surely precede it. *I can't think of anything but you.* She still couldn't believe those words had come out of Austin's mouth. Even more unbelievable, they could have come straight out of hers.

Much as she'd like to pretend otherwise, the sentiment had been mutual for so long. She'd put it down to a rivalry, the way he'd commandeered her thoughts that first meeting. Using the excuse of wanting to stay on her toes where Austin was concerned, she hadn't seen her infatuation for what it was. Now that those glimpses beneath his surface were no longer fleeting, but...extended and powerful? The truth wouldn't stay buried anymore. She'd fallen for Austin despite his past, his arrogance, his seeming lack of remorse. And getting to know him as more than an admittedly manipulative con man had only solidified her feelings.

But Polly had always been a realistic person. That personality trait was what had drawn her to computers in the first place. Once programmed, they didn't deviate. You could depend on the outcomes they provided, and if they froze or encountered a glitch, there was a tried-and-true method of fixing them. If she and Austin tried...holding... what if they didn't compute? Was there a method of fixing her when he walked away, his sights set on the next mark? The next...woman? Truth was, they didn't work together on paper. They were already a failed line of code. The time they'd spent together over the last few days didn't change the very important fact that he was a con. She was supposed to loathe him.

Somewhere along the line, though, she'd stopped. And looking at the man across from her, the father who'd been conned by Austin's ex-partner, she felt like the ultimate traitor.

"So eerily quiet over there." Drake gave her that familiar smile, the one where she could see the overbite he claimed made him accessibly handsome. "Makes me think this visit is more than some whimsical road trip."

Polly smirked at his sarcasm. They both knew she did nothing in the name of whimsy. But she appreciated his humor all the same. He'd even maintained it throughout her prison time and tangles with the law, when he should have been questioning his lot in life. After being swindled and left alone by his partner, he'd still managed to remain positive over having adopted a dud daughter. "I owed you a visit. It's been—"

"Three years." He lifted a white eyebrow. "But who's counting?"

"You, obviously." Polly sucked in a slow breath, wishing she could just sit there and enjoy her father's company and the familiar surroundings of Roanoke. There was too much on her mind that needed resolving, however, and so little time existed in which to accomplish it. "Dad, did you ever… was there anyone before Kevin who wasn't as good for you?"

"Women, you mean?"

She laughed. "Sure. Make me spell it out."

"I'm just funnin' you." His eyes twinkled in the midmorning sunlight. "But I'm also not going to accept some roundabout bullshit when we've always dealt straight with each other." He chuckled. "Dealt *straight*. Did you hear me?"

The pressure on Polly's shoulders was easing with each passing second, but something else replaced it. Regret? Yes. More than usual. *Why?* "You're right. That was some roundabout bullshit." She smoothed the napkin already resting on her lap. "The man who took your money—"

"You mean, the man you're after. The man you won't

stop going after, no matter how many times I tell you the past must remain in the past." He lifted an eyebrow. "That man?"

"Yes. Reitman." After she'd been sentenced for hacking into the government server, Drake had implored Polly to use her talent for something positive. All it had taken was an extended silence, and the man who knew her so well had deduced her next move. That it would include hunting down Reitman. He also knew Polly well enough not to expend any more energy talking her into ending her crusade, which only increased her love for him tenfold. Made it even more imperative that Reitman pay for what he'd done. The life and livelihood he'd stolen.

Polly's eyes were drawn across the street to the park, where a priest was surrounded by a dozen elderly women who were giving him very little space. Oddly enough, the sight lifted her mood.

"I've met a man in Chicago. A man who…he made his living stealing money. The way Reitman did." She couldn't tell him they'd stolen together. Saying it out loud was still too hard and somehow pushed her relationship with Austin over the line from *probably doomed* to *definitely doomed.*

Drake coughed into his first. "Any time you want to try to stop shocking me into an early grave would be ideal."

"I'm sorry." The waiter dropped off their coffees, but neither of them made a move to touch the steaming mugs. "With Reitman, did you ever feel like a veil dropped and you could see the real him?"

"Yes. But it was calculated. Something I ascertained when it was too late." Her father sighed and reached into his jacket pocket, searching for cigarettes she'd made him stop smoking at age fourteen. "There were also times the facade fell away and I saw something unsavory. I chose to make excuses or put my premonitions down to stress."

Polly thought back to her first encounter with Austin, then let six months of interactions play out like a movie reel. Memories of hot glances that caused a flush beneath her clothes. His voice speaking in her ear, saying just the right thing to keep her on edge, start her pulse skipping like stones across a quiet lake. Long before they'd met at the hotel, he'd been employing an effective brand of seduction. Until now, she'd chosen to ignore the little things, though. Austin slipping an umbrella into her hand on a morning when she'd forgotten hers, but disguising the kind gesture with a warm breath against her neck. Austin using work discussions as an excuse to accompany her home on the train, dropping *constant* innuendos along the way so she wouldn't notice he'd just wanted to see her into the building safely.

So many instances where he would negate a kindness... on purpose. As if it made him uncomfortable to be sincere, but he accomplished it in his own way that was almost too subtle to notice what he'd done. But never—*never*—had her gut told her Austin possessed the same evil as a man like Reitman. Would Reitman—or any irredeemable con for that matter—find his way to Chicago to watch over a daughter for whom he could never be a parent? Would he protect another person without the promise of any personal gain, as he'd done with her?

Lost in her train of thought, Polly reached for the sugar, intending to doctor her coffee—

Tea bags with pink tags. Two of them were haphazardly placed just behind the plastic container. "Did you bring these?"

She snatched them up, excitement drumming in her veins when Drake appeared just as surprised to see them. "The restaurant said they were out." Her father plucked one out of her fingers. "God, I haven't seen one of these in ages."

Austin was there.

Polly only half heard Drake speculating on the tea bags' mysterious appearance as she stood back from the table, felt the napkin flutter to her feet. Of course he'd come. Relief swept in and blanketed her, its instantaneous calming effect taking her by surprise. As soon as her legs straightened, she wondered how she hadn't felt Austin's presence before. It sat on the air, potent and crackling with dynamism. It attacked her stomach, twisting it in delicious knots as she scanned the streets, the other sidewalk diners.

When her gaze was drawn back to the priest, now surrounded by no less than twenty bickering women, Polly's upper lip curled.

"Dad, is it okay if I meet you at home?"

Chapter Sixteen

Austin really couldn't help being magnetic.

For the first time, though, he wished like fuck he could.

Extricating himself from the mob of women wasn't going to be easy, but a prickle along his spine told him time was of the essence—and a glance over his shoulder confirmed it. Obviously having discovered the tea bags, his almost-girlfriend was waiting for traffic to pass so she could cross the street.

Mine. Mine. Mine. Come to me.

Being made so easily should have disturbed him, but instead his heart seemed to be inflating at a rapid rate. Polly knew him. Even beneath a ginger hairpiece, fake teeth, glasses, and a priest disguise. If she hadn't picked him out among the pedestrian traffic and park-goers, he wouldn't feel this assurance now. Confidence that this monumental craving went both ways. Their awareness of each other went beyond what normal people felt, and he refused to classify her recognizing him in a crowd as a bad thing.

A woman named Bernadette was standing on his loafer, however, and another was tugging on his right sleeve, so he couldn't take the time to gauge Polly's mood. Be it good or bad, though, the last place he wanted to reunite with his erstwhile beauty was in the midst of a senior citizen parade. Not that they weren't quite sweet when it came right down to it, but Polly in polka dots trumped all, didn't she now?

"Ladies. I've so enjoyed this visit." He patted Bernadette on the arm, gently tugging his foot from beneath her practical white runner. "Afraid I've lost track of God's time, however. Have you seen it?"

That question provoked a round of laughter. He didn't have to turn around to know Polly was getting closer. Every hair on his neck lifted; his palms started to itch for contact with smooth skin. God, Austin hoped she was prepared, because he was going to fuck her into a different time zone. And in the middle of it, when he had her hovering right over an orgasm, he would demand she didn't take any more spontaneous vacations. Damn it all, he was a demanding almost-boyfriend. Felt *good*.

Austin really needed to ditch the group of women before one of them asked if he had a banana in his pocket.

"Do you ladies enjoy an afternoon cup of tea?" Austin extricated a handful of tea bags from his pocket, hoping Polly would forgive him, handing them out like tiny little lifelines. "I'm told it's just brilliant."

It wasn't quite on par with turning water to wine, but the distraction worked, allowing Austin to ease his way free of the group. He exited the park at a brisk pace, heading in the church's direction. Stopping to wait for Polly simply wasn't an option, because as soon as she was within reaching distance, it would be curtains. It occurred to Austin that he didn't technically have a plan beyond getting them both off the street. It appeared he would be improvising.

He couldn't very well walk into a church dressed as a priest. Not unless he wanted to go another endless round of questioning.

Just before Austin reached the church, he took a detour down a quiet residential block. Being that it was midmorning on a Friday, the good people of Roanoke would likely be working, a theory confirmed by the line of empty driveways. That wasn't to rule out a neighborhood watch or an eagle-eyed homemaker, though, so it behooved him to move quickly. Hearing Polly's boots approaching on the pavement behind him, Austin removed the false teeth from his mouth—not a sexy maneuver in front of a woman—and cut along a path separating two houses. He stopped outside the side door. No movement inside. No barking guard dogs, thank Christ.

Austin swiped the thin metal rod out of his back pocket—the same one he'd used to break into the stolen Lincoln—and inserted it into the lock. *Easy as one-two-three.* Polly reached him then, though, and he turned—*Jesus.* A gust of oxygen expelled from his body in a harsh rush. *She requires pleasure.* The evidence bloomed in her cheeks, reminding him of succulent watermelon. The tool was left sticking straight out of the lock, abandoned in the immediacy of the moment as he made a grab for Polly.

When she eluded his grasp, a low growl worked free of his throat. But it was cut off when she placed both hands on his chest, fingers curling into the material of his cassock.

Time suspended for a moment before she shoved him up against the door—*hard*—rattling the glass panes. Her brown eyes widened a little, obviously having surprised herself, and that sexy naïveté burned him alive. It would take little effort to overpower her, but he didn't want to. He exulted in her display of possessiveness, even though he was just as eager to turn it around on her, do some down and dirty handling of his own.

"You want to play rough with me, sweet?" He ran his tongue along his bottom lip. "Your favorite belt is wrapped around my waist."

Her soft, feminine moan filled the scant distance between them. "W-what are you doing here?"

Austin's gaze homed in on her mouth. "Dying," he rasped.

That watermelon shade deepened, spreading down her neck. "I m-meant, what are you doing in Roanoke?"

"Get us inside and I'll show you."

She loved him putting her in the driver's seat, could tell by the way she shifted on the balls of her feet. A ready stance. Instead of following through, though, she shook her head, hair brushing over her kiss-needy lips. "Austin. Tell me."

This honesty business was going to be the absolute death of him. It figured that his almost-girlfriend would be the one with the superpower to resist his advances. Fate was a cheeky bitch. "I'm here because you're here. Because I didn't want to know what Chicago felt like without you inside of it." *Blimey*, that felt good. His chest expanded with added room. "You were spooked yesterday. I could see it. It made me anxious. I needed to make sure you didn't ditch the plan and strike out alone, because that would be dangerous, and I don't allow danger a single breath in your direction." He swallowed his nerves, positive he was saying too much, but too revitalized by truth; he couldn't stop. "But mostly I just didn't want *distance* separating us. You're supposed to be close. I like having you *close.*"

"Okay," Polly breathed.

"Just okay?"

Telling the truth sucked.

Polly reached past his right hip and started to jimmy the lock with shaking fingers, her tits rising and falling. Her intakes of breath were deep, swelling her cleavage above the dress's neckline, pushing it up against his stomach. Right. Maybe the truth didn't suck. Maybe it was his new best friend.

The door opened, and Austin stepped backward over the threshold, distracted by Polly's aroused nipples, silently begging for one to make its way free of that polka-dot number. When his mental pleas yielded no results, he twisted his fingers in her dress and tugged down, giving him a peek of red as they moved into the house. When his back met the far wall, a flash of clarity told him they were in a dark, homey living room that smelled faintly of syrup, but then Polly went up on tiptoes and merged their mouths, slicing his consciousness in half with a hot, sensual knife. His instinct was to spin her around and fuck her into a screaming fit against the wall, but he tamped down the urge, sensing her desire to make the first move. And *Lord*, was he ever rewarded, when her left hand skated down his stomach to fist his cock through the black trousers.

"Ah, *God*," he groaned, thrusting his hips forward. "It's

always fucking hard now. It feels different in my underwear, rubbing and rubbing and needing to be adjusted." She gave him a tight stroke, and he slammed his head back against the wall. "You have me on a goddamn leash, Polly. What are you going to do with me?"

Using the hand that wasn't currently working his cock into a state of fuck-or-die, Polly traced his bottom lip with her thumb before pushing up and kissing him slow. So slow, descending his thoughts into sexual chaos. If her jackhammering pulse weren't audible, he would have thought she was toying with him. Making him yearn and pine with no end in sight. She could do it, too, if she chose. Only Polly.

She released his mouth, but he refused to open his eyes. Couldn't. In this exposed state, her beauty would rip him open like a knife through a feather pillow. "What the hell are you doing to me, Polly?"

Their heartbeats thundered in the passing silence. "Is this *you*, Austin?" He felt Polly's finger slip beneath the hairpiece's edges, sliding it from his head. Another crumbled brick from his wall. The glasses came next, dropped to the floor with a fragmented clatter.

If the world ended just then, he would have battled the heavens to the death for another minute in that stupid, syrupy house, with Polly. Nothing made sense but her hand working his cock and her sultry voice breaching the dimness. Unable to resist the call of her beauty, Austin cracked his eyes open and fell into an instantaneous trance. Their noses were almost touching, her breath warming his lips. Destruction. He was destroyed and...*made real* underneath her heavy-lidded gaze.

"There you are," she whispered.

Every brick in his wall disintegrated. An urgency to show her more, *everything*, thickened his blood. He reached for the priest collar and yanked it off, baring his teeth when she licked the swath of throat he uncovered. "That's right. Here I am, you goddamn siren." He rolled his forehead back and forth against hers, groaning when her grip tightened on his dick. "Come and get me."

"*Yes*." Her breath released on a sob, pushing up her tits, almost enough to spill completely from the dress. She used her teeth to spring open a button of his shirt. "Why did you come?"

It took him a second to stop staring at her mouth. "I needed to be here in case you got damp inside your panties, so you could ride me and make it all better. I'd drive across the country to feel you bucking on top of me. Making those adorable mewling noises as you slide up and down my cock. Or grind on my tongue. Whatever it took to make sure you get wet for what *I've* got every fucking time. Nothing else *can* or *will* do when it comes to satisfying my hot little mistress." *Fuck.* His willpower waned, just saying the title out loud. Austin ran a finger over her cleavage and yanked the dress down, allowing her braless tits to pop out, pretty handfuls for him to please. "You've been taunting me with these on purpose. Do you need them sucked, sweet? Maybe you'd like to slide me between them…?" He tilted his hips forward. "… that cock you can't keep your hands off of, hmm?"

Polly appeared flustered in her desire, eyes gone wide as saucers. As if she couldn't rule him with a single command. "Both. I want both."

In one fell swoop. Austin hooked an arm around Polly's waist and snatched her off the ground. He fell on her with long, greedy sucks of her tits, head going light at the taste of her, the fresh smell of lemonade. Not having her hand on his throbbing package anymore caused him physical pain, but she must have sensed it because her thighs locked around his waist, granting him mind-bending friction from her pussy. *Yes, yes, yes.*

Austin took a delicious pull of her nipple and let it go with a pop. "You understand how it works yet? You tell me what your body needs, and I make it happen." Hands dropping to her ass, he dragged the juncture of her thighs up and down his distended length, knowing she was seeing stars every time her clit met his fly. "Beat off in front of me, Austin. Fuck me hard and loud enough that my neighbors can hear your balls slapping me, Austin. Let me ride you until I've come three times. Yes to all of it, Polly. I'm *starving*."

"I want..." She was dragging in breaths, shoulders shaking, but he would give her no quarter. Giving her everything she needed meant pushing her when necessary. She'd taken control with the silk rope at their hotel room, but this was different. So much more had been revealed.

He swiped his tongue across her bottom lip. "You want what?"

"I *need* your mouth between my legs, please."

His grip turned punishing on her ass, a product of the heat she'd unleashed by saying she *needed* him. But it was also a chastisement. "You don't say *please* to me. I don't accept requests."

Austin twisted his hips as her pussy slid over his fly, and she cried out. "Oh my *God*. Get your mouth on me. I'm telling you to. *Now*."

Yes. Finally. He'd played this moment out in his head too

many times to count. Would she be lying down, showering, or standing above him the first time he put his tongue to work on her pussy? Would she like it fast or would she let him savor? It appeared karma hadn't completely turned her back on him, however, because his ultimate fantasy was ripe for the taking, and he wasn't going to allow a margin of time for her or Polly to change her mind. *Taste her or die.*

He let her slide down his body, but as soon as her feet hit the floor, he crossed his right arm between them, hooking around her hip. And he flipped her over, the way he envisioned when he wanted to come extra hard for his own pumping hand. But when the skirt of her dress drifted down and all that lay between his mouth and her honey was nude-colored lace, he almost laughed at how paltry his dreams had been compared to the reality of Polly. Dampness had caused the lace to mold around her center, revealing every nuance, dipping into the precious valley that ran down the middle.

Mine to worship. Mine to keep.

As soon as Polly's obvious shock wore off, her knees dropped to rest on his shoulders, positioning her lace-covered flesh in front of his mouth like an offering. "Oh…oh my God. *Please.*"

Austin rubbed his left cheek against her pussy, knowing from her gasp that she could feel his midmorning stubble through the thin lace. "I'm going to make you so sorry for keeping this from me. You'll wake up every morning needing my mouth before breakfast." He snared the edge of her panties, worrying the fragile material with his teeth until it started to snap and break apart. "You won't even have to ask, sweet. I'll already be yanking your ankles apart."

"Yes. *Yes.* Stop talking about it, just—"

He turned on a heel and lunged toward the wall, wedging her ass up against the hard surface and immobilizing her. After tearing away the remaining lace with his teeth, he greeted the new ruler of his world with a long, lingering lick that stopped just short of her clit. Once that tiny nub entered the mix and she started to beg, there would be no stopping to savor—and fuck—there was nothing on the planet that required more appreciating. Two more slow tastes and she began to squirm, hands working his belt like he'd known they would. He could still remember the way her gaze had dropped below his jeans waistband yesterday, the way her pupils had dilated. He'd been in a painful state of discomfort ever since, knowing—if only for a moment—she'd been hot to suck him off.

"Go on. Take it out." He stiffened his tongue and dipped it inside her, groaning at how tight a space he had to play with. "Take my cock out and see what a fucking state you've put me in, maddening girl. I'm not fit to be in public."

"Me either," she breathed, tugging on his pants until they fell to his ankles. "I can feel you watching me when you're not even there. Makes me so *hot…*"

Not knowing any other way to express what that honest revelation did to him, Austin closed his lips around her pink bud and drew gently once, twice, before lashing at her with his tongue in quick sideways strokes. Her thighs tightened around his ears, muffling the cries that flew from her mouth. When he felt her breath against his cock, finally free of his trousers, Austin growled against her shining flesh. "*Mistress.*"

Her hand circled his base, and Austin held his breath, releasing it in a heavy whoosh when his tip was enfolded between Polly's lips. It was over way too fast, though, replaced by an adventurous tongue. Any other time, he would let her explore and test him, but his balls were almost full to exploding with pressure.

"Let me have a suck, *goddammit*." Austin didn't know his own voice. He was a different man. His throat was thick, his vision hazy.

Polly's tongue traveled up the underside of his shaft in a slow, torturous lick. "You taste so good. Don't rush me."

A blinding light flickered in front of his eyes, produced by a sharp combination of pleasure and pain. *She doesn't want to rush? Give her a fucking reason to change her mind.* Desperate to feel the adorable flex of her ass, he slipped his hands between her round cheeks and the wall, squeezing as he teased her clit with several light strokes, before adding pressure to the movements of his tongue. Those muscles jumped against his palms, giving her away and drawing his balls up so tight he released a ragged moan. But he didn't stop his treatment of her sensitive nub, alternately worrying her between his lips and loving her with his tongue. Finally, her mouth closed around his dick and pulled hard.

God, yes. Yes, yes, yes.

Refusing to cease his quest to drive her to climax, his vile curse was relegated to his head where it echoed loudly enough to rattle his skull. Christ, would he ever stop being so desperate to come with Polly? His abdominal muscles were spasming with the effort to keep his seed from spilling. Never. He would never finish before her. His only option was to get her there quicker.

Austin traced the touch of his right hand over her ass, dipping into the space between her cheeks, placing his index and middle finger over her back entrance. Just a light presence. Until he tapped them over her puckered flesh twice to gauge her reaction. Her moan vibrated up his erection, pummeling him in the stomach. *That's right, you bad girl. I've got your fucking number.* A fact that became even more obvious when she gripped his bottom and yanked him toward her mouth, taking him so deep, Austin's eyes rolled back in his head.

He tapped against her harder, harder, until he was two-finger slapping her over the delicate entrance of her ass, never stopping the whipping of his tongue against her pleasure-needy button. Her fingertips clawed at his backside, thighs beginning to shake around his head. There was no way to stop the roll of his hips toward the perfection of her mouth, but she welcomed him with husky moans that turned into an abrupt scream.

Fuck yes. The orgasm racked her upside-down body, giving him the privilege of experiencing the climax along with her.

"That's it. Moan for me. Tell me how it feels to come with your ass in the air. It won't be the last time." He massaged her backside, spurring on her climax by stabbing his tongue inside her as she contracted. *In and out. In and out.* Christ, she had the most intoxicating taste. He could get drunk on her. "Now here's a tight pussy worth driving all night for. Wanted me to come and get it, didn't you, sweet? You might as well have rung a fucking dinner bell."

His own release was fast approaching, every muscle in his body drawing tighter than a bowstring. The permission he craved didn't come as Polly's body liquefied against him. She knew what held him back, knew what he wanted to hear. Only her green light would symbolize her total satisfaction, and he would never finish until he heard it out loud. The impish purring in her throat, her nonvocal denial, cranked his desire to eleven, while simultaneously driving him to the brink of madness. She tightened her lips around the base of his throbbing length and sucked her way up, so snug, so greedy for his breaking point, it took every ounce of remaining willpower not to let go.

Sweat dripping down his temples, shaking head to toe, Austin's voice came out sounding strangled. "I need to come so bad…"

The purring continued, her mouth venturing once more down his hard inches, tongue swirling around his flesh on the way back up. Austin's mouth fell open on a ragged groan, his intent to beg more, again, as long as she wanted. Then her palm slapped down on his left buttock and the room tilted around him. She smoothed her hand over the stinging area with a hum of concern around his cock before raining down another smack, harder than the first one.

"Jesus *Christ*, Polly." His head fell back, eyes staring blindly up at the ceiling. Euphoria tore through him, knees almost buckling beneath his impending annihilation. Punishment *and* reward. The conflicting actions blurred together until their meanings were the same. It felt like a turning point…an open door that led to a place free of guilt, and he ran through at full speed. A door Polly had opened. "Let me, let me, let me. Need to fuck it all into your cruel mouth. I'm *dying*. Ah fuck, it hurts so badly."

She released his tip, gave it a lick. "Say please."

The words scraped from his throat. "*Please, Mistress.*"

Her hand landed on his ass with enough force to jar his teeth. "Yes."

Austin hung on to Polly with one arm, bracing himself

on the wall with the other, lest he collapse. Breathing was an impossibility as the most fulfilling release of his lifetime shook his foundation, cracking it down the center. Even without the warm suction of her mouth, it would have been perfection, but she gave it to him, gave him her throat and fuuuuuck. Austin's shout emanated from the deepest pit of his soul, sounding distant to his ringing ears. It was too good, enough to capsize him. He gently tugged Polly's mouth away and let the rest of his essence land on the floor. A moment passed where he was freezing, or overheated, he couldn't tell, before he managed to turn Polly over. Then there was nothing, nothing, nothing, but wrapping her in his arms and falling against the wall with a *bang*, listing to the side, and lowering them both to the ground.

It couldn't have gotten any better, but it did, because she clung to him. Polly *clung* to him, like *he'd* been the one to wreck *her*. Everything and nothing made sense. Which was confusing. But he would figure it out when his heart wasn't trapped in his throat, beating with enough zeal to crush a windpipe.

"What the hell are we going to do about anything?"

Polly was silent a moment before she started laughing into his neck. A full, content sound that made Austin want to buy the house and live in it forever, just praying for an echo of that laugh. "You say the best things when you don't think about them first," she murmured.

Replaying that sentiment in his head on repeat, Austin cracked open one eye to see a black fur ball just beyond Polly's shoulder, watching them from his perch on the windowsill. "A cat was watching us that whole time. I don't know whether to be embarrassed or outraged."

"Be whatever you want. Just don't make a pussy joke."

A corner of Austin's lip turned up. "I wasn't even thinking about it. You've ruined me." He tightened his hold around Polly's huddled form. "When I promised you holding, this is not what I pictured."

She yawned against his shoulder. "I think the breaking and entering was a nice twist." A heavy passage of silence ensued—one that made him worry—but she broke it before he could descend into full panic mode. "I'm sorry I left. I was just…losing myself. In the planning, the strong-arming of our friends. I needed to take a breather." When she tilted her head back to meet his eyes, Austin had to bite his tongue to keep from shouting *I love you*. "But…I'm glad you came. I was so anxious all morning and right before…right before I saw you in the park, I realized it was from missing you."

Breathe. Breathe. Missing someone was a long way off from loving, so he needed to keep his shit together until she got there, too. And he had to have faith that she would. Otherwise what was the point of living anymore? "Polly, I don't want you to lose yourself. I can amend the plan to leave you out of it. I—"

"No." She shook her head. "No. I need to know I played a part in ending the pain he causes. I need to be involved or I'll always regret it."

Austin swallowed hard. "What if you regret *being* involved even more? I can relate to that, sweet. It's an ugly feeling and you're too beautiful to feel it."

Time seemed to suspend between them, a brutal ticking of time wherein Austin wondered if he'd said something wrong. In the end, she reached up and smoothed his eyebrow with her thumb. "Do you want to come meet my father?"

Chapter Seventeen

Amazing. The offer of meeting her father hadn't been made in some postorgasmic haze. And it was some *motherfucker* of a haze Austin had left her in. On the twenty-minute walk back to her father's condo, she'd kept expecting to get cold feet. After all, she was about to introduce Reitman's ex-partner to the man whose life had been obliterated by the very same con. On a scale of chess team captain to unemployed musician, Austin broke the suitable boyfriend scale in half. Then sank it to the bottom of the Chicago River.

But as they'd walked along a back route toward the condo, hands brushing several times before Austin had taken hold of hers with a muttered "grow a pair," she'd actually started to look forward to the introduction. Drake was an open-minded person who trusted her judgment. And if there were a few bumps along the way to pleasant, Austin knew better than anyone how to take a jab.

Polly frowned over at Austin, who was staring at

their joined hands out of the corner of his eye. She didn't
appreciate him having to take so many jabs, or that she'd
been the one to deliver them for so long. If everyone could
look a little deeper, the way she'd done recently, they would
see that he wasn't the sum of his arrogance. And he was
plenty arrogant, but he only used it to hide his generosity, his
need to please. Polly flushed at the last part. When they got
back to Chicago, she would set about rectifying everyone's
assumption that they could treat Austin like scum stuck to
the bottom of their shoes.

"What are you glowering at, sweet?" He lifted her hand
to his mouth, breathing on her knuckles. "Do we need to
break into another house and traumatize a second feline?"

Stomach twisting in a slow knot, she looked up at him
from beneath her eyelashes. "Not right this second, but I
reserve the right to make the request at a later date."

His grip tightened on her hand. "I told you, I don't
accept requests from you."

She welcomed the tingle of power in her limbs. The
more she grew accustomed to the rush, the better it felt. "I'll
tell you when I want it."

Austin dipped his chin. "Better. So what were you really
thinking about?"

The touch of vulnerability in his tone drew honesty out
of her. No more holding back. "I was thinking, I can't wait
for the next squad meeting so I can sit beside you again."
The words ached on their way out. "That I'm sorry I missed
the chance last time."

When she risked a look to gauge Austin's reaction, the
intensity she witnessed in his expression made her stumble
on the sidewalk. He pulled her close, so close, dropping his

forehead onto hers. "Say more things like that."

Polly gulped for air. "I liked sitting next to you, even when I didn't want to admit it," she admitted. "Last week, when I was waiting in your apartment, I stole your shaving cream because the smell comforts me. But it didn't comfort me when it wasn't on you. It was always you." His breath pelted her mouth in harsh pants, encouraging her to keep going. Sensing that her praise was affecting him in some important, unseen way. "I don't ever want you to disguise yourself *from* me or *for* me ever again."

"Okay," he whispered. "I hated the times I was unrecognizable to you, Polly. I always want you to recognize me."

"I recognized you today. I think I always will now."

His eyes closed briefly. "That was the best feeling I've had in a long time." He sucked her bottom lip into his mouth and released it gently. "Not counting the times you've had your hands on me. Or the times you've looked at me or spoken to me. Or drank the tea I brought you." Her top lip got a turn in Austin's mouth. "You *are* the feeling."

If she stood on the sidewalk letting his mouth play with hers another minute, she would be under Austin-hypnosis. With a commendable effort, Polly stepped back, ignoring his protesting growl. "Is my father the first you've been introduced to?"

Austin narrowed his gaze, snagging her hand once again as they started to walk. "What do you think?"

Polly bit back her hesitation. "I told him about you." She glanced over. "About your chosen career."

His visible surprise was fleeting, but she suspected he was internalizing. "Should I be glad that you told your father about me? Or worried that this meeting is doomed before it begins?"

"I think he'll surprise you."

"Well." He laughed under his breath. "If he's anything like his daughter…"

She realized he'd pulled her to a stop outside Drake's condo and gave him a look, registering for the first time that he'd sat outside waiting for her, dressed like a priest. "You could have picked a more comfortable stakeout disguise."

He smirked before turning serious. "I didn't feel anything while I was sitting here. I hated you being out of sight. I always hate it."

Polly couldn't swallow around the sudden heaviness in her throat. "Say more things like that."

"My things aren't nice like yours."

"Let me decide."

He looked to the side, his Adam's apple rising and falling. "Sometimes when we go an entire week without a squad meeting or a case, I…sit in the back of your diner while you eat breakfast. Just to see your face. And to make sure no one's with you."

Polly had to struggle to hear him over the pounding pulse in her ears.

"I like the way you move to stay fresh in my mind. So I can recall it any time I want to see you, but can't. I like the feeling we're sharing something, even if you didn't know it. And I like knowing you order breakfast at random after barely looking at the menu. It's so unlike you. Why do you do it?"

Afraid the maelstrom of feelings whirring inside her chest would show in her expression, Polly ducked her head.

"Everything else in my life is a file icon on my computer screen. Sometimes I like not knowing what's coming. But I have to resist ordering the blueberry waffles every time, because they're my favorite." She turned and headed up the path toward the condo, sensing him directly behind her. It should have bothered her that he'd been watching for months without saying a word. It should, but it didn't. In a way, it even soothed her, knowing she'd never truly been alone. Austin had been there, fighting the loneliness off without her knowledge or appreciation.

When they reached her father's door at the far end of the complex, Austin curled a hand around Polly's elbow and pulled her to a stop, his frustration visible. "If I've said too much, it's down to your encouragement. I just wanted to keep holding your hand and now I'm not." He glanced at the appendage in question, as if he wanted to take it, but wasn't sure she'd allow him. "How do I hold it again?"

She knew he wasn't referring to the present. That he meant beyond today. The future. And it scared her, because she'd never thought past settling her score with Reitman. But he was scared, too, even if he didn't admit it out loud. This trip to Roanoke had proven one crucial fact, however, which was that they needed each other in a way that transcended a vocal explanation. So they would be scared together and figure out what came after Reitman when the time came.

"You could hold my hand without touching me," she said, struggling to keep her voice steady. "You're holding it right now."

He stared off into the distance, jaw flexing. Trying to downplay and not pulling it off in the slightest. "Blueberry waffles, is it? I would have guessed something more practical, like a cheddar cheese omelet and wheat toast." When their gazes reconnected, the gravity behind Austin's knocked her back a step. "I need to eat waffles with you, Polly. I need to know that we have breakfast in our future—normal things that make you happy—or my next breath doesn't mean shit."

"We'll have breakfast." She took a step closer, and Austin met her halfway. "But never having normal will be what makes us happy."

He leaned down to growl against her mouth. "I'm going to fuck you senseless at the first opportunity, you realize."

Halfway through his declaration, the door swung open to reveal her father, whose smile didn't waver, even though Polly suspected he'd heard far too much. "Coffee, anyone?"

Austin put a respectable distance between them, looking sheepish for the first time since Polly had met him. "Tea, actually." He reached into his pants pocket and drew out a fistful of her favorite tea bags, handing them to her confused father.

"That was your doing back at the café?" her father asked.

"Indeed." Polly could see the moment he decided not to act the part of doting boyfriend—although she knew he definitely had a seamless golden boy act in him—and decided to be real. Be Austin. "I had to find a way to make her need me. She doesn't need anyone or anything…and I worked with what I had. Because I need her. And so I bought a fuck-ton of tea bags and I'll dole them out when I feel like it. Until I'm sure she'll come back to me with or without them. You'll both need to employ patience."

Her father split a wary, but slightly bemused, look between them. "Shall we have that tea now?"

Polly laughed and slipped inside, waving at Austin to follow. When she reached the kitchen, she turned to watch Austin venture into the homey condo the way an art expert walks through a museum. Cataloging the nuances of each family picture, making deductions based on her father's decor choices. She was more eager than ever to pick his brain, to find out how it worked without the biased windshield through which she'd viewed it before.

"This isn't the place where Polly lived when she was younger," Austin said conversationally, straightening his right sleeve with a tug of the wrist.

When he didn't continue, her father quirked an eyebrow in her direction and went to light a fire beneath the kettle. "How did you come to that conclusion?"

"It's impractical for a young child. Ground floor with no gate between the front door and the pool." Austin shivered. "Can I assist you with anything?"

"I think I've got it."

Austin slid onto the stool beside Polly. "Am I to see school pictures of Polly with missing teeth? Or a ballet recital video? I'd be satisfied with either."

Polly had the simultaneous urge to punch Austin in the shoulder and hug him tight. His lord of the manor behavior might be irritating on the surface, but it meant he wasn't hiding. And that made it wonderful. "You'll see nothing of the sort. I was born with all my adult teeth and the battery died on the camcorder. Every single time."

"Now. That's not entirely true," her father turned from the stove to say. Gone was his affable expression, replaced with one that said *business time*. It was so unexpected that even Austin gave a low whistle that was cut off when her father continued. "But you have to *earn* the right to see those things, and you've got a long way to go. I'm not a man who judges others without getting to know them, mind you, but I think you know that you're a special case."

Austin nodded, his confidence visibly slipping just a touch. "I do know that. Please feel free to ask me anything you wish."

Her father blew out a breath. "Well. I'll have to make a list, won't I?" He lifted the tea bags to his nose and smelled them. "Since I want Polly to come back without an extended hiatus next time, I'll only ask one question and save the rest until then."

"Please," Austin prompted, folding his hands on the breakfast bar.

Drake looked shaken for the first time in a long, long time. So shaken, it forced Polly to fight back tears. "I—we knew. Kevin and I, after five minutes in her company, that we would have to stand back and watch her life unfold. That we couldn't unfold it for her. So I know better than to interfere with what she deems her life's mission. I trust her. Which is why *you* are in my house right now." He picked up a mug and set it back down with a *click*. "I can feel something coming. Tell me my daughter won't be hurt."

Austin was silent for long moments, void of all sound save the flame roaring beneath the kettle. "Polly is the most capable woman I've ever met. I never wanted to be the macho asshole that steps in and plays the hero, because she's her *own* hero. And even knowing that, knowing I'd go side-by-side with her into any battle, I would accept my own death before I allowed her injury. Protecting her is something that gives me purpose, and it doesn't listen to logic." His penetrating stare hit her with the force of a cannonball. "She's untouchable as long as I'm breathing."

The teakettle started whistling, continuing until her father flipped off the burner, although Polly was only semi-aware of the action. Because Austin. He captivated her so completely, movement was impossible. *Love him. I love him. I love him. I love him.*

Her father cleared his throat. "Tea, anyone?"

• • •

Polly woke to the sound of heavy breathing. Hers? Between her legs, a thrumming beat echoed with delicious persistence. Her palms sweated, even though the air conditioner bathed her body. The passenger-side window of the car vibrated beneath her head, signaling the car's movement, but it was nothing compared to the rasping intakes of breath picked up by her left ear. *Not* her breaths.

Cracking an eyelid open, she saw that evening had fallen and they'd exited the interstate, now winding their way through the streets of Polly's neighborhood, Logan Square. Attempting to get her bearings, she rolled her neck and sat up, muffling a gasp in the sleeve of her borrowed jacket when the seat belt rubbed over her stiff nipples.

The sound of labored breathing once again filtered through the residual exhaustion fogging up her head, bringing her attention to Austin where he sat in the driver's seat. Her spine snapped straight at what she saw. His upper lip was beaded with perspiration, his jaw tight enough to shatter. He stared straight ahead, navigating the streets with a white-knuckled grip on the steering wheel.

"You were moaning in your sleep," Austin said, so low she could barely hear him over the car's engine. "Moaning my name...rubbing your legs together. For *me*. I called you mine in your father's house, and you've accepted me. You... want me back."

They slowed to a stop at a red light and he turned eyes that blazed on Polly. Sleep fled as they tracked a path over her exposed thighs, telling her without looking that the dress had ridden up in her sleep, or perhaps she'd lifted it herself, tempting him even in an unconscious state. "I should have pulled over, hiked up that meet-the-parents dress, and fucked you against the side of the car. But I liked hearing you need me. No, I...I love it. I *love* it. Your needs are *my* needs. And I won't breathe or think or sleep until I've satisfied them. Twice."

Polly had grown damp during Austin's speech, the seat's leather upholstery pressing against the underside of her mound. Her own breathing matched the tempo of his now, their urgency in sync as he gunned the car through the green light. Polly was thankful for the encroaching darkness because in her current state, she would feel indecent in the light of day. The dream she'd been having came back to her in graphic snippets, turning her nipples to tight peaks inside her dress. "Nothing looks familiar," she breathed, watching her neighborhood speed by. "Nothing looks the same anymore when I feel like this."

She wasn't making any sense, but Austin's hand left the steering wheel to squeeze her knee, telling her without words that he understood. And that was all that mattered. Finally, they turned down her block, bringing her building into view. Employing the same precision with which he did everything, Austin parallel parked alongside the curb and exited the vehicle to open her door. She studied his offered hand in fascination for a moment, amazed that it appeared to be an ordinary hand when she knew how he could use it.

"Help me breathe, Polly," he grated.

Polly shook herself and slid her fingers onto his palm, gasping when he yanked her out of the car, into his side. He hastily locked the doors and led her to the building's entrance, his footsteps brisk and familiar. But different. Because everything was different now. The way he'd been watching her ever since his declaration in her father's kitchen...it wasn't simply lust and fascination anymore. At first, Austin had appeared a little unsettled by his own vehemence, but it hadn't been long before his demeanor had begun to *own* the words. Grow more powerful within them. Primal possessiveness had been present in every mannerism, every flare of emotion in his eyes.

As soon as they were off the street and ascending the stairs, Austin's touch was beneath her dress, one strong hand molding her bottom.

Polly stumbled on the stair, gripping the wooden banister for balance. "I can't concentrate on walking when you're doing that."

"I drove the last forty miles with you moaning *fuck me Austin* from the passenger's seat." He swatted her backside. "You can make it three flights."

Dented pride spread a blush down her neck to shade her chest, but it was cut with perilous arousal. Since their physical relationship had begun, she'd been the one making the calls. Saying she'd enjoyed being in charge was a vast understatement, but *this* Austin, the demanding one who was abusing her bottom in his grip on their way upstairs? The one who commanded her libido at will, without apology? Yeah, she was starving for *him*, too. A week ago, this kind of treatment wouldn't have flown with her—not from Austin—but she trusted him now. Trusted him enough to let the control he'd granted slip from her hands into his.

A wave of anticipation speared up her legs to manifest between her thighs as they stopped outside her apartment door. Austin's gaze was riveted on her neck, but he didn't devour her the way she expected. His hesitation was obvious in the taut lines of his frame, although he clearly wanted to pounce. *He still thinks it has to be on my terms.* She couldn't wait to strip him of that notion.

They both flinched when the peephole across the hallway darkened, a wooden floorboard creaking. Either Erin or Connor was watching, their vigilance typical for any of the wary squad members, and serving Polly's new purpose at the same time.

Refusing to second-guess the impulses that felt so right, Polly pressed her back up against the door and beckoned Austin closer. There was only a momentary flare of surprise before he pounced, forcefully conforming his rigid body to her softer, pliant one. "You crook your finger at me, little Mistress," he breathed at her temple. "You better have a satisfying demand to make when I get here."

Hyperaware they were being watched, knowing this was her chance to claim Austin as her man in front of the squad who'd made him persona non grata, Polly traced her mouth across Austin's stubbled cheek. "I can make demands," she whispered, their mouths brushing. "But only if it pleases *you*."

Austin ceased breathing, but the rest of him pulsed with urgent, renewed energy. "What is this?" His voice was rubbed raw. "Don't play games with me when I'm this hungry. My life's plan starts and ends with getting my cock inside you."

Swaying under the tingling blast of desire, she positioned her mouth over his. "If you're so hungry, maybe you should kiss me."

A line snapped inside Austin. He devoured her like a starving man, dry-humping her against the door as his tongue invaded with greedy strokes. She never wanted him to stop, could hardly think past how easily the bulge pushing between her legs could drive her to a climax. But she had to focus. There was so much that needed straightening out. Without breaking the kiss, Polly fumbled with her keys, turning them in the lock, allowing them both to crash into the apartment. Austin kicked the door shut, rubbing a hand over his swollen mouth. His eyes were bright, feverish as he strode in her direction.

Polly held up a hand, halting him in his tracks. "W-wait."

Attention locked on her like an unrelenting magnet, Austin unbuttoned his shirt and threw it to the ground. His lip curled in satisfaction when Polly gulped at the sight of his magnificence. "You take ownership of me in front of *them* and then ask me to wait? Do you have any idea how eager to please you I am right now? After what you did?"

"Yes, I know," Polly whispered, reaching behind her back to unzip her dress. She let it flutter into a pool at her feet, emboldened when Austin's smirk crumbled. She hadn't been wearing a bra, and after he'd destroyed her panties with his teeth, had zero coverage to speak of. "I know you want to please me, but you deserve to have me just as desperate to please you. And I am."

Apprehension shaded his expression, but his bravado found its place just as quickly. A potent dose of nerves assailed her. Why was he ignoring her obvious efforts? Had she waited too long to give him the same trust he'd given her? Nothing could stop her from watching as Austin made short work of his belt. His movements were uncharacteristically clumsy as he lowered the zipper and drew out his substantial erection, teeth clenched as he fisted it. "Is it to your liking, Mistress?"

Polly worked to calm her breathing, to no avail, her head light with the temptation of him. It would be so easy to take the offered reins and continue along the same albeit gratifying path, but they couldn't exist inside it forever. She didn't want to. Not when they could be something even *better.* Something lasting. "I gave myself an orgasm before I left for Roanoke." Her confession released in a single gust of breath, her words stunted by the anger that instantly shuttered his features. "After the way you touched me in the hallway, I had to—"

"Excuse me?" Austin moved toward her in slow, measured steps that were far more daunting than a full, barreling sprint might have been. His nudity made him larger, more real. *Right there.* Raw, sexual male animal with a score to settle, and the utmost capability to do it. When he reached her and didn't stop, Polly had no choice but to back away until her bare bottom was wedged against the kitchen table—halting her progress. "That rule was set in goddamn stone," Austin enunciated. "I was very clear. Break it and all bets are off."

"So?" Lust dug its claws into her stomach. "What are

you going to do about it?"

His head tilted to the left. "Turnabout is fair play, don't you think, *sweet*?" Polly's mouth went dry as he fisted his fat erection. Roughly. His thumb circled the head as he completed a choking slide of his grip. Such a tiny detail, and yet it caused yearning to weigh down her loins. An all-consuming requirement to be filled by his steel flesh. Have her body thrust into. Austin made a sound of misery at whatever he saw in her expression, closing his eyes. "I can't even look at you while I fuck myself or I'll spill everywhere before you'vc had a chance to suffer."

Heart twisting, Polly shook her head. "You don't want to make me suffer."

"*No*, I don't." Austin shouted, releasing his distended arousal to advance on her, coming so close she bent backward over the table. "*I don't*. But what else do I have? You stole the only way I know how to keep you."

"No. No, that's *bull*, Austin." Her instinct was to hold him, pull him close, but if they touched in this state of frustration, they would give in to their attraction, and nothing would get solved. "You said all bets are off? Fine. That's what I want."

"I don't understand," he said, voice vibrating. "I thought you wanted control."

"That's what you told yourself, but it wasn't just about me. You needed me to punish away your guilt, and I won't do it anymore." Swallowing her dancing nerves, Polly slipped her fingers into his hair and looked him in the eye. "What you gave me...I love how it made me feel. How it brought us together. But I won't *ever* do it again—not until you stop feeling like you deserve it. You don't."

She couldn't read him for long, scary seconds, his face

carved from stone as he scrutinized her. Relief filtered into her chest when he finally responded. "You have no idea what I'd do to become even slightly worthy of you, Polly. Even if every failed attempt shaved five years off my life, I'd jump in headfirst every time."

God, she was staggered under the weight of that confession, but it was a weight she wanted. Needed. "You don't *have* to do anything. You're already there," she breathed, shaken. But it wasn't enough. "I don't always want to be in control. Sometimes I need...*really* need it to be you."

Fire sparked in his eyes, his nostrils flaring. She felt rather than saw his hands curl into fists at her thighs before they lifted to grasp her hips in an unforgivable grip. "Shall we start by evening the score, then?" Her world blurred into a series of colors as Austin spun her around, shoving the upper half of her body face-first onto the kitchen table. She only had time to glimpse the wooden cooking spoon she'd left on the table a second before he picked it up, the movement almost thoughtful. His heat left her only a moment before she felt the unmistakable sensation of smooth wood sliding down her back. It lingered at her bottom a moment before Austin struck it against her flesh, eliciting a sharp *slap*. "I will still receive the occasional punishment, when it's what you need. But there will be times where I reciprocate. Are we in agreement?"

"Yes," Polly managed, excitement careering through her veins. "Agreed."

"That's very good, sweet, because I've already got one lined up." Austin's fingers tangled in her hair, holding her cheek down against the cool surface. Again, the spoon landed with a *smack* against her backside. "This is for being born with an ass that turns men, including me, into animals."

Her fingers curled on the table. "Y-you're punishing me for something I have no control over?"

"I never said my reasons were rational." With one wing-tip-clad foot, he nudged her feet wider, leaving her with nothing to hide. "When it comes to you, I don't possess a single rational thought. I'm 100 percent fucking irrational over you."

When she felt the concave smoothness of the spoon cup her core, a perfect fit, she whispered his name, eyes squeezing shut. "Austin…"

"Symbolic, isn't it? Since I'd eat your pussy for every meal?" He flipped the spoon over, moving it in a gentle sawing motion, smoothing the wood over her clit. "But we were talking about this ass of yours, and I'm far from finished. It's flexing for me right now. Do you even notice it? Or did the gods build that feature into you hoping it might torture me to death?"

"I don't know. I don't know."

The spoon cracked against her flesh, bringing forth a rush of moisture between her legs. "I've made a study of your ass, sweet, and it's not enough to say men want to fuck you when they lay eyes on it. No. They want to *rut*. They want to take you on your hands and knees in the dirt, in front of their friends." The spoon hit the floor, bringing Polly's head up, but she had little time to prepare before he applied a condom dug from his pocket and drove his thick length inside her, robbing her of anything but the ability to scream. "Were you aware of that, Polly?" His words were growled into her hair. "Were you aware of men coveting you in such a way that I suffer, just watching you walk down the street?"

"No," she croaked, reaching behind to grab his hip and urge him to move. Instead, he clasped her wrist and pinned it at the small of her back.

"You've attracted the scariest animal of all, haven't you?" He reared back and gave her several rough thrusts, driving Polly to the brink. As if he sensed her impending climax, Austin slowed his movements. She began to protest until she felt his mouth lay a soft kiss at the center of her back. "You've attracted the kind of animal who won't rest until he's mated you for life."

Her breath shook out, tears swimming in her vision. Austin slid his forearm beneath her belly, lifting her up and back against his damp, heaving chest, cradling her like a precious treasure. She felt his tongue and lips kissing her neck with such passionate focus, she went up on her toes to get closer, giving him the angle he needed to drive himself into her with measured pumps, hips rolling behind hers with breathtaking skill, his erection pushing deep, thick, *deep*. His arms were wrapped so tightly around Polly's body, her breath escaped in hiccups that were echoed by his throaty groans. But she didn't care about her lack of oxygen, because one big hand massaged its way down her stomach to tease her clit, stroking in time with their undulating bodies...and the storm broke. It didn't crack like lightning this time, but was even more devastating, submerged as it was in honey. Release moved through her, rich and full, like a distant rumble of thunder. Her stomach and thighs shook uncontrollably, tiptoes straining to hold her weight on the floor.

And all the while, Austin's voice in her ear praised her,

prolonging the bliss. "That's it. Milk it so tight. Buck your hips back a little so I hit that clit...ahhh, that's how we do it. Make me feel those little clenches in my sleep. Make me crave more of that pussy. *All day*."

The drain of tension was immense, but it didn't last—not completely—because Austin hadn't finished and she wanted him sated along with her. She pried his arms from around her body and dropped forward, bracing herself on the table and lifting her backside. "Take me, Austin. Use me."

"Never. *Never*, Polly." He pinned her to the table with a swift ramming of his hips, a broken sound passing his lips. "But I can't...I can't come slowly like you did. Not yet. The pleasure...it's new to me. I think it might always be new to me—and you gave me that. You're the only one." His lips brushed over her shoulder. "Tell me you understand that when I fuck you this hard, I'm cherishing you."

"I understand," she gasped when Austin started to drive home. Over and over. The table rocked and creaked beneath her, sweat dripping from her forehead onto its surface, whimpers and cries of ecstasy filling the room. She reached orgasm once more before Austin yanked her hips back, ground himself against her bottom, and came with a shout of her name.

Chapter Eighteen

Austin and Polly walked down North Rush Street side by side, holding hands. He would never get used to that. If he ever got used to Polly wanting to hold his hand, he would convince her to leave him, because she didn't deserve someone who would take her for granted. The words "I love you" sat on his tongue like a chocolate coin, still wrapped in foil. Such sweetness existed inside, but there was a metallic taste because now wasn't the time for professions of devotion. Not when Polly needed to be prepared for the unexpected. He *needed* her to be prepared, because he couldn't be actively involved. Sidelined while his own con played out. While the love of his life made a deal with the very devil.

The Four Seasons got larger and brighter as they approached. Reitman would be inside by now, pretending to drink champagne, trading his full glass for an empty one every so often, staying sharp while everyone else's senses dulled.

They were arriving late on purpose. Making an entrance. It was risky considering they weren't invited, but important people never showed up on time. And tonight, they were the biggest game in town. Bowen, Sera, and Henrik were waiting for them a block from the venue, ready to go, if quite grudgingly. He'd managed to tear himself away from Polly long enough this afternoon for a conference call with his squad mates, reviewing details one by one until each step could be repeated in their sleep.

Some calls were made while Polly slept. He didn't like having secrets between them, but in order for her to be convincing, they were necessary. He consoled himself with the personal vow that after tonight, he would never keep a single secret from her as long as he lived. *Please God, let me have the opportunity to stick around and carry out that promise.*

Austin looked down at Polly, trying not to make it obvious that he was memorizing every one of her beautiful features. "Red hair suits you, sweet, but if you don't mind, we'll be burning that sodding wig later. I don't like changing any part of you."

She tilted her head, peeking up at him from beneath her false eyelashes. "Now you know how *I* felt all those times."

"I suppose," Austin said quickly, before he could profess his undying love. It was an amazing—*amazing*—thing to believe someone when they spoke, without question. He had that with Polly, which meant she truly didn't like him being in disguise. She liked the man beneath, despite his past. Hell, despite his present. He was an unforgivable asshole and they both knew it, but she wanted him in spite of it. The list of what he wouldn't do to protect that was blank.

She deserved better. Total honesty. He couldn't give her that just yet, but he could give her the closest thing, even though it might discolor him in her eyes. No, it *would*. There was no *might* about it. But he couldn't let her go into tonight without a clear picture of the man on her team. Him. Before Polly, he hadn't been a good man, and she needed to know the worst of it.

Austin pulled Polly to a stop, just outside the glow cast by a streetlight. She rubbed her painted red lips together, looking up at him expectantly, but the damning words wouldn't come out of his mouth.

His atypical hesitation must have tipped her off that something bad was coming, because her shoulders sagged an inch. "What is it?"

"Polly, I...you should know that Reitman is retaliating against me for a good reason. After I found out about Gemma in São Paulo and he took off with the money—"

Alarm flared in her gaze. She lifted two fingers and placed them over his mouth, shaking her head. "Not now, Austin. Don't do this right now."

She didn't understand. *Couldn't* understand. What if he didn't get another chance? He circled her wrist and tugged her hand away from his mouth. "It has to be now. You should know whose team you're playing on."

"I *do* know." Confidence laced her tone. "I *know* who you are. I've done some terrible things in the past, too. Taken what I can do at a keyboard and ruined lives with it, telling myself those people deserved their comeuppance for what they'd done. But one of those people could have been you. Or Bowen. Or Erin, Connor, Henrik. If I'd known who

I was affecting, I would have thought twice." She stepped closer, getting right in Austin's face, making his heart boom like back-to-back explosions in his chest. "We are not the sum of our past deeds. There are gray areas and straight-up mistakes, but we can't let them define us. Okay? Whatever you did won't change what I know. And I know *you*."

"Oh God." Austin dropped his forehead down to mesh with hers, rolling it side to side, absorbing warmth, strength. "Oh God. What are you doing with me? Why are you saving me like this?"

"You know why," Polly whispered, her voice carried away on the wind.

He wanted to snatch the words back and immortalize them somehow, because they were as close as he ever expected to come to a declaration from Polly. The chocolate coin on his tongue grew heavier, but instead of unwrapping it the way he longed to do, he clutched her arms tight, so tight. "Listen to me. You go in there and do exactly as we planned. I *will* be there, even though you can't see me." He shook her a little. "Remember this." Austin paused to make sure he had her attention. "I never go into a job unless I know for sure that I can win. Repeat that for me."

She nodded. "You never go into a job unless you know for sure you can win."

A man stepped out from between two parked cars, just behind Polly.

"Neither do I."

Austin's muscles tensed, preparing to throw Polly behind him. When the newcomer stepped into the light, showing Austin his identity, the tension didn't ease, but his fear for Polly's safety took a nosedive. His relief was so intense, it took him a moment to breathe again.

Captain Derek Tyler. *I've been expecting you.*

The captain joined them in the shadows, giving the sight of Austin embracing a redheaded Polly a speculative once-over. "Going somewhere?"

I knew I was right never to underestimate him. "You must already have some idea, since one of your officers has been following us for five blocks," Austin drawled. "Where do you *think* we're going?"

"I'm not here to answer your questions."

"In that case, we're just out for a stroll." Austin turned and tucked a bemused Polly into his side, massaging her hip in a silent signal to relax and trust him. "Just about to bring Polly home, in fact. Fingers crossed she'll give me a good-night kiss at the door."

Derek's expression remained stoic. "We both know I was aware of your connection to Reitman when I hired you, Shaw. It's not a coincidence that he's a block away at the Four Seasons right now." The captain waited while that sank in—although it didn't—because Austin had already been waiting on Derek's intervention since the initial meeting regarding Reitman, well aware he was playing the clock. "One phone call and I can have an extradition warrant to arrest him. I already have uniforms outside the hotel. That would throw a wrench in your plans, wouldn't it?" Plans he should have been made aware of—clearly that was the captain's subtext.

"You don't want to give Reitman to another state for questioning, or you would have brought him in by now," Polly said, hitting the ground running, even though she hadn't been expecting Derek. "Nothing will stick to him. And then you'll have lost your chance to punish him for breaching Chicago city limits."

Austin slapped a hand over his heart. "This *woman*."

Polly was silent a moment, cogs turning in her gorgeous head as she formed conclusions and filled in answers. She would have gotten there sooner, but she'd likely been too stunned in the squad meeting over Reitman to notice Derek's behavior. "You gave Austin the case for a reason. You *need* us to get Reitman."

Derek lifted a dark eyebrow. "And you both needed me to stay out of prison. Cutting me out to settle some fucking vendetta isn't an option."

"What would you like to know, Captain?" Austin asked slowly. "If you're not putting the kibosh on our operation, am I correct in assuming you want in?"

The captain nodded in Polly's direction, smirking when Austin tightened his hold around her. "You're not going along with this for Austin's sake. You've got skin in the game, too." A beat passed. "Reitman appears to be the one thing you two have in common. It took some digging since you erased your fathers' financial records going back twenty years, Polly, but Reitman's name was listed in the physical police report. Not everything is stored in a database."

"I don't like the way you're speaking to her," Austin said, his voice cracking like a whip. He was showing a weakness—his feelings for Polly—when they needed a solid front, but protecting her came first. Apparently his protectiveness extended to her feelings. The idea of her aching on the inside was intolerable.

Derek split a look between them, his cop mind working overtime. "Well played, Polly. Using Austin's little crush on you to help settle a score."

"That is bullshit. You insult us both by suggesting it," Polly responded, hitting Austin with a meaningful look. He knew what she was asking, so he gave a simple, stiff nod, trying not to acknowledge the tidal wave of insecurity spurred on by the captain's claim. "This is for Austin as much as it is for me. Reitman is using his proximity to Austin's daughter to bring Austin out of the woodwork."

Derek's surprise was brief, but there nonetheless. Everything clicked into place on the captain's face, like a blurry pond going perfectly still. "Gemma Klausky is your daughter," he muttered, his attention on Austin. "I'm assuming you're not close."

That statement hit his mark, not that Austin let it show. "No. But Reitman has already stolen a small fortune from her family. The least I can do is not let it happen again."

"Especially since you helped steal it the first time around. Am I right?" Derek tacked on, nodding when Polly stiffened against Austin's side. "Right."

Derek checked his watch and returned his arm to his side, the movement stiff. "What was the desired outcome tonight?"

It was obvious what Derek wanted to know. Were he and Polly planning on retaliating against Reitman by ending his life?

Good question. Justified, too, considering they were a pair of ex-cons. Unfortunately, it was a question Austin didn't have an answer for. Yet. Because Austin knew Charles Reitman better than anyone in the world. And there wasn't a chance in hell of the man being taken alive.

It would all come down to *who* pulled the trigger.

"We get what we came for," Austin answered, steel in his

tone. "And you get your man. Beyond that, we're not willing to share. I'm more than happy to take Polly home right now and call tonight a wash. It would be a dreadful waste of my genius, but I will endeavor to recover."

A tense silence passed, Chicago wind funneling down the sidewalk.

"My officers will stand down, but they'll be ready to move at a moment's notice." Derek grated, already unclipping the two-way radio from his belt. Relief lifted its head inside Austin—after all, additional protection for Polly tonight was why he'd intentionally allowed Derek to remain on their trail—but panic ensued at the captain's next words. "But I'm sending over an officer to put a wire on Polly."

"Absolutely *not*," Austin snapped. "You have no idea who we're dealing with. If he sees or even *suspects* she's not legit, he'll...he could..."

Polly pressed her lips to Austin's cheek when he couldn't continue. "He won't. You have to *trust* me."

His instincts screamed for him to shoulder Polly and make for the closest train station. But he couldn't. They were in it. Too late to turn back now. And part of him was glad he would be able to hear what took place, so he would know if Polly needed him. If she did, he would be removing her from the situation in seconds. "Make damn sure it's a female officer putting the wire on her."

"Start talking," Derek prompted after barking a terse command into his radio.

"We don't have much time," Austin said briskly. "Driscol and his missus are waiting for us. Oh, and the disgraced cop you thrust into our midst."

"Jesus," Derek muttered. "I'm going to regret this."

It was quite possible they all would.

. . .

Polly felt an invisible caress between her shoulder blades and knew it was Austin, watching her. Until now, she hadn't been nervous. She trusted Austin, trusted the plan. But right before they'd parted ways, he'd kissed her. Not *just* kissed. He'd separated them from the group, tugged her into a doorway, and feasted on her mouth. He'd been so thorough, making savoring noises in the back of his throat, branding her with his tongue. She couldn't stop replaying it in her head, remembering his expression as he'd pulled away. There wasn't a name for how he'd looked at her. Or if there was, she hadn't come up with it yet.

There was no time, either. As Austin had reminded her over and over, she was playing a role. Breaking character wasn't an option.

Bowen walked ahead of her on the sidewalk, a careless arm thrown around Sera's shoulders, although Polly knew his attitude was far from casual. He'd made it clear if he sensed a hint of danger, Sera would be out of there in seconds and heads would roll. Polly sensed that Sera's provocative attire wasn't doing anything positive for Bowen's nerves, either. Sera wore a black corseted dress with a slit running all the way to her hip. Paired with a short blond wig, the getup rendered the undercover cop virtually unrecognizable.

Initially, when Austin had pegged Bowen as the closest member of their group resembling a con, she'd been skeptical. But like had recognized like, apparently, because Bowen's swagger and confidence were exactly what they needed to project. In his expensive suit, he was every inch the cocky boxing promoter. Smooth with just the right amount of cunning in his eyes.

Henrik was to her right, clearly unhappy at being the epicenter of their strategy, especially since he'd been informed of Derek's involvement. Polly understood that sentiment all too well. The captain had given them a second chance, and they'd gone behind his back. It would take them a while before they earned his trust back, if ever. She didn't hold out any hope of Henrik ever trusting any of them, however. Not after she'd unearthed the only tool that would guarantee his participation.

When they reached the glass double-door entrance, a hotel employee stepped back to allow them entry, unable to hide his interest in their ostentatiously dressed party of four. Polly checked the urge to tug her dress's neckline higher, preferably up to her neck. Heat stole up her cheeks when she remembered Austin putting her into the garment, the way he'd dragged his tongue across her chest, his gaze locked on the swells of her breasts the entire time.

"I'm going to press these together later and slide my cock between them," he'd said. "Other men will look tonight, sweet. They'll want to touch. But you know your servant touches them best. And so do they." He'd blown cool air across the damp path left behind by his tongue, turning her nipples erect. "*My* mistress."

Polly pressed a hand to her stomach, trying to still the cyclone of need.

It turned out the memory was exactly what she needed, because suddenly, the hotel's interior wasn't intimidating. It was...sexy. Luxurious. Lit with tasteful lamps, the lobby bespoke elegance with a hint of edge, achieved by the seductive strains of modern jazz. She and Sera were drawing the attention of the male clientele, as planned, while receiving reproachful once-overs from the conservatively dressed women who frequented the upscale hotel. Bowen eased the sting, however, by sending winks in their direction.

Henrik's surly expression—whether intentional or not—garnered a different kind of attention. With his size and authoritative demeanor, he was intimidating under normal circumstances, but his lack of smile was in such contrast to the amused, half-drunk expressions worn by Sera, Bowen, and Polly, he stood out. They followed scripted signs through the lobby and down a wide, lushly carpeted corridor where big band music signaled the event.

Just before they reached the entrance, Polly tucked a hand inside the crook of Henrik's arm, well aware of any possible eyes on them. Reitman was just inside those doors, marking the first time she would see him since the nightclub. God, had it really only been a matter of days? "Your animosity is showing," Polly murmured to Henrik, smiling as she said it.

"Good." His jaw flexed. "Tonight, I'm a fallen cop who's been reduced to fighting for money. Not that far off when you think about it. I don't have much of a reason to smile."

Polly wanted to reassure him things would get better, but the words would have been empty. "You have every right to hate me for digging into your business, I—"

"The only person I hate is myself. For not seeing it coming. For needing the information you found in the first place. But I do. I need it." He looked irritated with himself for revealing too much. "Your smile is slipping, Polly."

He's right. Polly mentally shook herself, putting her game face back on. Austin was probably shitting a brick, listening to her talking about anything that didn't pertain to Henrik's upcoming boxing match.

A man stood with a clipboard just outside the partially ajar door, watching the foursome approach with an expression of awe and apprehension. Before tonight, she'd never stopped to wonder what their band of ex-convicts presented to the world, but they were nothing short of daunting in street clothes. Throw in party attire and a fuck-off attitude and they were a force. She could hear Austin's accented voice in her head. *Walk in like you own the bloody place. For all they know, you* do *own it. Nine out of ten people abhor confrontation, so be someone they want to avoid. No one holding a clipboard is desperate enough to keep their job that they'll fight you about entering a party where you clearly belong.*

Bowen turned to Polly and Henrik, speaking loud enough for Clipboard to hear. "Just one quick drink, I swear, then we'll get back to my place."

"Thank God," Polly returned, leaning into Henrik's side. "I've been to so many of these fundraisers lately, I should be nominated for sainthood."

Sera threw her a skeptical look. "Uh. I think it's safe to say that last night knocked you out of the running."

Three of them burst into laughter, Henrik being the sole holdout, as Bowen jerked open the ballroom door. They didn't pause on their way into the noisy event, ignoring the suited gentleman's muttered request to see an invitation. Polly trailed a finger over his chest as they passed, cutting him off.

And just like that, one obstacle was down.

The biggest one lay ahead.

Inside the semi-crowded darkness, playing the carefree party girl was easier than it had been in the lobby. For one thing, there were a lot of boobs on display, not just her own, although she could feel eyes traveling over her as they filtered through the guests on their way to the bar. *My mistress.*

Polly lifted a glass of champagne from a passing tray and tipped it to her lips, allowing the healthy swallow to slide down her throat. Immediately, the music sounded louder, the risk of their actions more pronounced. There were approximately two hundred guests at the function, wealth projecting from each of them. Reitman would see them as marks.

As if the simple act of thinking the man's name had produced his location, Polly saw Reitman in her peripheral vision. Adrenaline spiked in her veins, but she sipped the champagne to keep it contained. She counted to ten, then performed a slow perusal of the dance floor and seating area, only allowing her gaze to pause on Reitman for one-tenth of a second. He was tapping an empty champagne glass against the side of his leg, a speculative expression molding his features as he watched their group fan out at the bar. Bowen hopped up on a leather stool, dragging Sera into the space between his outstretched legs, all while ordering a round of drinks. Polly made a mental note to have a discussion with Derek about their underutilization of Bowen during undercover operations.

Henrik crossed his arms and stood at Bowen's elbow while Polly swayed in a circle to the music. The other guests gave them a wide berth, speaking in hushed tones behind their beverages. Honestly, they were taking hiding in plain sight to the next level, although their behavior wasn't inappropriate. Just *loud* as hell without saying a single word. They made small talk with one another, throwing out innocuous topics to keep them appearing animated. All the while, she could feel Austin's presence just outside, listening to her, speaking to her even though she couldn't hear him.

They had been inside the ballroom for four songs when Reitman sidled up to the bar beside Bowen and Sera. Not one of them so much as blinked, merely continuing to laugh at the story Bowen had just finished telling. A story about him stealing a chicken off the back of a truck in Brooklyn and putting it in his grade school teacher's desk, although Polly had no idea whether or not it was true.

"Should we have another drink here, or head out?" Bowen asked the group, already reaching for his wallet.

"Out," Polly sighed, echoed a second later by Sera.

Henrik's bored expression was his only response.

"Excuse me."

That was the first time she'd ever heard Reitman's voice. It sounded like a shiny nickel. Harmless. Years of resentment twisted like a wrench in her sternum, but she fought to ignore the pain and focus. Reitman smiled at each of them in turn, before nodding at Bowen. "Mind if I buy you and your friends a drink?"

Bowen traded a suspicious look with Henrik. "Is there something we can help you with?"

Reitman didn't show even a hint of alarm at the instant animosity. "I hoped we could talk." He tipped his now-full champagne glass in Henrik's direction. "You've got a fighter's stance. Anyone ever tell you that?"

A subtle change transformed the air at the bar, making the group feel pressed in close, rather than in a loose circle as they were. This eventuality was exactly what they'd wanted, but now that it was upon them, Polly felt an almost-giddy need to make an excuse and leave. No. No. Years of strategic choices had led her to this night, and she wouldn't abandon her cause now. It wasn't only *her* cause anymore. It was Austin's. The friends they'd involved.

"I've been told that a time or two," Henrik finally answered, tight-lipped.

Bowen laughed, breaking just enough of the tension for Polly to draw a breath. He passed Reitman a conspiratorial look. "We weren't exactly invited to this little shindig, so you'll excuse us for not being warm and fuzzy." He scratched a spot beneath his right eye. "Who knows? You might have been security."

"I'm about the furthest thing from security," Reitman returned smoothly. "And hotel security would take one look at your friend and make for greener pastures. No one wants to tangle with a dirty cop turned prizefighter."

Henrik remained still as a statue. Sera and Polly laughed nervously, but Bowen only appeared speculative as he watched Reitman. "That's right. I heard there would be action at this party. Is that still the case?"

A reed-thin woman with a cap of blue-black hair bumped hips with Reitman, before dropping a noisy kiss on his cheek. "Hey, babe. You left me hanging back there. Where's my drink? I'm going to *die*."

Polly just managed to maintain an expression of mild interest, but jealousy prowled like a caged animal in her stomach. Why hadn't she expected this? Isobel had just joined them. Reitman's mark. The mother of Austin's child.

Chapter Nineteen

Austin thought he might be sick. He'd known Isobel would be at the event, but he'd banked on Reitman's shaking her long enough to arrange a deal with Bowen. He'd considered the possibility that she and Polly would come face-to-face, but it was an altogether fucked-up difference to hear his girl's breathing change, her heartbeat dull to a soft pound via the wire taped between her breasts. Goddammit. Having this situation so far out of his control was unacceptable. She was upset, and he was stuck in a bloody panel van with a gaggle of cops. How had he gotten here?

He took a deep breath through his nose and focused on later. Later. Later. When he would have Polly beneath him in bed. She would be stiff at first, still fresh from sharing oxygen with someone with whom he had a past. A child. If the shoe were on the other foot, putting Austin in the same room with an ex of Polly's? He'd have the man in a chokehold already, whether it were rational or not. His hands fisted and shook just imagining it. If Polly felt even a fraction of that…

Focus on tonight. She wouldn't want to be soothed, but he'd give her no choice except to listen. She would hear the words he'd been holding back, again and again, while he rocked into her. There would be no satisfaction for him until she believed him. That life before her was unbearable. That he'd been hiding under a series of identities until she'd made it all right to be…Austin.

He just needed to hold on to tonight. It was almost over.

Bridling his apprehension as much as humanly possible, Austin tuned back in to the voices interspersed with static. Derek grumbled something to an officer wearing a headset, who turned a series of knobs, making the conversation clearer.

"Ah, here's your drink." A beat passed. "Isn't that your friend Shayna?" Reitman, obviously talking to Isobel. A muffled female response followed, to which Reitman replied, "Sure, go catch up. I'll join you in a few minutes."

Some static intruded, clearing just in time for Bowen to speak up. "I have to say, man, seems like you've already got a good thing going. Sure you want to take this action?"

Reitman laughed, but there was an underlying note of tension. "Why don't you let me worry about that?" The tinkling of glasses. "You might be the first fight promoter I've met to question cash in any form."

Austin could picture Bowen spreading his arms, chip on his shoulder all but visible beneath his suit jacket. "Maybe I don't need it."

"I don't trust my money with people who *do* need it."

Derek whistled through his teeth. "Smart motherfucker."

Austin nodded. "Don't assume you've seen the tip of

his iceberg. Imagine how intelligent one must be to be *my* mentor."

The technician turned to Austin with a raised eyebrow, but he only shrugged and went back to listening in on the exchange. He could hear Bowen and Henrik having a low discussion, obviously feeling out Reitman between each other.

"Now these two stick out like sore thumbs..." Reitman was speaking. To Polly and Sera? "You ladies stand out for a different reason. It's a pleasure to be in such beautiful company."

"Thank you." Polly giggled. "Pretty smooth, aren't you?"

Austin could practically feel Reitman's grin through the wire. "Sometimes. But I can be rough when the occasion calls for it."

Bile burned in Austin's throat. "*Fuck.* I want this over."

"This is your show, in case you've forgotten," Derek said. "We could have done this by the book if you hadn't kept me in the dark."

"Keep believing that, if it helps your badge stay shiny."

Bowen's voice filtered through the speaker. "Fight is two nights from now, but we don't give out a location until two hours before the bell, for obvious reasons. It'll be posted on this website and will go dark after thirty minutes." Austin imagined the business card he'd crafted being slid across the bar. "Our boy has three-to-one odds in his favor. These cats are lining up to bet on an ex-cop with nothing to lose." Silence passed. "A shit-ton of money will be lost when he takes the fall, but it won't be us losing it. If you've got the cash up front."

Reitman cleared his throat. "I'm good for it."

"Well, then," Bowen said, backed by the sound of glasses being tapped together. "Fucking mazel tov."

"You're not good for it until we *see* it." Henrik's voice rumbled amid the crackling connection. "I'm not lying down based on your word. We don't know you from Adam."

"He still talks like a cop," Reitman said, amused. "I don't expect blind faith. But one of you will have to come along with me to pick up my offering. I can get away long enough to make one stop, but not two."

Bowen's sigh wasn't overdone, just a touch irritated. *Not bad.* "If it has to be right now, I'll go." A yelp from Sera, following by the musical notes of feminine laughter. "Much as I don't want to let this girl out of my sight."

"No." Despite his negative answer, there was a smile in Reitman's voice. "*She* comes with me. I'll let you know where to pick her up."

A frigid wind blew through Austin, icing every inch of his insides. Breathing ceased to be an option. Which girl? Polly? No. *No.* What the fuck was happening?

"Me?" Polly laughed, Sera joining in. "I said you were smooth, not lucky."

Reitman wasn't laughing. "As we've already established this evening, I play winning odds. And four against one is a losing bet, especially when my money is on the line." No one spoke for a moment. "I'm not picky about which girl comes along, but I get the feeling no one's prying *her* out of your cold, dead hands," Reitman continued, obviously referring to Sera. "So the redhead comes with me and gets the two-fifty. Real easy."

"Not happening," Bowen said. "It's all of us, or the deal's off."

Austin slumped back against the van wall, making a silent but fervent promise not to be an asshole to Bowen in the future. At this point, he just wanted Polly out of there so fucking bad, weight bore down on his chest, crushing his lungs. They would regroup. Do it by the book—

"Whatever. I'll go," Polly broke in, speaking in a hushed tone, pushing straight through Bowen's repeated protests. "You can't turn down that much money. Take his wife's name and phone number and call it if you don't hear from me in half an hour. Fair?"

"She's smarter than she looks," Reitman observed. "Maybe you should listen. She's already contemplating how many dresses she can buy with the winnings."

"Look, it's settled," Polly said. "No big deal. One quick ride so we can get this party back on track. Take the number."

Austin knew what Bowen and Henrik were thinking. With Polly wearing the wire, they would be able to hear everything. They would have him on illegal gambling charges as soon as he handed over the cash. Not to mention, Chicago PD was outside, prepared to follow Reitman's vehicle. But they didn't know Reitman like Austin did. There was blood in the water, and no one could see it but him.

"Get Polly out of there," Austin croaked, forcing words past the squeeze in his throat. "He's made her. I don't know how, but he's made her."

"I'm not getting that." Derek appeared skeptical, but not dismissive. "He's covering his ass. And we're going to cover it, too, as soon as they're on the road."

Austin lunged toward the van door, but Derek wrestled him back. "If he sees you, this entire operation—or any others—will be blown. You think Polly wants that?"

Austin heaved Derek off of him with a growl. "I want her *alive* to be mad at me." He was shouting and didn't give a fuck. His heart was going to explode inside his chest if he didn't get eyes on Polly *now*. "I'm getting her out. If you try to stop me, I will kill you all."

Two guns were drawn on him. "Wrong thing to say," Derek said, gesturing for his officers to lower their weapons. "You can either sit down and be an asset in this operation or I can have you taken downtown to wait in a cell to hear the outcome."

There was only one factor in play that kept Austin from tearing the van apart from the inside out—and he hoped to God he hadn't misplaced his faith. *I never go into a job unless I know for sure I can win.* When he'd told Polly that, he'd meant it. If tonight were the one time that oath failed to be true, he wouldn't allow himself to see tomorrow's sunrise.

• • •

Polly waited for Reitman outside the hotel's back entrance. He'd gone around front to retrieve his car from valet parking, after which he would swing around and pick her up, since they couldn't be seen leaving together. She truly expected Austin to come storming down the dark, narrow street any moment, asking if she'd lost her mind. Maybe she had. But letting the whole ruse drop when so many people were counting on the outcome seemed worse than a car ride with Reitman. His logic had made sense to her, his lack of desire to be robbed or overpowered by two men he didn't know. They were so close to the finish line, derailing now wasn't an option.

Her decision might have been different if the captain hadn't supplied her with a gun, in addition to the wire. The department-issued piece weighed her purse down in a manner both comforting and unnerving. Polly's wits were her weapon of choice in every instance. Having the option of violence, whether it was unlikely or not, started a pulse ticking behind her right eye. Made her depth perception feel off, the way it does in abstract dreams.

Trying not to think about her squad mates' obvious disapproval over her choice, Polly ran a finger down the wire between her breasts, between the unbuttoned opening of her coat. It was comforting, knowing Austin could hear her. But she couldn't say what was on her mind with God knew how many officers listening, so she kept quiet. When headlights illuminated the street, Polly straightened from her casual lean against the wall. He slowed to a stop at the curb in a silver Mercedes, reaching across the console to push open the passenger door.

"Such a gentleman," Polly murmured, sliding onto the leather seat and closing the door. "Silver car for a silver fox, huh?"

His smile was tighter than it had been inside. "Sure."

Polly crossed her legs and dug through her purse for a piece of gum. "How far away are we going?"

"Not far."

All right. That wouldn't really help the officers listening. She'd been hoping for a neighborhood, at least. She resisted the urge to check the rearview for any headlights following them. "You're a real conversational—"

"It was the way you danced," Reitman interrupted. "I didn't get a good look at your face that night at the club, but I remember the way you danced. Same way you danced tonight. All hips and no shoulders. Not that I'm complaining about the hips."

Before he even finished speaking, Polly was considering a grab for the door handle, prepared to dive out of the car, if necessary. Her decision was split between that dangerous idea and removing the gun from her purse, but two things happened at once, preventing her from following through on either. Reitman locked the passenger-side door. And he cocked a gun at her, holding it down in his lap with the hand not occupied steering the car. Her breath echoed so loudly in her ears, it almost drowned out the passing traffic. Shit. *Shit.*

"Oh my God," Polly breathed, dropping the stick of gum to hold up both hands. "What are you doing?"

"You know, I'm a little ashamed to admit I was all in. Word of the unsanctioned match came from someone reliable. The dirty ex-cop story checked out. You had me. I was going to hand my hard-earned money right over." A muscle jumped in his cheek. "It was so good, in fact, that I *know* my ex-partner is involved. Where's my old pal Austin hiding?" He scorched her with a look. "Hmm?"

"I don't know what you're talking about," Polly whispered. "I don't know who that is. Just…please. I want to get out."

"Ding dong, motherfucker." Another gun was cocked in the backseat, whipping Polly's head around. *Erin?* Her blond hair was stuffed inside a black skullcap, her right hand pointing the gun through the seat, straight at Reitman's back. "Save your applause. It might be a Mercedes, but the locks weren't even a challenge."

To Reitman's credit, he didn't even flinch at Erin's unexpected arrival. He didn't take the gun off Polly, either. "It would appear the pupil has become the teacher," he murmured. "Well played, Austin. He always was able to get beautiful women to do his bidding."

Erin moved into a cross-legged position, jingling the bells on her combat boots. "I do no man's bidding, but I owed Austin a favor for procuring this gorgeous baby for me." She lifted the gun an inch. "Plus Polly is the only one who doesn't comment on my table manners. I'm keeping her around."

Reitman remained silent a moment, continuing to drive out of the downtown area. From the corner of her eye, Polly could see the streets were becoming less and less populated. "What's your plan?" Reitman asked tightly. "Do you really think I'll take you to the money now?"

"You will if you don't want a bullet in your back," Erin replied, sounding bored. "We would find it eventually, without your *ass*istance. But I'd rather not shoot you because it would upset Connor." She lowered her voice to a sly whisper. "That's my *boy*friend."

"Yeah?" Reitman took an easy left turn, putting them on a quiet block. Too quiet. A prickle rose on Polly's neck, exacerbated by the hard note in Reitman's voice. "What are you going to do about the gun I have pointed at your friend? It's not going away any time soon."

Erin laughed, the sound cutting off abruptly when Reitman cocked the gun. Polly had no option but to make a grab for her own weapon. In one deft motion, she jammed a hand into her purse —

Reitman swerved the car to the right. *Hard.*

If Polly hadn't been wearing a seat belt, Reitman's maneuver would have sent her flying through the windshield. The vinyl strap dug into her neck, body lurching forward as tires squealed. With a sense of dread, she felt the heavy purse slip off her lap, dropping down near her feet. As soon as the car came to a jarring stop, Polly released her seat belt and went up on her knees, looking for Erin in the backseat. *No. God, no.* Her friend was slumped lengthways across the back seat, clearly unconscious. Blood had already begun to well on her left temple.

"Whoops," Reitman said, his gaze momentarily distracted in the rearview mirror. His lips were curled in a smile. "I kind of liked her, too."

Polly ignored the roaring in her ears, diving for Erin's gun where it lay discarded in the footwell. It was a risky move with Reitman's weapon still leveled in her direction, but she was banking on him wanting to draw out Austin. If Reitman had anything in common with the man she loved, it would be the requirement for satisfaction, answers, knowledge. And right now, Reitman had nothing.

That hope did little to comfort her as she closed a hand around Erin's Ruger and shot back into the passenger seat, expecting a bullet to rip through her skin the entire time. Her relief came in the form of a shaky sob when it didn't happen. Then it was just Polly and Reitman, pointing guns at each other across the car's front console.

Silence stretched for a heated moment before Reitman spoke. "Austin Shaw, huh? Do you have any idea what kind of scum you've teamed with?"

A sharp stab of anger made her grip tighten. "I would say that's the pot calling the kettle black, but Austin is nothing like you."

"Oh no?" A dark glint entered his eyes. "You know, we might be grifters, but there's an honor code among us. We leave family alone. It's not much, but it puts us in the eighth circle of hell, rather than the ninth."

Polly shook her head. "You're the one using Austin's daughter to draw him out. After stealing money Austin tried to *return*."

Reitman scoffed at that. "There's not a con alive that would work a job for two months and walk away without a dime, family or not. That's how I knew Austin had lost his edge." He jerked his chin at Polly, the gun. "Or so I thought."

"What's your excuse for being in Chicago now?"

He tilted his head. "So there's a limit to our Austin's honesty with you, is there?" Polly ignored the lead weight in her stomach and waited for Reitman to continue. "Money is one thing. This, here, *tonight*, this is something I understand. I welcomed Austin getting back at me for double-crossing him. But what he did?" Reitman ground his teeth together. "An eye for an eye."

This is what Austin had been trying to tell her, but she hadn't wanted to know. She'd been so confident it wouldn't make a difference in their relationship—she still had faith it wouldn't—but the lack of knowledge now put her at a disadvantage she couldn't afford. Erin was in the backseat losing blood and needed medical attention. That was her priority now, not an explanation of Reitman's vendetta. Where the hell was her backup?

"That motherfucker seduced my daughter," Reitman gritted out, stalling Polly's rapid-fire thoughts. "He found her down in Texas. Gained her trust and then took her money, the way *I'd* taught him." He swiped his free hand over his mouth. "That money went to Isobel to replace the money I took from Austin's kid. I'm here to get it back, and then some. If anyone understands an eye for an eye, it's Austin."

The gun shook in Polly's hand, but she steadied it. Okay. She'd known it was going to be bad. But it was out in the open now and they would deal with it. So Austin hadn't wanted to get the money back from Reitman for his daughter. That debt had already been replaced. Did he want it for Reitman's daughter instead? To right a wrong? She wouldn't know until they were face-to-face. Ignoring the jealousy trying to wing its way through her breastbone, Polly chanced a glance at Erin in the backseat. God, there was so much blood. About two minutes had passed since she'd been injured, and she needed medical attention immediately.

"Look, I just need to get my friend to a hospital—"

Reitman lifted the gun on a laugh. "A hospital won't be useful to either of you."

Just out of view, tires screeched to a stop.

Chapter Twenty

Austin could barely hear over the fear screaming in his head. He jumped out of the van before it stopped moving, arms raised over his head, turning onto the darkened block where Polly, Reitman, and Erin occupied the silver Mercedes. The last five minutes would forever hold first place as worst in his life. A gun being drawn on Polly, the Mercedes swerving, listening to her being blindsided by his disgusting past deeds. Deeds he'd somehow known would come back to haunt him, but hadn't known when.

How could he have known he'd someday have someone to live for? To be better for?

Polly shot him a fearful look through the windshield. *Don't be scared, sweet.* He tried to communicate with a nod that there was nothing to worry about. He'd taken care of everything. Knowing he'd been prepared for every eventuality did nothing to lessen the blow of seeing a gun pointing at Polly. Rage braided his intestines together like a pretzel, so tight, an explosion seemed inevitable. No. *No.* He needed to be calm and see this through. It had taken some serious convincing for Derek to allow Austin to trade himself for Polly. Erin's apparent injuries had sealed the deal and took precedent now.

Austin stopped at the front bumper of the Mercedes, resisting the need to search Polly's face for a sign of how she felt about him now. Now that there was no question whether or not he deserved her.

He didn't. He never would. But he could give her what she'd come to Chicago for. He could be her champion just this once.

"Charles," Austin shouted, loud enough to be heard through the glass. "You're not going to shoot a *girl*, are you?" He shook his head. "Poor form, old chap."

Austin could see Reitman trying to piece together how he'd gotten there. How he'd known where they would be. He would never put it together that Austin was working for the police. There was no way of him finding that out. It would be too much of a leap for him to make at a moment's notice. Austin was banking on Reitman's assumption that he'd followed them in his own vehicle, which was presumably parked just out of sight in the alley.

Keeping his weapon trained on Polly, Reitman opened the driver's side door and elbowed it open. "Do us both a favor and don't pretend you would shed a tear if I pulled this trigger."

Austin shrugged, striving for nonchalance even though his heart wanted to rip straight through his chest, propelled by fury. "It would be unnecessary. You came to Chicago for me, and I'm standing right here." *Don't look at Polly. Don't look.* "If it's money you want to replace what I took from your daughter, fine. I just want you off my back. Let's go somewhere and have this out like men."

Reitman narrowed his eyes. "Put your weapon on the ground."

Only allowing himself a momentary hesitation, Austin slipped his weapon from its shoulder holster and laid it on the ground. He lifted both pant legs and the back of his untucked shirt, turning in a circle so Reitman could see he wasn't hiding anything. Reitman tilted his head in Polly's direction and Austin nodded, giving her a brief glance. "Lower the gun, babe." He'd never called her that before and hoped it would signal her somehow. Furthermore, it was a generic nickname, one he'd used countless times over the years, that wouldn't seem odd to Reitman. Would make Polly just another mark in his eyes, when she was the furthest thing from it. Polly's arm had started to shake from holding the gun, and the sight made Austin's throat ache. "Jig's up. Put *down* the gun."

Her lips formed the word *no*, but she eventually dropped the weapon. As soon as it went down, Reitman retrained his gun on Austin and climbed out of the vehicle slowly. "So here we are. Finally reunited."

"Spare me the sap, if you please."

Reitman chuckled. "I took a chance, bringing you out of the woodwork this way. Gambling on the assumption you could worry for anyone but yourself." He gave Austin a disgusted once-over. "That little girl will never know your name. And it'll be the best thing that ever happened to her."

"Maybe. But you're the worst." The wire taped to Austin's chest glowed hot. "How much are you planning on taking Isobel for?"

"All of it." Reitman's stance loosened, the way it did when he was bragging. "We're the survivors of the wreckage you left behind, Isobel and I. It's almost too easy." He shrugged. "When I'm done, your child will be as penniless as you left mine."

There. Along with the recorded deal made back at the hotel, that added confession was all Derek needed to arrest Reitman. In exchange for immunity and Derek agreeing to trade Austin for Polly, Austin had agreed to reveal everything about his time with Reitman, once the man was in custody. Yes, he was breaking code. Turning snitch. And given a choice every day for the rest of his life, he would make the same decision to protect Polly. Give her what she wanted.

Austin's eyes connected with Polly for the barest of moments. God, he hated not knowing what she was thinking. When he would see her again, if ever. Once her mission in Chicago had been accomplished, would she see *him* as a valid reason to stick around? With a great force of will, Austin forced his attention back to Reitman. "I presume the money is in the car?"

His ex-partner didn't flinch. "What was that?"

"The money you intended to wager on the match." Austin tipped his chin toward the car. "In the well of the boot…stuffed in a duffel and taped inside the spare tire. Am I right?" When Charles still didn't react, Austin laughed, but it was forced. He could see Polly casting anxious glances at Erin, where she still lay in the backseat. "We both know you have it with you. Never could go five feet without that much cash. Afraid someone like you might make off with it."

Reitman gave a disbelieving eyebrow lift. "I assume you

have a point?"

"Not so much a point, as a strong fucking suggestion." Austin's voice turned to steel. "Take the money from the trunk and let the girls leave in the car. You came here for me, so here I am. You want to put a bullet between my eyes, here's your chance." He ignored Polly's flinch inside the car. "You have your money, your precious revenge…and I can die with a clear conscience, knowing I've sent them to safety. Are we in agreement?"

There was a tense standoff that seemed to go on forever, but in reality was likely only fifteen seconds. Finally, Reitman bent to the side and popped the trunk before backing toward it, Austin still in his gun's sights. He could hear Polly sobbing inside the car and refused to look, loathing that her obvious distress put a smirk on Charles's face. Austin's ex-partner was out of sight for a mere five seconds before popping back into sight, holding a black duffel bag in one hand.

Austin had no choice but to nod at Polly, his stomach pitching at the stark misery in her expression. *Go*, he mouthed, trying his damnedest to appear reassuring. She reached a hand out to him, but it dropped like it weighed a ton. Tears poured down her cheeks as she dived into the driver's seat and gunned the car in reverse, barely giving Reitman enough time to move. *Good girl. Get Erin to a hospital.* He knew before the car even hit the avenue, she would be on the phone with Connor.

Begging fate to give him another chance to hold Polly, Austin aimed the wrath he could no longer contain at Reitman. "Letting her go was the smartest decision you ever made. One more second of that gun in her face might have signed your death warrant." Austin took a menacing step forward. "There's still a chance to sign it, if you don't pull that trigger soon. I'm running out of reasons not to kill you with my bare hands."

"So eager to die, aren't you?" Reitman's confusion was rife with blood lust as he caressed the trigger with his index finger. "Suits me."

Reitman pulled the trigger.

Nothing happened.

Austin released a pent-up breath, silently thanking Erin for remembering to remove the bullets from the gun Reitman kept in his glove compartment. "Maybe next time," Austin murmured to Reitman, just as the police van's engine roared to life and burned rubber onto the street. Another vehicle blocked the far end of the road, giving Reitman no option for escape.

Using Reitman's confusion to his advantage, Austin scooped up the bag of money and left the scene at a brisk pace, ignoring the insults being leveled at him via his ex-partner, who was currently being wrestled to the sidewalk by Derek. No time to stay and enjoy the sight, however. He had work to do.

· · ·

Polly stared at the scuffed-up hospital wall, jolting when a voice droned over the hospital loudspeaker. *What am I doing here? I should go home.* Erin had been released — how long ago? At least an hour. She'd been diagnosed with a mild concussion, and the doctor had wanted to keep her in the hospital overnight for observation, spurring an absolute panic attack on Erin's end. Yeah. Being kept anywhere really wasn't the escape artist's thing. After repeated promises from Connor—who'd looked on the verge of an anxiety attack himself—that his Navy SEAL background qualified him to care for his girlfriend's concussion at home, Erin was discharged.

Throughout the entire scene, Polly had been a presence for Erin, but she'd been useless, only able to see Austin staring down the barrel of a gun. *You want to put a bullet between my eyes?* Cries of denial had risen repeatedly in her throat at the memory, her phone remaining hatefully silent inside her purse. Not delivering any news. Not telling her if Austin was still alive. Until finally, *finally*, the phone had rung.

Polly had been terrified to answer upon seeing Derek's number. *No.* She wanted Austin. She wanted her conceited, inappropriate, secretly amazing Austin. Just before the call could go to voicemail, she'd answered. When Derek told her that Reitman had been taken into custody, she'd nearly collapsed, thinking it was confirmation that he'd shot Austin. *Is he dead? Is he dead?* She remembered her words bouncing off the shiny linoleum hallway floors outside Erin's hospital room.

Her body had surrendered to relief when Derek explained that Reitman's gun hadn't been loaded. That Austin had been suited up with a wire and sent in as a trade for her and Erin. Six hours later, no one could find Austin, nor had anyone heard from him. There'd been no mention of the money from Derek, which meant Austin had it. He'd taken it and gone.

Now there was a very real insecurity attempting to break through her utter joy over Austin being alive. It was taking all of her concentration not to let the insecurity win. If she stood up and went home, walking and boarding the train would require her to let her mental guard down. Which was why she was frozen to her chair, feeling rather than seeing hospital guests passing by like fuzzy specters.

Austin hadn't taken the money and left her behind. She couldn't allow it to be a possibility. But the fear remained, growing stronger. Gaining speed. She felt painfully alone, trapped inside some undiscovered realm where everything was the opposite of what she'd known twenty-four hours prior.

Sitting there would solve nothing, however, so Polly stood on shaky legs, traversed the hospital corridor, and walked into the pitch black of predawn Chicago. The buzz from the fluorescent hospital lights stayed with her as she walked. And walked. Without any real idea of where she hoped to end up. She needed to end up in Austin's arms. She needed him to be standing outside the hospital doors with an explanation, but when he didn't appear, she began looking for him on every street corner. At every bus stop. Passersby were few and far between at this time of the morning, but she double-checked to make sure none of them were Austin, waiting for her in a disguise, with a concise explanation for where he'd gone.

When Polly realized where she'd ended up, she started walking faster. Their hotel. Perhaps he hadn't known where to find her. Perhaps he was waiting in their room. Even as her brain dismissed that hopeful logic, she was jogging through the lobby and riding the elevator up, fumbling in her pocket for the wallet to extricate the key card as it ascended. Somehow before she'd even turned the door handle, she knew Austin wasn't on the other side. There was no electricity, no intuition or pumping excitement she always experienced when he was close.

Polly pushed open the door and stopped. But his *scent*... it hung in the air. Fresh. Like he'd just been there? Or was that her exhausted, desperate mind trying to conjure him any way possible?

Her gaze was drawn like a magnet toward the bed, where it was silhouetted by the outside streetlight. Images lambasted her from all sides. Austin's head falling forward with the belt's first strike. Their mutual groans as he took her hard, unrelenting in his quest for her pleasure, so intent on her every reaction.

That man had felt something for her, hadn't he? It hadn't been a game. She didn't care about the money anymore and would have told him, had she been given the opportunity tonight. She only wanted Austin. Had it been the same case for him?

Polly slapped at the light switch, a ceiling fan illuminating the room from above with a soft glow.

On the bed. What—

Tea bags. Hundreds, maybe even thousands of them were waiting in a mountainous pile, their pink tags waving in the fan's breeze. Polly was across the room in a millisecond, scooping up handfuls of the familiar brand. Distressed whimpers fell from her lips because she didn't know what they *meant*. Was this Austin's way of saying good-bye? No, *please.*

She pinched one of the bags between her thumb and forefinger, noticing for the first time writing on the pink tag. In Austin's confident scrawl were three bold words. *I love you.* Tears fell from her eyes as she picked up another bag and saw the same words. He'd written them on every single tea bag. Her chest constricted to the point of agony. *Dammit.* Why wasn't he there to tell her himself?

Polly's phone went off in her purse, making her jump a full foot in the air. She scrambled to get it out, refusing to pause and wipe the moisture from her eyes. Not Austin. Her father.

"Hello?"

A drawn-out, heavy sigh greeted her. "You're okay."

"Of course I'm okay." She flopped down onto the mountain of tea bags, sending a dozen of them to the floor. "Why...why are you calling?"

Her father didn't say anything for a moment. "The money. I woke up to go for my run and there were just... *stacks* of it on the kitchen table. I assumed it was you."

"No." Polly's eyelids fluttered shut, nuzzling her cheek against the fragrant tea bags. "Austin. It was Austin."

"Right." She could hear him pacing. "What am I supposed to do with it, Polly? Pick up where I left off? That's not an option for me. Not anymore. Not without..."

"I know. I think I knew all along it wouldn't solve or repair anything. I just needed to fix the wrong. The way you two fixed mine." Her hand felt heavy as she lifted it to massage her forehead. "We'll figure something out, all right? I just need some time."

"Where is Austin now?"

"I don't know," she whispered. "Maybe he was never here at all. Maybe I've been asleep this whole time, dreaming him up."

"Polly." Her father sounded worried. What was there

left to worry about? Over. It was all over. "You need to get some sleep."

Sleep was overrated without Austin to hold her.

There will be holding, Polly.

His vow played on a loop as she drifted into unconsciousness.

. . .

Polly didn't recognize any of the waitstaff in the diner. It was midafternoon, not early morning as it was when she usually came. She would still be asleep in the hotel room if a hotel clerk hadn't knocked on the door to remind her checkout time was 11:00 a.m. Unable to leave the hotel without the possibility of returning, she'd called Drake and asked him to book another night on his credit card. The fact that he'd done so without asking any questions only made her love him more.

Acknowledging love for anyone or anything was like prodding an open wound with a fireplace poker. Would she ever be able to feel the emotion again without experiencing such blinding loss?

She slid into her usual booth, waving away the offered menu with a polite but strained smile. "Coffee, please."

The tea bags were still in the hotel room where she'd left them, although the aroma clung to her clothes like a layer of smoke, haunting her. Austin had hijacked the tea's comforting qualities and made them bitter. Bitter and rife with confusion. She'd woken up positive he'd been saying good-bye. Not just with the tea bags, but back in the street with Reitman. How else should she interpret the regret plaguing his handsome features?

A waitress stopped beside Polly's table, placing a plateful of blueberry waffles in front of her. For an interminable stretch of time, all she could do was stare, the implications trickling in slowly, like a dam giving way. The thudding in her chest picked up its pace until Polly felt as if she'd just finished a marathon. She didn't realize she was standing until her hip bumped into a table across the carpeted aisle.

Austin was there.

I need to know that we have breakfast in our future— normal things that make you happy—or my next breath doesn't mean shit.

Where? She'd been so preoccupied upon entering the diner she hadn't felt him. Now, though, when she was allowing herself to feel, energy spun around her in a tight funnel. Customers were looking at her strangely, but she noticed only in passing. She was too busy scanning faces, searching for Austin in the bustling afternoon crowd. When she saw him in the far back corner, the brim of his hat pulled down low over eyes that blazed in her direction, her legs were moving before her brain could catch up, making her stumble.

Austin jolted on his seat, reaching out for her with a startled curse, but she'd already recovered. Two more steps and she'd thrown herself across the booth and into his arms. Arms that banded around her so tightly, she knew instantly that she'd betrayed him by worrying. By doubting.

"Ah, sweet. There you are. Jesus, there you are." He yanked her onto his lap, laying kisses along her jawline. "A day is too long to go without holding you. I could feel myself beginning to fade into nothing. I'm *nothing* unless you're with me."

"Where have you been?" She found his hat offensive for covering even an inch of him, so she knocked it off his head. "I thought you left. I thought—"

Austin pressed their mouths together, cutting her off. "No, you didn't. You didn't really think that, Polly." He searched her eyes, as if looking for some unknown answer. "I was giving you a chance to leave *me*."

The energy funnel churning around them slowed to a crawl. "What?"

His gaze cut to the side. "What Charles told you about me...I've done things I'm ashamed of, Polly. I'm not the kind of man you can be proud of." He rubbed his thumb over her collarbone, studying it so closely she wondered if he was memorizing the shape and texture. "I needed to give you my love. And then let you decide if you wanted it."

"I don't want it," she whispered. "I need it."

His head pitched forward for a moment, as if he were praying, before it lifted again, hitting her with the full force of his happiness. He cradled the back of her head in a gentle hold, his breath striking her lips in relieved gusts. "Oh, thank God. I gave you one night." His laughter embodied the same exhausted frustration she'd felt until being enfolded in his arms. "I was only able to manage it because there were things that needed accomplishing. Things I'm hoping made me slightly more deserving of you, Polly. But I'm still not even close."

Her hands lifted of their own accord to frame his face. "You took the money to my father." Swallowing the desire to avoid an uncomfortable topic, she forced herself to keep going. "Did you send the other half to Reitman's daughter?"

Austin gave a single, pointed nod. "It doesn't excuse my actions. I'm not sure anything will." A multitude of emotions swam across his face, regret and hope chiefly among them. "I want to make up for everything I've done. Repay my debts. It's the only way I can justify allowing myself to be a part of your life."

"Austin—"

"It's going to take some work." A heavy silence passed between them. "Will you help me?"

Polly took a moment to think about what Austin's request really meant. Returning money to the people—mostly women—he'd conned over the span of a decade. Could she do that? It would mean setting aside any and all jealousy, not turning a blind eye on Austin's past, but acknowledging each and every aspect of it. Was she big enough a person to handle that?

Yes. Neither of them was strong enough to accomplish such a difficult task apart, but together they were formidable. One hundred feet tall. For so long, she'd hated him for being a con. Now, here he was, wanting to make amends for the actions she'd condemned. If anything, she felt pride in his decision. Not trepidation or anxiety. As long as Austin was by her side, there wasn't a damn thing she couldn't handle. His love was hers. No one else's. And that wouldn't change. She'd never been more confident in that fact as she was right at that moment.

"I'll help you. We'll do it together."

No sooner had the words left her mouth than Austin crushed his mouth down on hers, his tongue parting her lips on a deep moan. A single brush of his thumb over the exposed skin of her waist, a subtle roll of hips, and Polly almost lost the ability to reason. Or remember the fact that they were in public. When Austin finally pulled away a minute later, they were both gasping for breath. "Polly, tell me we're going to be together. Tell me I'll wake up beside you tomorrow morning."

"We will. You will." She savored the fervent prayer he whispered against her lips. "You told me you loved me on a pile of tea bags," she murmured, heart twisting inside an invisible fist. "It was romantic, but I needed you to be there. To hear you say it."

Austin tilted her chin up, hitting her with eye contact that robbed her of the ability to inhale. "I'll love you straight through into the next life, Polly Banks." He tipped her head to the side and planted a hot kiss beneath her ear. "And the next one. And the one after that…"

Oh, she was going under. But before she could drown in Austin's sensual spell, she pressed a hand over his heart. It was pounding. "I love you, too, Austin. Everything you are. Everything you'll do. I love you."

Epilogue

Henrik pounded his boxing gloves together, wishing it were a bare-knuckle fight so it would hurt more. Make him *forget* more. Shouting of various volumes blended together behind him. Everything blended lately. He was living in a flip-book that went back to the beginning every morning. Wake up, go through the motions, repeat the following day. It was all black and white to him.

Maybe that was why he'd decided to go through with this unsanctioned fight, even though his participation was never supposed to happen. It had only been the setup for Austin's con. Yet he'd found himself unpacking the cardboard box containing his old boxing gear, laying it on the kitchen table where he passed it for hours, considering. When the time had come to make a decision, he'd realized it had already been made.

He was one sorry fuck. Living in a shitty one-bedroom in Arcadia Terrace. Friendless. Jobless. And he'd gotten that way over a girl with whom he'd exchanged one single goddamn sentence. One.

He'd been just outside the park on his lunch break, leaning against the hood of his police vehicle and scanning the sports page. He'd never know what made him glance up, but the sports page had been forgotten in his hand. A green dress. She'd been wearing an emerald-green summer dress that made her hair shine like burnished red-gold in the sunlight. Ailish had run those hazel eyes over Henrik's badge before giving him her undivided attention.

There had been shadowed rings beneath her eyes. Fatigue in the set of her shoulders. But nothing could have detracted from her stunning beauty. It outshone everything in the vicinity. Made the birds' chirping sound dull and desperate. He could remember commanding himself to breathe, but only being able to manage a quick pull of oxygen the entire minute he'd encountered her.

Looking back, he knew even if they hadn't exchanged that one sentence, he still would have fallen for her. Right then. One look and he'd sunk to the lowest ocean floor, unable to hear a sound, save her husky voice.

Do you *ever wonder which side you're really on, Officer?*

She hadn't been mocking him. She'd truly wanted to know. The distress in her tone had gripped him by the throat, rendering him incapable of responding. She'd moved on before he could formulate an answer. Or help her, as every bone in his body demanded. *Save. Fix. Mine.*

So a month later, when she'd been implicated in her father's crime? He'd made up for that day in the park when she'd silently begged for his help.

Or. Or, it was possible he'd imagined the entire exchange.

Seen it for something it wasn't. And he was legally insane. Probably something he should have considered before staking his career in law enforcement on it.

Across the ring, Henrik's opponent was smiling, but he wouldn't be for long. One thing he knew from being a Chicago cop was this: a wounded animal was the scariest animal of all. A wounded animal came at you with triple the strength. Triple the determination. And Henrik was wounded as hell. He wasn't just an animal tonight. He was a motherfucking monster.

The spectators were out for his blood. He could hear the word "cop" being spat like an epithet behind him. Didn't they know he was one of them now?

Henrik estimated he had another minute until the bell rang and he could release the aggression pounding inside his temples. He actually felt bad for the other guy and the way he'd feel tomorrow. If anyone deserved a good beating, it was Henrik. After all, his aggression was directed squarely at himself. No one else.

He'd compromised himself for the girl.

And then he'd lost her.

Her location was pinned to his refrigerator at home, courtesy of Austin's late-night delivery, during which the cocky Brit hadn't said a single word. If Henrik were capable of feeling pity for anyone else, he might have felt it for Austin as he stood outside Henrik's door, pale and agitated, muttering words beneath his breath. Or a name, rather. *Polly.*

Yeah. Pity wasn't exactly in Henrik's arsenal at the moment. He needed to distract himself from the insane compulsion to drive to Ailish's location. To make sure she wasn't in danger. Or being held against her will. God help everyone within swinging distance if she was hurt or scared.

This girl with whom he'd exchanged one sentence.

The bell rang and Henrik punched himself in the head with his right fist. Then his left. As he closed in on his opponent, his agonized growl rent the air.

. . .

Austin shut off the shower spray and flattened his palms on the slick tile wall. Frigid water ran down his face and chest, making his skin feel tight. The cold shower hadn't helped his aroused state — not in the least bit. Between his legs, his flesh hung heavy, ready. In the five months since he'd moved into Polly's apartment, now *their* apartment, his existence seemed to ebb and flow in varying states of need. Upon waking most mornings, he didn't hesitate to tuck Polly's ass against his lap and fuck her into a heightened state of wakefulness. It served her right for giving him no respite from the wanting of her, even in sleep.

But they had been up all last night working on a project. A project that would bring him slightly closer to atoning for his past. Polly and her dexterous fingers needed their rest. So he was being a conscientious boyfriend and letting her sleep. The situation — meaning his rigid cock — was not helped by the fact that no matter where he paced in the apartment, her naked, slumbering form seemed to be visible.

Austin flipped the cold water back on, wincing at the icy blast. His state could be remedied if he focused on a vision of his Polly and stroked himself off...if he didn't consider it sacrilegious to expend pleasure anywhere but inside her lithe, beloved body. She hadn't requested he keep himself only for her; it was merely a personal rule. And while he'd stopped forbidding her to touch herself, he knew she followed the same personal dictate. One he frequently rewarded her for, some days on an hourly basis.

He stuck his head directly beneath the shower spray and attempted to focus on something else. Anything to distract him from the knowledge that Polly's delectable backside was peeking out among their bedsheets like a tight little trophy, begging for him to come win it. Remind her whose name was engraved permanently on those smooth cheeks. *Fuck.* Austin's hand curled into a fist on the shower wall. By sheer force of will, he prevented himself from giving in and jerking the flesh dying for attention.

Something else. Think of something else.

In addition to Polly's nude body, his need this morning sprang from the ever-present desire to reassure her just how thoroughly she owned him. They'd spent the night tracking down one of his past marks, now living in Denver, and arranged for a transfer of funds. The woman was only the third on a long list that required repayment. Each time he and Polly fulfilled another debt, his shoulders felt lighter.

He and Polly had waited until after Reitman was formally charged with several felonies, including illegal gambling and extortion, before going to Derek and explaining their mission. In addition to their work on the undercover squad, they were now assisting state witnesses in maintaining their low profile while awaiting trial. Much like she had done for Bowen and Sera, Polly not only consulted with Chicago PD about how best to protect witnesses, she actively kept them invisible on the web and necessary financial databases.

They were paid for their side work. And the proceeds went to filling the potholes in Austin's past. Not a second passed during the day when Austin wasn't in awe of Polly. The selflessness she continued to display. That she was fulfilled by making a difference in the people's lives that had been wronged.

She saved him a little more each day.

Austin's role in their side business had been vague in the beginning. It had taken quite some time to gain the same trust Polly had received from the officers Derek arranged for them to work with. His unique expertise had finally been put to use creating new identities for witnesses who were required to leave Chicago for good after testifying. After spending years transforming himself into different people, Austin had proven himself invaluable to those witnesses. And it felt damn good to be doing something positive. To be anything other than the villain of someone's story.

Polly's father hadn't kept the money Austin returned. He'd donated it to the adoption agency that had brought him Polly. And maybe Austin still had a bit of villain left inside him after all, because he would steal the money all over again just to see the look on his girlfriend's face when she learned of her father's actions.

When the bathroom door creaked open outside the shower, Austin stopped breathing. His right hand lifted on his own to shut off the cold water, bathing the bathroom in silence, except for Polly's footsteps. Through the power of distraction and freezing water, he'd managed to reduce the swelling at the juncture of his thighs, but knowing Polly was close, he immediately rose to full mast.

There was something about the drawn-out cadence of her

steps, the way she didn't call out to him. *Polly wants to be in charge.* Intuition sparked, telling him she'd been pretending to sleep. Making him wait on purpose. They might trust each other enough to exchange power, depending on the ebb and flow of their mutual needs, but when Polly took the lead, *fuck* did he benefit, especially knowing his chance to return the favor wouldn't be long. Often it was only a matter of moments before he became the aggressor. And when that happened? *Jesus,* the screaming could echo in his head for days.

Austin's eyes slid closed when she climbed into the shower behind him, his raspy inhales calling to mind the shake of a rattlesnake tail.

Leather ghosted over Austin's hip, and his groan of anticipation echoed off the shower walls. It had taken some time to convince Polly that he didn't consider the belt a punishment anymore, but a way to express the trust they'd built for each other. Nothing calmed the quiet in his head more than holding Polly, but there was sex in the snap of leather. It was honesty with a bite—and on occasion, his Polly needed to do some biting. Fulfilling that need for her was his ultimate fantasy, so he gladly allowed it.

God, he loved the woman. Loved her strengths, her vulnerabilities, and everything in between. By some twist of fate, she loved him, too. Every time she said it, he still asked her to repeat herself.

Now Polly placed her fingers lightly on his chest, trailing them down to his belly, where they lingered. "I missed you. I missed hearing you love me before I'm even fully awake. I miss you when you're in the next room."

A vise cranked tight around Austin's throat. This woman.

She made him feel secure and out of control at the same time. "I love you so much I can't see straight. I'll tell you a thousand times tomorrow morning to make up for it."

"I love you, too," she whispered, her breath drifting up his spine. "Endlessly." By the time she wrapped his dick in a tightfisted grip, he was shaking with anticipation. "Did you touch it?"

"No, I didn't touch," he managed. "I saved it for you."

She ran her thumb in circles across the thick head. "Thank you."

They both groaned when Polly gave him his first full stroke of the day, a rough squeeze from root to tip. Austin's breath shuddered out. "What does my little mistress need from me today?"

Her tongue licked moisture from his back. "I want you to take me back to bed and wake me up properly." A tight jerk of his cock wrenched a growled curse from his throat. "After."

His breath fogged the slick shower tiles. "After?"

She removed the perfection of her touch and a second later, the sound of leather slapping wet flesh, coupled with his groan, split the air.

The corner of Austin's mouth edged up into a dangerous half smile.

"If it pleases you, Polly."

Acknowledgments

This was a hard book for me to write. Not because I don't adore Austin and Polly and their story. I do. *Muchly.* I think because it was my first time writing a hero in a submissive position that I started doubting my decision to take the risk. And then I doubted it more…and hey, a little more. The ever-fabulous community of romance writers surrounding me on social media, at conferences and via email are what pushed me through on this one. So I would like to thank them. All of them, even the mean ones. (Kidding!) Just *listening* to you share common frustrations is enough motivation to push through a rough patch, because it's a reminder that we're ALL taking risks on a daily basis and making shit work, even when we're scared it won't.

Good hustle, ladies.

I would also like to thank my husband, Patrick, and daughter, Mackenzie, for being my foundation and the reason I get up in the morning. I love you guys.

I would like to thank my editor, Heather Howland, for loving this book right along with me and helping make it super shiny.

I would like to thank Aquila Editing (aka Eagle) for beta reading this book and convincing me it was fit for public consumption. (PS: Sending your meal tray down to the basement in twenty minutes…)

Thank you to Bailey's Babes for being the bomb.com and so damn supportive. I want to gather you all to my bosom and rock to and fro.

Thank you to the bloggers and reviewers who continually pick up the books in the Crossing the Line series and devote their time to reading/reviewing my work. I never take it for granted that you will – and it means everything to me when you do.

New York Times and USA TODAY bestselling author Tessa Bailey lives in Brooklyn, New York, with her husband and young daughter. When she isn't writing or reading romance, she enjoys a good argument and thirty-minute recipes.

www.tessabailey.com